"I shall make you a promise," Jared said.

"If you find a lady I can love as much as my father loved my mother, I shall marry her—and if she has a fortune so much the better...."

"You will look for a wealthy bride?"

"You will look for one for me," Jared said, and his expression was once again inscrutable. "Present the right lady and I will marry her."

"Oh..." Hester looked at him. He seemed to be serious for once. She did not know why she felt reluctant to agree, but he was clearly waiting for her answer. "I shall try...."

"Good," Jared said, settling back and closing his eyes.

Hester frowned. How annoying he was! They were just beginning to get to know one another and now he was refusing to talk to her. And after he had thrown her into confusion by kissing her in such a way that it made her pulse race. He really was too bad! She bit her bottom lip, feeling at odds with herself. She should be pleased that he had almost given his word to stay and marry an heiress if she could find the right one, but somehow she had an awful sinking sensation inside.

* * *

The Unknown Heir
Harlequin® Historical #269—October 2009

Author Note

This is a special year for authors, readers and lovers of romance. Harlequin is sixty years old, and this is certainly a cause for celebration. No other publisher has consistently given us the high-quality romance fiction we have come to expect and love from Harlequin.

As an author, I am thrilled to write for a large international company that retains its family atmosphere. Regency stories continue to flourish, and in this anniversary year I am proud to be contributing *The Unknown Heir*. I hope you will continue to enjoy my books throughout this year and the years to come.

I really appreciate my readers and love to hear what you think of my books. You can find out more about me at my Web site, www.lindasole.co.uk.

The Unknown Heir
Anne Herries

HARLEQUIN®

TORONTO • NEW YORK • LONDON
AMSTERDAM • PARIS • SYDNEY • HAMBURG
STOCKHOLM • ATHENS • TOKYO • MILAN • MADRID
PRAGUE • WARSAW • BUDAPEST • AUCKLAND

Recycling programs
for this product may
not exist in your area.

ISBN-13: 978-0-373-30578-0

THE UNKNOWN HEIR

www.eHarlequin.com

Printed in U.S.A.

ANNE HERRIES

Award-winning author Anne Herries lives in Cambridgeshire, England. She is fond of watching wildlife, and spoils the birds and squirrels that are frequent visitors to her garden. Anne loves to write about the beauty of nature, and sometimes puts a little into her books—although they are mostly about love and romance. She writes for her own enjoyment and to give pleasure to her readers. She invites readers to contact her on her Web site: www.lindasole.co.uk.

Available from Harlequin® Historical and
ANNE HERRIES

*Banewulf Dynasty
**The Elizabethan Season
†The Hellfire Mysteries
††Melford Dynasty
‡The Horne Sisters

Chapter One

Hester Sheldon placed the vase of perfect chrysanthemums on a table in front of the parlour window, gazing out at the sodden grass and dripping trees that fronted the beautiful old house. Shelbourne had been built in the reign of Queen Anne and had all the grace and beauty of its period, though it was looking faded and had suffered some fire damage recently. Hester loved her home, but of late a dark cloud seemed to hang over them, for the family had been deeply affected by the death of her step-father some months previously. The tragedy had quite possibly led to the Duke of Shelbourne's illness, and it was these things that made the house she adored seem so empty at times.

'Miss Hester?'

She turned as the housekeeper came into the room, prepared to deal with whatever might be asked of her since the burden of the estate had fallen on her shoulders these past weeks. Lady Sheldon had been delicate since the death of her husband, and the duke was unable to do more than advise her from his bedchamber.

'Yes, Mrs Mills? Is there something wrong?'

'His Grace has asked that you go up to him as soon as you have a minute, miss.'

'Yes, of course. I shall go now,' Hester said. 'And my compliments to Cook, Mrs Mills. The beef was excellent last night. Grandfather particularly remarked on it.'

'I am sure she will be pleased to hear that, miss.'

Mrs Mills stood back for Hester to leave the room, shaking her head as she went into the hall and up the stairs. It was hardly fair the way they all expected Miss Sheldon to do everything these days. Not that she was a girl, as she had passed her twenty-sixth birthday, and it was unlikely that she would marry, which was, in Mrs Mills's opinion, a proper shame.

Hester was smiling as she went quickly along the landing to the stairs leading to the top floor of the west wing, which held the duke's private apartments. He seldom left them these days, because his illness had taken the strength from his legs and he had to be carried down the stairs—something he did not enjoy. She knocked and was admitted by the duke's valet, who smiled at her.

'How is he this morning, Simmons?'

'Oh, much the same as usual, miss. He will be all the better for seeing you.'

Hester went through the duke's private parlour into his bedchamber as he had not yet been allowed to get up for more than an hour or so a day. She had been anxious that he might have suffered a relapse, but he actually looked a little more healthy, which brought a smile to her face.

'What can I do for you, Grandfather?'

Although not a blood relation, she had always been encouraged to think of him as her grandfather. The child of her mother's first husband, who had sadly died soon after she was born, Hester had been adopted by Lord Sheldon and given his name when her mother remarried. She had loved him as the only father she had ever known, and the duke was in all respects but one her beloved grandfather.

'Nothing for the moment,' he said. 'I wanted to tell you that I have sent for the heir. If he agrees to come, it may make a difference to both Lady Sheldon and you, Hester.'

'Yes, of course. We might have to retire to the dower house, perhaps.'

'Not while I live,' the duke replied. 'But it is all in the air at the moment. As you know, I made inquiries about him and they were favourable. He seems to be in possession of a fortune… Heaven knows, we could do with some of that money here, girl!'

'Yes, sir—but he may not wish to use his fortune to help restore this house or the estate.'

'Well, I have persuaded Birch to go out there,' the duke told her and frowned. 'He must be told of his duty to the family. He may not be presentable, of course—but I dare say you could knock him into shape for us, Hester?'

'I am not sure I understand you, Grandfather.'

'He will need to learn English manners. I have no idea what sort of schools they have out there these days, but I dare say he may have some rough edges. His father was a riverboat gambler, as I understand it, though he must have done all right for himself.'

'I am willing to offer my help if he wishes for it, of course,' Hester said, looking doubtful. 'But he is Amelia's son and she will surely have taught him his manners.'

'Perhaps,' the duke said. The mention of his favourite child's name made him frown. She had run away to marry the man of her choice against his wishes and it had taken him a long time to forgive her. 'Well, see what you can do for him if he comes, Hester—of course, he may not…'

'If he does not wish to live here, he might give up his right to the title, sir.'

'And then there would be only Mr Grant to deal with,' the duke said and sighed. 'Why weren't you a boy and born to my son, Hester? If I had the money, I would break the entail and leave this place to you. You love it and none of my sons ever cared a hoot about the estate—and as for my half-brother's grandson…' He shook his head in disgust. 'I should turn in my grave if he became master here. He is a pompous idiot!'

Hester laughed softly. 'Do not upset yourself, dearest. You know that I have no right to inherit. Besides, this American heir may be everything you could wish for, especially if he has a fortune.'

'Well, Birch will sound him out. He cannot leave for America until a week or so after Christmas, but we must hope that his journey will be successful. I wrote to the heir as soon as your father died, but he has not answered my letters.'

Hester was silent. She knew that the duke was hoping that the heir would come over to take his rightful place as the next in line for the title, but she could not truly see what he could gain from it, particularly if he was already in possession of a fortune.

'I hope he comes for your sake, dearest,' she said. 'But if he doesn't, we shall manage. We always do…'

'We manage,' the duke said and thumped the bed. 'If I had my legs again, I would sort things out, but as it is I am helpless. If you ever decide to get married, this place will go to the devil.'

'Well, I have no intention of it,' Hester reassured him. 'I shall not leave you, dearest Grandfather. If the heir comes…' She left the sentence unfinished, because as yet they could not know whether or not the heir would wish to leave his home. 'We must wait and see what happens.'

* * *

'You—the heir to an English duke?' Red Clinton threw back his head and laughed deep in his throat. 'Don't make me laugh, Jared. You are kidding me, aren't you?'

Jared looked at his cousin, a lazy smile playing over his sensuous mouth. 'It sounds crazy, I know, but my mother ran off with my father when her family rejected the marriage. Pa didn't have much going for him then…'

He glanced round the richly furnished room above the gambling club he owned in New Orleans. It had been his father's legacy to him when he died, all that remained of the fortune Jack Clinton had amassed when he was younger. Jared's father had built a home fitting for the daughter of an English duke after making his fortune gambling on the riverboats that plied the Mississippi River, but it had been sold when she died, most of the money lost the way it had come. Jack Clinton's heart had been buried with his wife, and he had become reckless, neglecting his son, drinking and gambling carelessly until all he had left was a gambling saloon. After his death of a heart attack, Jared had taken what he'd inherited, swearing that he would never end the way his father had, and had since increased his wealth many times over. He was now much richer than his father had ever been, respected and admired by the highest in New Orleans society; he had recently been approached to enter politics by some of the elders of the city.

'I thought the family refused to have anything to do with her after she ran away with your father,' Red said. 'Why have they decided they want you now—after all these years? Isn't there anyone else?'

'It seems not. There were three sons and about four grandsons as I recall. A heck of a lot of people must have died for the title to come down to me.'

'Hell!' Red swore half a dozen times and pulled a wry face. 'What are you gonna do? You live like a king here— why would you want to go and live in some draughty old mansion that's probably about ready to fall down over your head?' He tipped his head to one side, the left eyebrow raised in inquiry. 'Or is the family dripping in gold?'

'I very much doubt it,' Jared said. He grinned, looking much like his more handsome cousin for a moment. They were both tall, strong men with broad shoulders, slim hips and the athletic look of men who had passed out of West Point with first-class honours. Both were rich men, both attractive in their own way, though of the two Red was the most striking, his hair a flaming torch as a ray of sunshine touched it. Jared's hair was a darker shade of auburn, his features harsher and less attractive when in repose. Only when he smiled was it noticeable that the two were cousins. 'The lawyer's letter was all about the honour of the family name. Apparently, it is my duty to go over there and set things to rights.'

'You mean they've got wind that you're as rich as Croesus and they want some of it,' Red drawled, his top lip curling in disgust. 'You're a fool if you do it, Jared.'

Jared nodded because his cousin was echoing the thoughts that had been running through his head for the past week since the latest letter arrived.

'What's more, they seem to imagine I need a lesson in manners,' he said. 'They are sending someone to talk to me and take me back on the ship to England. I have been advised that I should leave the purchase of any new clothes I might need until I get there. Apparently, a female cousin is going to teach me what to wear and how to behave in society.'

'Well, dang my hide!' Red exclaimed, a huge grin spreading over his face. 'Think you're an ignorant hillbilly, do they?'

'Well, the lawyer didn't quite say that, but that's about the size of it,' Jared agreed, amused by his cousin's unaccustomed language. 'He is coming today. I was wondering where to receive him.'

'What do you mean?' Red asked, puzzled. He glanced around the large room, which was furnished with the finest French furniture from the Empire period and contained treasures that a lot of Jared's neighbours would give their eye-teeth to own. 'You've plenty of property you could choose to receive him in. Why not this place? One look should disabuse their agent of any erroneous ideas they happen to have formed of your education and standing in American society.'

'Yes, I dare say it would,' Jared said, a wicked glint in his eyes. They were somewhere between green and blue in colour and at that moment the expression in them was both deep and mysterious. 'But it makes me angry when I think of the way the old man treated my mother. He was a martinet by all accounts and he could afford to ignore her, because he had all those sons and grandsons. It must have given him some grief to realise that I was the only one left to him.'

'Yes, I suppose so,' Red drawled. Knowing his cousin well from the time they spent at military academy together, he knew that some devilish plan was lurking behind that look. 'Going to tell me any time this week? Only I've got a pretty girl waiting for me to show this afternoon.'

'You know that shack down by the river?'

'The warehouse you bought last week?' Red's eyes narrowed. 'You were going to pull it down and build new, as I recall.'

'Fortunately, I haven't got around to it,' Jared said. 'Do you think your lady love would mind if you were a little late for your important meeting, Red? Only you can do me a favour if you will.'

'No problem,' his cousin said. 'Sue Ellen looks beautiful when she's angry. She may shoot me on sight, but I guess I'll take the chance.' He raised his brows. 'So what is the plan?'

'I'm going to meet Mr Birch there in the river shack,' Jared said. 'I'll dig out some of Pa's old working clothes and give him a fright. Since he's expecting me to be ignorant and disgusting, I may as well give him what he wants.'

'Good,' Red said and grinned broadly, loving the plan. 'Where do I come in?'

'Well, I think they may have done their research,' Jared said. 'But they made a big mistake. You see, I'm a no-good gambler, like my father, and last month I lost everything to you.' He smiled at his cousin. 'Think you can do that for me?'

'Yes,' Red said and laughed. 'I reckon that will teach those aristocratic relatives of yours a lesson—but what then? You won't actually go over there, will you?'

'Well, that depends,' Jared said. 'I'm curious to see what happened to all those sons and grandsons, but I'm still thinking about it.'

'Well, take your time making up your mind,' Red told him. 'If they have sent someone all this way, they want something—and they need it desperately.'

'Yes,' Jared agreed, his eyes narrowed, angry. 'I am certain they do.'

'Thank you for coming to me before you see Grandfather, Mr Birch,' Hester said when she greeted him in the parlour at Shelbourne. It was spring, some months since her grandfather had first told her of his intention to send for the heir, and Mr Birch's recent letter had shocked them. 'Your letter upset him and I have wondered if the heir can possibly be as terrible as you suggested. Grandfather's reports all indicated that he was wealthy and reasonably well educated. Didn't he go to an exclusive military academy?'

'It appears that he was thrown out halfway through his training, because of his drinking and gambling,' Mr Birch said and sighed. He had worked for the Duke of Shelbourne since he first became a lawyer and his loyalty was unswerving. 'It is the cousin—Mr Roderick Clinton—who has all the money, and he is really quite a gentleman, even if he does use some odd words occasionally. Now that would have been easy enough for you to correct, Miss Sheldon—but I fear Mr Jared Clinton is beyond your help. He lives in the most appalling shack and his clothes…' He shuddered at the memory and the appalling smell that had clung to the heir apparent when they first met. Only his duty had kept him from turning tail in the first instance. 'I managed to get him looking fairly decent for the journey to London, but he refuses to buy anything further, even though I assured him the duke has opened an account for him at Coutts Bank. It seems that he did have money until recently and lost it at the tables when drunk. He told me that he has to learn to control his bad habits before he can take anything from the duke.'

'Well, at least he seems to be aware of his duty to Grandfather,' Hester said, her sigh even deeper and more heartfelt than her lawyer's if that were possible. Her glossy dark hair was drawn back in a severe knot at the back of her head, which did nothing for her features. She was, however, elegantly dressed, though the colours she chose were usually of a subdued hue. There had been so many tragedies over the past few years, including the death of her stepfather and half-brother John, and she had grown resigned to remaining at Shelbourne House to comfort her mother and Grandfather, neither of whom cared to go into society these days. 'I suppose that is something. And since most of my step-uncles and cousins were gamblers, I suppose we cannot look for our American heir to be an exception. I was afraid it was too good to be true when the report came saying that he was industrious, honourable and clever.'

'If only you had been born a man,' Mr Birch said. 'You are everything that this family needs, Miss Sheldon. I have always thought the female line had all the common sense in this family.'

'You forget that I am no blood relation to the duke,' Hester told him. 'I love Shelbourne as if he were my true grandfather, and he loves me, but that is as far as it goes.'

'Yes, I had forgotten for the moment, but I am sure that no one could have a more loving granddaughter, Miss Sheldon.'

'I wish that there was some way in which I could protect Grandfather,' Hester said. 'The male line of this family are cursed, Mr Birch. For years I believed that the old story was a myth, just a foolish tale, as my step-uncles were profligate gamblers and drinkers—but since Papa died and then there was John…' Her voice broke as the grief welled inside her.

'It is just a tale,' her lawyer assured her. 'It is true that the family has been unfortunate for the past few years. Your stepfather's brothers all carried the illness passed down through their mother, Miss Sheldon—an inflammation of the lungs, which often proves fatal.'

'Yes, perhaps you are right.' Hester sighed. 'Grandfather had such hopes for the new heir. It seems he is doomed to disappointment.'

'Well, he seems healthy enough. He is a gambler and he told me himself that he drinks more than he ought, but he seems disposed towards his duty because he did not drink more than a glass of wine at dinner on the voyage, and he refrained from gambling. His speech is a little...' Mr Birch hesitated, wondering how best to prepare her. 'American, I think is the best way to describe it...but I dare say you might be able to do something about that, and you could direct him to the right tailors, Miss Sheldon. You have always had perfect taste and he could do no better than to listen to you.'

'If he will listen,' Hester said doubtfully. 'I have not found gentlemen normally accommodating in that respect. Papa certainly never listened to Mama on any subject— and if he had, he might never have lost so much money at the card tables. And then you know he might not have started drinking so much, taken that fever and died as he did, but when John died it broke his heart. He was never the same again after that because he knew he could not have another son. Mama's health would not have permitted it, you see.'

'Most unfortunate,' Mr Birch agreed, nodding in sympathy. 'You can only try, Miss Sheldon. What little there is left of the estate depends on the heir at least making an effort to bring the family fortunes about. If we can make him respectable, we can marry him to an heiress.'

'And then what?' Hester asked. 'Mama was an heiress, but Papa gambled all her money away as well as his own. She has only the settlement her father insisted on when she married him and that is scarcely enough to clothe us both decently. But, as you say, a rich marriage is the only solution. Grandfather is determined on a ball to introduce him into society.'

'Not yet, Miss Sheldon,' her lawyer begged with a little shudder. 'If he were seen in good society as he is...all chance of his finding an heiress would be gone.'

'Is he really so awful?' Hester said, wrinkling her brow. 'I was not born when my aunt ran away with her American gambler, but I have heard that she was an intelligent, beautiful lady.' How could her son be the ignorant, coarse man the lawyer had described? Surely there was some mystery here? 'I think I should see him before Grandfather does, Mr Birch. I shall come back to London with you and stay with my godmother. Perhaps I can at least make him look presentable before he comes here.'

'I think that is a good idea,' Mr Birch said. 'I was hesitant to suggest it—but since you have done so, I can only applaud your devotion to duty.'

'Duty?' Hester shook her head. 'In truth, I care little for what becomes of the heir, sir. I wish only to make Grandfather's last few months as easy as possible. I know he blames himself for what has happened to the family, and I would find a way of giving him peace of mind if it is possible.'

'Your generosity of spirit is everything that one could wish for in a daughter,' the lawyer said. 'Your mother and grandfather must rely on you for so much, Miss Sheldon. It is a little unfair on you that they entertain so little these days.'

'I have been given so much love,' Hester replied with a serene smile. 'I did have my Season before Papa died, you know. I did not take and I fear it is too late to think of marriage now. I am content with my life as it is, sir.'

Mr Birch sighed inwardly, for he knew that an intelligent woman such as Miss Sheldon undoubtedly must be wasted in that mausoleum of a house. However, he knew her too well to imagine she would ever think of disobliging her mother or the duke, and was therefore doomed to remain a spinster.

'So, the prodigal son is not everything you had hoped,' Lady Sarah Ireland said, casting a critical eye over her

goddaughter. She thought it a great pity that Hester had
not married when she was younger, because she was a
charming, sensible girl and deserved a home of her own.
She was at the beck and call of the duke, who had grown
selfish in his old age, Lady Ireland believed. In truth, she
had never liked Shelbourne, but she did like Hester, who
was related to her through Hester's real father, and she had
tried to persuade Hester to come and live with her in
London more than once. 'Well, I dare say you can teach
him some society manners, Hester, but it is a pity about
the money. It would hardly have mattered how he speaks
if he still had a fortune.'

Hester shook her head at the elderly lady, of whom she
was very fond. 'That remark was a little cynical, dearest
Godmother, but I know you meant it well. In society, most
things are forgiven one if there is a large enough fortune.'
She sighed and glanced at herself in the great oval mirror
that hung on the wall of Lady Ireland's elegant salon. 'As
you are aware, Grandfather still has the house and the land,
possibly because his sons died before they could force
him to sell, but there is very little money. Had the heir not
gambled his money away, he might have helped restore the
house. The west wing needs a large amount of money
spent on it if it is to be restored to its former glory.'

'Yes, for it was sadly damaged by fire last year, was it
not?' Lady Ireland frowned. 'It was fortunate for the duke that
you were there and happened to have gone down for a book.'

'Yes, that was fortunate,' Hester said, her smooth brow
wrinkling. 'I smelled the smoke and roused the servants.
It was contained to the ground floor, but had it really
caught hold…' A shiver ran through her, for she knew that
they might all have died in their beds, but particularly the
duke, whose apartments were immediately above where
the fire had started.

'Have you ever discovered how it happened?' Lady Ireland asked. 'Was it merely a careless servant or…?'

'I wish that I could answer you,' Hester replied, looking anxious. 'I cannot think it was started deliberately, for who would do such a thing? If Grandfather had died…'

'But the heir was at that time living in America, was he not? I dare say he had not been told he was the heir, for your father had been dead only a few weeks, and the duke waited some months before sending for him, I believe?'

'Yes.' Hester furrowed her brow. 'Grandfather did make some inquiries regarding the entail. I think if it were possible he might have had it legally broken, but it proved too expensive. You see, there is actually another heir. That meant he would have had to settle two claims rather than one, for Mr Stephen Grant would have had a claim if the heir died. Grandfather gave up then, for it would have beggared the estate to pay them both.'

'Is that so?' Lady Ireland raised her brows. 'I did not realise that the duke had any other relations. I thought it was just you, your mother and the American heir.'

'Grandfather had a half-brother, the son of his father's second wife,' Hester said. 'They quarrelled many years ago and he lost touch with Philip. He was vaguely aware that Philip and his wife had a daughter, but the families did not visit, and he knew nothing of Philip's grandson until recently, when he sent a polite note asking if he might call.'

Lady Ireland frowned. 'And did he call? Have you met him, Hester? What manner of man is he?'

'Oh, quite the gentleman,' Hester told her. 'I think Grandfather found him acceptable, if a little irritating.'

'Irritating?'

'Mr Stephen Grant is a man of the cloth,' Hester said. 'He is everything that is proper in a gentleman, ma'am—and he is entitled to call himself by one of the lesser family titles, as

Grandfather reminded him, but he considers it inappropriate for a man of his calling, and prefers to be just Mr Grant.'

'Is there any fortune in the family?'

'Very little. I believe he has a small trust fund set up by his father, before he died, but his grandfather was disowned by the family at one time, and I understand that what money there was may have been lost at the gaming tables. Mr Grant despises gamblers.'

'He sounds a more sound character than the heir,' Lady Ireland remarked. 'What did the duke have to say?'

'He said Mr Grant was a prig and a fool,' Hester said, her lips curving into a naughty smile. At that moment she looked younger than her years, and, in the eyes of her fond godmother, very pretty. 'At that time, he was pleased with the reports of the American heir.'

'Ah…' Her godmother nodded. 'It is a shame that Mr Clinton did not match up to the initial reports, for the family needs some good blood—a man who might have put a stop to the rot. However, you must cut your coat from the cloth you have, Hester. When did you say you were to meet him?'

'Very shortly,' Hester told her. 'Mr Birch is bringing him here this afternoon for tea.'

'Oh, so we shall see for ourselves what manner of man he is,' Lady Ireland said. 'I do hope he at least looks presentable, Hester—but I fear you will have your work cut out before you can present him to society.'

Jared Clinton stared at himself in the elegant wall mirror in the bedchamber of the exclusive hotel. He disliked what he saw, for the coat was ill fitting and not to the standard he was accustomed to wearing. His linen was decent, but it lacked quality and felt uncomfortable. For two pins he would have given up this charade and unpacked the clothes he had, unknown to Mr Birch, brought with him. However, the lawyer's disapproving manner at their first meeting had angered him sufficiently that he was determined to carry the masquerade through. Besides, he had no intention of shelling out a fortune in order to prop up some crumbling mansion for a family who had once disowned his mother.

Who the hell did these people think they were? He had been given a lecture about what he owed to the duke and to the family name. Apparently, there was some old dragon who was prepared to teach him some manners, which the lawyer had made clear were sadly lacking. He needed to acquire some town bronze before he could be introduced to society as the duke's heir. Jared had begun this deception as something to amuse himself and his cousin, with no intention of obliging the lawyer by coming over to England. However, his childhood memories of a beautiful English lady, who had sung songs to him and told him about the wonderful house she had grown up in, had somehow come to the fore and made him curious to see his birthright for himself.

'Surely, you won't really go over?' Red had been incredulous. 'You know it's only the money they want, don't you? You might fool some crusty old lawyer for a short while, but you'll never be able to keep it up—and why should you? There's nothing for you over there, Jared.'

'Nothing but the satisfaction of seeing that arrogant devil beg for my help,' Jared replied, a gleam in his eyes. 'He disowned my mother because she ran off to marry my father. I think the duke owes me an apology for what he did to her, if nothing more.'

'You won't decide to stay there?' his cousin asked. 'You have all this here—and we need you. I need you, Jared.'

'Now that is funny,' Jared replied, grinning. 'You need me telling you what to do like a hole in the head. If you had nothing of your own, I would point out the advantages of my selling up here—you could buy the property and increase your own holdings in the business.'

'Damn it! I don't want that and you know it,' Red said, an angry glint in his own eyes now. 'I have more land and property than I need already. Folk round here have been expecting you to run for Congress—this year senator, in a couple of years who knows. You could be the next president.'

Jared laughed. 'Not my game, cousin. True, I've had a certain amount to say about the way things are run here, but I am content to keep my efforts at a local level. However you—you could go a long way.'

Red shook his head. 'Well, I suppose if you are determined to go, you must, but take care of yourself. You won't have me to watch your back over there.'

'If I feel the need, I'll write,' Jared said drily. 'I don't expect to stay long. I just want to take a look and see how things lie.'

'I wouldn't want to be writing your obituary,' his cousin said, suddenly serious. 'You said there was some mystery about the way all your male relatives died over there, didn't you?'

'Yes. I asked the lawyer about that, but he wasn't having any of it—natural causes and a couple of accidents—but I shall keep an open mind on that one.'

'You do that,' Red said, 'and, if you need me, I'll come.'

'The cavalry to the rescue?' Jared chuckled deep in his throat. 'We had some good times, cousin. Keep an eye on this place for me—and if anything happens to me, you are my executor.'

'That's a heck of a consolation!' Red said. 'What am I going to do if you don't come back? I can't run your empire

alone, cousin. Besides, it would interfere with my plea-
sures.'

The memory made Jared smile. His cousin was also his
best friend and he could not help wishing he were here,
though he knew it was foolish to feel so apprehensive
about the meeting with his mother's relatives. He had an
odd feeling that he was being drawn into something he
would regret. Perhaps it would have been better to stay at
home and ignore his grandfather's demands. But he had
never been a quitter and he wasn't about to start now.

Some of the tension had drained out of Jared by the time
he went downstairs to the hotel reception area. He was just
in time to see the lawyer walk in the door, noticing his
quick frown of disapproval. It made Jared smile inwardly.
The odd feeling of unease had passed, his natural resili-
ence bouncing back. He was going to enjoy himself this
afternoon; he hadn't met a female he couldn't charm yet,
be she sixteen or ninety-six. He didn't think this Miss
Hester Sheldon would be an exception.

Hester stood up as she heard footsteps in the hall
outside her godmother's salon. She walked over to the
window, glancing out at the gardens, which were in full
bloom with spring flowers, for some reason unaccountably
nervous. She had made light of the whole thing to Lady
Ireland, but truthfully she knew it was very important that
the heir should be presentable. Unless he could charm
himself into the good graces of one of this season's
heiresses, it was likely that the duke would have to begin
selling off some of the land—or, worse still, the west wing
might have to be closed off and abandoned until the money
could be found to restore it. And what her godmother had
no idea of was how much she had come to love Shelbourne, even though it could never be hers.

'Mr Birch and Viscount Sheldon, madam.'

Hester heard the announcement, but did not turn immediately. She did not know why she was so reluctant all of a sudden, but it might have been her fear of disappointment.

'Well, ain't this a real pretty place, ma'am,' a voice with a pronounced southern twang said behind her. 'I'm right pleased to meet you, Miss Sheldon, though I ain't rightly sure what I'm supposed to call you, ma'am. Are you a cousin?'

'I fear you have mistaken me for my goddaughter,' Lady Ireland said in what sounded like cut-glass accents to Hester's practised ear. 'Hester, my dear. I believe this is your cousin.'

Hester turned, a shock running through her as she looked into eyes that were at that particular moment more green than blue, his hair a rich shade of auburn, his skin darker than she would have expected in a man with that colouring. He was tall, broad shouldered with a face that looked lived in, a squared chin and deep crinkles at the corners of his eyes. He must be in his late thirties, older than she had imagined, though of course his mother was just seventeen when she ran away from her home.

Hester would normally have explained that she was not a true cousin, but for some reason her throat had dried and she had difficulty in speaking at all. She wasn't sure what she had expected, but somehow it wasn't this man with his air of self-assurance that accorded ill with the clothes he was wearing. He looked good as he was—dressed decently, he would be magnificent, and that was due to his build, because some of the fops who patronised the best tailors in London would never look one-tenth as good as he did at this moment. She cleared her throat, going forward to offer her hand.

'I am not sure what Mr Birch told you about us, my lord,' she said. 'You actually have several titles to choose from should you wish to change yours—but Grandfather thought it might be too daunting if you found yourself being called the Marquis of Shelby, which you could be if you chose, so he has given you the title that was once Papa's.'

'If you don't mind, ma'am, I prefer to be known as Jared Clinton. I've never considered myself a member of the English aristocracy.'

'No, perhaps not,' Hester said, taking a grip on herself. Her pulses were racing, which was foolish because she was always in complete control of herself when in company. To lose her composure now would be ridiculous. 'I must welcome you to London, sir. The duke is looking forward to meeting you and presenting you to his friends as the heir. I dare say Mr Birch has told you that an account has been set up for you here in town. You might wish to purchase a few clothes—the kind of thing you would be expected to wear in society. If you should wish for it, I shall be delighted to help you purchase your new wardrobe.'

'Well, I reckon that's right nice of you, ma'am,' Jared said, a glint in his eyes. She was standing in sunlight and he could not see her face clearly, but she was dressed well. He had been prepared to treat gently the elderly lady he imagined had been dragged from her bathchair to rescue him, but what was he supposed to learn from a girl like this? 'But I wouldn't want to be a trouble to you, dragging you all over town—unless you can put up with a hillbilly like me? I ain't never been to London before and I cain't wait to see the sights. Red is just going to hog my ear when I get back, wanting to know everything I seen in this little old town.'

'It would be my pleasure to accompany you—at least to those places where a lady is permitted to visit. I am not sure whether we could find someone who would put you up for a decent club, but after Grandfather has seen you, I dare say he will ask one of his friends to do the necessary.'

'Hog damn, if that ain't right decent of you, cousin.'

'One thing,' Hester said, frowning slightly. 'That phrase you just used would not be accepted in polite circles. If you wish to be accepted by the best people, it might be as well to moderate your language, if you can.'

'What phrase would that be, Miss Sheldon?' Jared asked, his eyes wide and innocent.

'I imagine she meant hog damn,' Lady Ireland intercepted. 'Please come and sit down, sir. I have rung for tea.'

'That's the milky stuff they keep sending me at the hotel,' Jared said. 'If you don't mind, ma'am, I would rather not. Coffee, if you please, or something stronger.'

'Madeira, then,' Lady Ireland replied promptly. 'You may not know the wine, sir, but I assure you it is much drunk by gentlemen of taste.'

Jared thought of his well-stocked wine cellar at home, which held some of the finest wines from France and other countries, but held the biting retort back, knowing that he had invited this kind of thing by pretending to be something he was not.

'You are too kind, ma'am. I was thinking maybe I'd try some of your cute English ale, but this…what did you call it—Madeira?—that will do just fine.'

He became aware that his cousin was staring at him. She had walked out of the sunshine now and he was able to see her face properly for the first time. He realised that she was not quite as young as he had thought her—perhaps twenty-four or -five, but as yet unmarried, for her finger was ringless. He wondered why, because she was not unattractive. Not pretty, but pleasant to look at, he thought, her hair a soft brown and her eyes what some people called hazel.

'Will you not sit down, sir?' Lady Ireland inquired as Hester took a seat on the small sofa. 'How do you like what you've seen of England so far?'

'It rains a lot,' Jared answered, deliberately obtuse. 'I cain't say as I've been far as yet, ma'am, but what I've seen is kind of cute.' He winced at his own drawl and wondered what his mother would say if she could hear him. He sounded like one of the uneducated young men who came to his cousin's estate looking for work from time to time.

'Cute? I dare say that is meant to be a compliment,' Lady Ireland said, looking down her long nose at him. 'I think what you meant to say is that you haven't had time to see a great deal, but you like what you have seen so far.'

'Yes, ma'am, you could say that,' Jared replied. He got to his feet instantly as a young maid came in carrying a heavy tray. 'May I help you with that, miss?'

'Oh, sir, my lord…' The girl looked flustered as she set the tray on the stand beside her mistress. 'So kind…' She met his gaze and blushed, a little smile on her lips as she hurried from the room, clearly embarrassed by his attentions.

'You do not need to stand up for a servant,' Lady Ireland told him. 'And you do not offer to help her with her work. I dare say you are not aware of it, Lord Sheldon, but it isn't done in polite society.'

'Where I come from, a gentleman always stands for a lady,' Jared replied without thinking. 'And that tray looked heavy. At home my father would have expected his son to help if the tray was too heavy for a servant. He believed in equality for all.'

'You are in England now…'

'I don't think it matters,' Hester said, because she had seen the flash of anger in the heir's eyes. She was rather pleased that he had shown himself to have good manners, even if his politeness was misplaced. 'Mr Clinton erred on the right side, Godmother.'

'Well, yes, I suppose he did,' Lady Ireland agreed, looking at her in surprise. 'I was merely trying to help. I should not like you to suffer a severe set-down, sir. You will find that many society hostesses would give you the cut direct if you used some of the words you have here today—and they will snigger behind their fans if you jump to your feet every time a maid brings in a tray.'

'They may do as they please, ma'am,' Jared replied, a note of steel in his voice. 'A lady is a lady where I come from—and that little girl was struggling with that tray.'

'As it happens, I agree with you. She should never have attempted it. I shall have a word with my butler. He ought to have come himself or sent two maids. Madeira, sir? I believe you will find it agreeable. Please help yourself from the decanter. Mr Birch, will you have tea or join his lordship in a glass of Madeira?'

'If I may, I should enjoy a glass of wine,' the lawyer said. He had been standing silently, watching the American heir with a puzzled frown. He had noticed it once or twice before—that unpleasant twang disappeared when the viscount was roused to anger or passion. Could it possibly be assumed? But why would he do that? Surely he would wish to make a good impression on his English relatives? Unless… Mr Birch decided that the viscount would bear further investigation. It might just be that the American had been having a joke at his expense. Oh, dear, how very embarrassing that would be: the duke did not suffer fools gladly!

'Yes, of course,' Lady Ireland said, smiling at him. 'Do please sit down, sir. I had forgotten you for a moment, but you are welcome to join us. Hester, my dear, you would like tea, of course?'

'Yes, Godmother,' Hester replied, a slight smile on her lips. The heir had spirit, she thought with satisfaction. He might wear dreadful clothes and come out with some very strange phrases, but all in all, he wasn't anywhere near as bad as the lawyer had painted him. 'I shall join you in a cup of tea.' She refrained from saying that she often shared a glass of Madeira with her grandfather when they were alone.

She was about to get up to receive her cup from her god-mother, but Mr Clinton anticipated her. He was already on his feet, pouring the wine for Mr Birch and himself, but he left his own glass standing to pass her the tea. She noticed that he lifted his coat tails when he sat down, and the way he held his glass—and she noticed that his nails were short and very clean.

Something wasn't quite right here, Hester thought. Mr Birch had spoken of the heir as being ill mannered, badly educated and uncouth—but that did not describe the man now sitting on her godmother's chair. He had chosen a sub-stantial, square-seated, Chippendale elbow chair, which was one of the few up to his weight, and he looked very much at home. She had also noticed that his accent was missing when he asked the maid if he might help her. Why?

Why would he possibly be pretending to be something he wasn't? Hester's curiosity was aroused. If he had been an ill-educated man pretending to be a gentleman, she would have assumed it was because he wanted to impress his relatives and make sure of his inheritance when the duke died—but why pretend to be an ignorant oaf when he was, in fact, a gentleman?

Hester had no idea, but the slip had made her suspicious. If he were honest, he would not have tried to deceive them, therefore he must be up to something. She decided not to demand the truth at once. She would go along with his masquerade for the moment and see where it led them.

'You must call for me in the morning, sir,' she said, giving him a smile that was as innocent as it was false. 'We must begin to collect your wardrobe and I am sure we shall be pleased to show you something of the city—shall we not, Godmother?'

'I sure don't want to drag Lady Ireland all over the place,' Jared said, giving her a smile that set Hester's heart racing. 'Would it be proper for you to accompany me without your godmother's escort?'

'Well…' Hester saw a gleam in his eyes and realised he was testing her. 'If I were a young girl, I should say not, for we hardly know one another, but since I am nearly seven and twenty—and we are cousins—I see no harm in it, sir.'

He grinned at her then, and Hester's heart jerked. She knew he was feeling very pleased with himself and wondered just what she had let herself in for, but it would not have suited her pride to withdraw.

'I think we shall begin with a visit to Lock's,' she told him. 'The one thing a gentleman cannot do without is a supply of good hats.' She glanced down at his boots, which her expert eye recognised immediately as having been made by an expensive bootmaker, even if they had seen better days. She knew at once that her suspicions were correct. He was acting a part—but why?

'I bow to your superior judgement,' Jared replied without a trace of the awful accent. Hester looked into his eyes and knew that she had walked straight into his trap.

Chapter Two

'Well, what did you think of him?' Lady Ireland asked after their guest had left them. 'His clothes were awful, of course, but that isn't too much of a problem for you, Hester. He has an unfortunate habit of speech, but I dare say you may cure him of it in time—' She broke off as she saw the gleam of laughter in her goddaughter's eyes. 'What is so funny?'

'Did you not see through his act, dearest?' Hester asked. 'I am certain that that awful accent is assumed. He is pretending to be something he isn't, though I cannot say why he should wish to deceive us.'

'Pretending to be something he isn't…' Lady Ireland frowned. 'Well, yes, I can see why you think it, because in some ways he was very much the gentleman.' A look of annoyance entered her eyes. 'That is so ridiculous! Why would he do such a thing?'

'I am not sure,' Hester said, 'but I believe he has some personal agenda of his own and I dare say we shall discover it in time.'

'Why did you not challenge him if you thought it?' Lady Ireland was annoyed. 'I consider it to be most rude of him.'

'Yes, in a way,' Hester said. 'If he means it as a jest, then I suppose it is quite amusing—but if there is something more sinister…'

'Sinister?' Her godmother frowned. 'What reason could he possibly have that might be sinister?'

'He cannot know that Grandfather's health is precarious,' Hester replied. 'He need only wait a few months, a year or so at most—but perhaps he thinks there is more money waiting for him to inherit.'

'Oh, no! You cannot possibly think he…' Lady Ireland looked shocked. 'He did not appear to be a greedy, grasping sort of man, despite his odd manners. I believe he may be playing a practical joke on you, Hester, though I cannot see why he should wish to do such a foolish thing.'

'If it turns out merely to be a jest, I shall be relieved,' Hester said. She looked her godmother in the eyes. 'I have never been sure that my brother's death was an accident, and the fire last year may have been deliberate. If I am right and someone did try to kill Grandfather…'

'But surely…' Lady Ireland frowned at her. 'It could not have been Mr Clinton. He was in America.'

'We do not know that for sure. Besides, I dare say that he could have paid someone to do it.'

'No, no,' her godmother said. 'I cannot think so harshly of him, Hester. Even with that accent and those strange expressions, I quite liked him. I am usually thought to be a good judge of character, my dear.'

'Yes, I liked him too,' Hester said, a rueful smile on her soft mouth. 'But I shan't if he has come here to upset Grandfather!'

'You must not pass judgement too soon, Hester.' Lady Ireland smiled at her. 'Now, let us think of something else if you please. We are going to a soirée this evening, and I think I shall rest for an hour before I change. What do you plan to do, dearest?'

'I believe I shall change in an hour or so,' Hester told her. 'In the meantime, there is a letter I wish to write.'

'Then I shall leave you to amuse yourself.' Lady Ireland got to her feet. 'Do not be too anxious for your grandfather, my love. I think you will find that he is still able to take most things in his stride.'

Hester nodded, looking thoughtful. She went over to the pretty little writing desk that stood by the windows and sat down, taking paper from the top drawer and a quill from the enamelled tray. She dipped the nib in the ink and began to write, then stopped and frowned, screwing up the paper. She had thought she might write to Mr Grant, because he had seemed a very honest, sensible man when he came to visit, but something made her change her mind.

She frowned over her fresh sheet of paper. Lady Ireland was very kind, but she was not a gentleman, and Hester felt that she needed the support of a male relative. There was only one man she knew who might help her—her mother's cousin by marriage, Mr Richard Knighton.

Mr Knighton was a man of three and forty. Hester knew him well as he was the only male relative she had on her mother's side, and he had always taken an interest in her— at least he had been kind to her for the past few years. Mr Knighton was unmarried, an attractive, personable man, and she knew she would see him that evening. She returned the paper to the desk drawer and stood up. She would go into the garden for a few minutes, because she needed to think.

Jared looked at the evening clothes the hotel valet had prepared for him. He had spoken to the manager, asking him where he might find a gentleman's club that would accept him as a temporary member, somewhere he could spend an hour or two in company, and perhaps play a hand of cards if he chose. He was not a hardened gambler like his father, but he could enjoy a game of skill occasionally. He actually enjoyed a busy social life and had many friends both at home and abroad.

As a young man he had travelled to Europe, widening his experiences of the world and sowing his wild oats. At seven and thirty, he looked his years and perhaps more, for his face had the craggy appearance of a man who loved working outdoors. Despite his huge fortune, Jared was never happier than when he working hard at some physical task, and often chopped wood for the kitchen stove at his home. Yet he could add a long list of figures in his head without use of pen or paper, and he was well read in the classics and history, as well as taking a keen interest in the sciences. His one besetting sin was that he became bored easily, and he was already bored with staying in his hotel room. He wished that Red had been with him. Together, they would have found something to amuse themselves. As yet he had been disinclined to go far at night, for he was not one to drink alone, but his patience was at an end, and he could no longer remain cooped up like this—nor would he! So the hotel manager had recommended a gaming club at his request.

'It is not the quality of White's or Brooks's, sir,' he explained politely. The manager of the Cavendish was no fool and he was of the opinion that clothes did not always indicate a man's true worth, and a few gold guineas in his hand had told him that his guest was richer than he might appear. 'But it is frequented by gentlemen looking for something more…exciting. One word of warning, however—be careful not to play too deep, because there are a few sharks waiting for the unwary.'

'I thank you for your warning, though it is not necessary,' Jared said. 'My father was a gambling man on the Mississippi, sir, and he taught me a few tricks.'

'I thought you might be an American, sir,' the manager said, nodding his satisfaction. 'You have a slight accent, though it is not always discernible.'

'I dare say you have guests from all over the world,' Jared said. 'Perhaps even a titled gentleman now and then?'

'Oh, yes, quite often. They come here when they wish to be discreet, sir.'

'Would you have heard of Lady Ireland—or Miss Hester Sheldon?'

'I know the name of Sheldon, sir, though not the lady herself. I believe Viscount Sheldon may have been her father. He used to visit us occasionally, though the poor man has been dead some months now. I believe the old duke is unwell himself—Shelbourne, they call him as the head of the family. Tragic really—it must be hard to outlive all those sons and grandsons.'

'Yes, perhaps,' Jared replied. 'Thank you, you have been helpful.'

Jared's expression was thoughtful as he began to dress for the evening. The manager had not elaborated on the tragic deaths of his male relatives, but Jared had a feeling that there might be more to the story of tragedy in the family than was commonly known. Yet, as far as he could tell from what Mr Birch had told him, there wasn't much money in the family—at least by his standards. A couple of hundred acres of land and an ancient pile—surely not enough to kill off a succession of rivals?

Maybe they *had* all died from natural causes or from accidents. It was possible, of course—simply an unlucky family. He would take things as they came, keep his eyes and ears open just in case—but this evening he intended to enjoy himself. It was good to be wearing his own things again, to feel the superb fit of beautifully tailored clothes.

He wondered if he should put Miss Sheldon out of her misery and turn up decently dressed the next morning, but a little imp on his shoulder prompted him to leave her in the dark for a bit longer. Besides, he might just buy himself a few things while he was here; he had been using an English tailor for years, though he usually did his ordering in New York.

Of course it wasn't his first visit to London, though he hadn't told Mr Birch that—he had visited several times, the last just over a year previously. He hadn't stayed long, because he had been en route to Paris to sort out a problem with some business interests he had there. Not many people knew it, but he owned a chain of exclusive hotels, including ones in Paris and London, as well as several in America. He had chosen not to stay at his London hotel, because the staff knew him well, and it would not fit with his present image.

A smile played over Jared's rather sensual mouth. Compared to his cousin he might not be considered handsome, but he had something that appealed to ladies of all ages. He liked them and they knew it, which was why he could usually take his pick when he wished for female company. He had known many beautiful women, and counted some of them amongst his past mistresses, but there was something out of the ordinary about Miss Sheldon. He had to admit that her taste in dress was impeccable, though he would have liked to see her in brighter colours. Her gown that afternoon had been a soft dove grey, which suited her well, cut on simple lines, but with an elegance that told him it had been fashioned by an expert. She had been wearing a large and exquisite cameo set in gold at her bodice, but no other jewellery. It was strange that a girl like that, clearly intelligent and of good birth, should not be married or even engaged. Perhaps she was not inclined to marry, he thought, dismissing her from his mind as he went out to the cab the manager had summoned for him.

He would not think about her again this evening. He wanted male company, a glass or two of good wine and perhaps a pleasant game of cards...

'You are just the person I wanted to see,' Hester told Richard Knighton at about the same moment as Jared was setting out on his quest for some entertainment. 'I have a problem and I need someone to listen.'

'Delighted,' Knighton said, bestowing a smile of considerable warmth on her. 'Do you wish to retire to somewhere quieter—or shall I call on you at home?'

'I am staying with my godmother,' Hester told him. 'The London house has been closed since Papa died, as you know. I think it may be opened again soon, but it depends on the heir.'

'Ah, yes, I believe your mama mentioned him in her last letter.' Richard Knighton's grey eyes narrowed as he looked at her. 'You are surely not worried that he will displace you in the duke's affections? He would never see you left penniless.'

'No, it is not that,' Hester replied. 'Both Mama and I have a small allowance, and we could live in the dower house, though Mama says that if anything happens to the duke she will retire to Bath. She has friends who live there and we visit once a year, as you know.'

His gaze narrowed. 'You know that both your mother and you would be welcome to stay at my country home should you feel a need, Hester.'

'How kind you are,' she replied. 'I think I should come to you if I were in trouble, Richard—but I do not anticipate it. My godmother would love me to live with her, and Mama has many kind friends—but no, it is Grandfather I worry for, not myself.'

Richard's brow arched. 'I know his health is precarious, but there is no immediate concern, I believe?'

'No, at least I hope not,' she said. 'But I am afraid the American heir may not be…honest.'

'In what way?'

'Oh, I cannot tell you now, for my godmother is beckoning me to her,' Hester said. 'Will you call tomorrow for tea?'

'I should like that very much,' Knighton said and, taking her hand, bowed over it. 'And now I must leave you to the company of your friends, for I have another appointment. Expect me tomorrow, my dear. I shall look forward to it, as I always do.'

Hester nodded, watching as he walked away. She was glad she had chosen her mother's cousin as her confidant rather than Mr Stephen Grant. Mr Knighton was a man in his middle years and she felt at ease with him. Indeed, he had always been kind to them and, since her stepfather's death, had visited more frequently. She believed she could talk to him about the things that were worrying her.

It was late when Lady Ireland called for her carriage to take them home. She had met several of her close friends that evening, and, seeing that her goddaughter was in good company, had lingered beyond her normal hour. She glanced at Hester in the dim light inside the carriage.

'Did you enjoy yourself this evening, my dear?'

'Yes, it was a pleasant evening,' Hester replied. 'I always enjoy myself when I stay with you. I met several friends.'

'I saw you talking to Mr Carlton and Sir John Fraser,' Lady Ireland said. 'Sir John is such a pleasant gentleman, do you not think so?'

'Yes, I do,' Hester said. 'But so are Mr Carlton and Lord Havers.'

'Ah, yes, Lord Havers. The gossips say that he is about to propose to Miss Castle.'

'Yes, I have heard that, but I do not know if it is true,' Hester said. She glanced at her godmother in the poor light. 'It matters little one way or the other, because I do not wish to be married.'

'I have never understood that,' Lady Ireland said. 'Would you not enjoy being the mistress of your own home? Surely you must wish for a husband—and children?'

'Perhaps, I am not sure,' Hester told her and wrinkled her smooth brow. 'Had I been asked when I was eighteen, I might have said yes, but I have become settled in my ways. Mama cannot be bothered with the running of a large house these days. Papa's death left her feeling… delicate. Grandfather still orders the estate as much as he can, of course, but he leaves the house to me. It would be ungrateful of me to desert them, do you not agree?'

'As it happens, I do not agree,' her godmother told her. 'Your grandfather has enough servants to see to his comfort—and your mama could well do her share if she tried.'

'Yes, perhaps,' Hester agreed and laughed softly. 'But you see, I enjoy looking after them, and the house and the servants. It really isn't a trouble to me.' She glanced out of the window as they passed by a house from which a great deal of light was to be seen streaming into the street. It was, she supposed, one of the fashionable gaming houses that gentlemen liked to frequent. At that moment a gentleman was on the point of leaving, standing for a second or two in the full light of lanterns and a torch one of the links boys was holding aloft. She saw his face clearly, and noted the fact that he was fashionably dressed before the carriage swept by. 'Was that—?' She broke off as her godmother turned to her inquiringly. 'Did you see that gentleman just now?'

'Which particular gentleman?' Lady Ireland asked. 'We passed a rather noisy group of them a moment ago. Coming, I dare say, from that club we passed just now.'

'I thought it was Mr Clinton,' Hester said and frowned. 'It was a little odd.'

'He does look a little odd,' Lady Ireland admitted. 'But, as I said earlier, once you take him in hand he will do, Hester. I imagine he will pay for dressing.'

'Yes,' Hester agreed. She decided against telling her godmother that the man she had just seen needed no help from her. If it had been the heir—and she had seen him so briefly that she could not be certain—it meant that he was playing a deep game, as she had suspected. Was there something sinister about him? A shiver ran down her spine as she thought about the various accidents that had happened to the Sheldon family over the past few years. Supposing they were not accidents, but deliberate acts to bring about the situation that now existed? Could the American heir have been behind some of the accidents that had befallen her family?

Jared left the Carrick Club and began to walk in the direction of a hackney cab that had drawn up a short distance from the club. It was a pleasant night, the sky lit by a sprinkling of stars, and he might have been inclined to walk had he been certain of his way. As he was not well acquainted with this part of town, he thought it might be best to take advantage of the cabs that waited for paying passengers. His head was clear for he had drunk no more than a glass or two of wine, and he had spent an enjoyable few hours playing piquet for a few hundred guineas with some gentlemen he had met at the club, winning just slightly more than he lost. He was deep in thought, undecided whether to go on with his masquerade the next day, and it was only an ingrained instinct that warned him at the last moment.

Turning suddenly, he found himself confronted by a burly rogue armed with a stout cudgel. The man's arm was raised, as if he had been about to strike from behind. Jared acted to save himself, flinging himself at the rogue and catching his arm in a powerful grip that caused the other man to cry out in pain. Seconds later, the rogue found himself suddenly twisted off his feet and thrown head over heels, landing on his back on the hard pavement. He stared up at Jared, a dazed expression on his face as he struggled to understand what had happened to him.

'What did yer do that fer?' he asked in an aggrieved tone. 'I weren't doin' no 'arm.'

'I suppose you were not about to crack me over the head in the hope of stealing my purse?'

'Fair go,' the man whined as he struggled to his feet. 'I were only tryin' to earn an honest crust, me lord.'

'I do not think the watch would consider assault and robbery an honest way to earn your living, rogue.' Jared's gaze narrowed suspiciously. He had pulled a small pistol from his greatcoat pocket and held it cocked and ready. 'Or perhaps it wasn't money you were after?'

'He said I could keep whatever I found in your pockets,' the man stated, eyeing Jared's pistol nervously. 'You ain't goin' ter shoot me, are yer?'

'Give me one good reason why I shouldn't,' Jared said coldly. 'If you try to escape custody, I would be well within my rights to shoot you in the leg. Such wounds turn bad in prison and you might die there, alone and untended.'

'I might be of use to yer, me lord,' the man said, beads of sweat on his brow as he looked into Jared's eyes, because he didn't doubt that he would shoot if provoked. 'I could tell yer somethin' that might save yer life.'

'Indeed?' Jared's brows arched. 'Why should I believe anything you say?'

'It weren't yer purse he wanted,' the man said with a crafty leer. 'He wants yer dead, me lord.'

'Who wants me dead?'

'I don't rightly know his name, sir—but I could tell yer where he lives when he's in town. He thought 'e had me fooled, but Harris Tyler knows a thing or two about fooling hisself.'

'You are saying that someone paid you to crack me over the head?'

'That be the truth of it, me lord. He said he didn't care how I did it, but I was to kill yer ternight.'

'And how did you know who you were to kill?' Jared wasn't sure whether to believe his tale. 'Where did you meet this man?'

'A gentleman, he were, me lord, just like you. He came looking fer me at the Crown and King in Cheapside; it's where I hang out, see—and he told me there were twenty guineas in it if I done you in.'

'He gave you my name?'

'No, me lord, just took me to your hotel. We followed you here, sir. He told me to wait until you came out, as you'd likely be two parts to the wind and easy prey.'

'He did, did he?' Jared frowned. 'Did he give you your money, rogue?'

'No, sir. He said he would come to the Crown and King termorrow at eight of the evenin', and give it me then.'

'And yet you know where he lives?'

'I know where he went after he left me 'ere,' the man said. 'I followed 'im, see—I like to know things about a cove who offers me money to do murder—but I can't swear to it that it were 'is house. There were others comin' and goin'.'

'Possibly a house party,' Jared said. 'Well, Tyler, if that is your name. I think you had better take me to the house, and then we'll see. As you said, it is possible that you might be of use to me, but we should get one thing clear from the start. I may use you, and I may pay you if you serve me well—but I make a bad enemy. I would not advise you to get any ideas about double crossing me.'

A shudder went down Harris Tyler's spine as he looked into the icy eyes of his former victim. 'If I'd known what manner of man yer were, me lord, I wouldn't 'ave tried nothin'…cross me 'eart and swear to die.'

Jared smiled. 'I doubt you have a heart, Tyler—but if you don't want to die, keep faith with me.'

'It's me missus and the little 'uns,' Tyler whined. 'Sick she's been and no money for the doctor.'

'And I was born yesterday,' Jared replied in a pleasant tone that belied the threat beneath. 'I'm giving you one chance, Tyler—and you can start by telling me anything you can about this man, and by showing me where this house is.'

'Well, sir, I did notice one thing when his head was turned from me, sir. He has a small scar behind his left ear. You can't see it most of the time, but his hair was tied with a bow, and when he turned his head I saw it for a moment.'

'A scar behind his left ear?' Jared studied his face. Was he inventing the scar—had he invented the whole story? For the moment he would go along with it, because there were only a handful of people who knew he was in

London. A rogue attacking him in the hope of robbing him was one thing, but a mysterious man who had paid for him to be murdered was quite another.

Hester sat at her dressing table, brushing her hair. It was thick and reached to the small of her back when she let it loose from the strict confines to which she habitually consigned it. With her hair loosely waving, and in the soft light of the candles, Hester looked younger than she was, a wistful expression in her eyes as she stared unseeingly at her reflection.

It was very strange that she had been on the point of writing to Mr Grant earlier that day, she thought, and wondered what had brought him to town. She had discovered his letter waiting for her in the hall on their return that evening. It was a very proper letter, informing her that he was in town for a matter of a few days and would be happy to be of service to her in any way he could. She had only to send for him, because he was staying at the Carrick and would call on her before he left town. She would reply to it in the morning, but for the moment she was not certain what she ought to say to him. Would it be proper of her to discuss her worries concerning the heir?

She had no such doubts about talking to Mr Knighton, because she trusted him to keep her confidence, and she had known him for most of her life. She did not know Mr Grant well, and though he seemed sincere, he might not be the best person to speak to about Mr Clinton. After all, should anything happen to the American, he would be the next in line to inherit. Mr Knighton, on the other hand, had nothing to gain from such a tragic occurrence.

Hester closed her eyes, determined to put it all from her mind. Lying here worrying would not help her. She would spend the morning with the American heir. If he continued with his masquerade, she would ask him why he was trying to deceive her.

Hester was ready and waiting when Jared arrived the next morning. She noticed that he had abandoned the ill-fitting clothes he had been wearing the previous day. His coat was a little shabby, but she could not doubt that it had been tailored by an expert; his boots were old, but discernibly of good quality, and his breeches fitted him well. His shoulders were broad, his body lean and strong looking, his face attractive rather than handsome. She decided that her godmother had been right—he would pay for dressing.

'Well, sir, are you ready to be fitted for the outfits you will need if you are to be introduced into society?' Her eyes challenged him, meeting his so boldly that he was momentarily startled. He could almost think that she had seen through his disguise—and yet how could she?

'I am not sure that I can afford to patronise the best tailors,' he prevaricated, knowing that he might be recognised at some of them.

'You must have good hats and boots,' Hester said. 'Besides, Grandfather has opened an account for you at his bank. You may spend what you wish within reason. He will make you an allowance for other things once you have settled on a proper sum between you, but you must have a decent wardrobe.'

'Must I?' Jared's eyebrows rose. What he had learned from Tyler the previous evening had put him on his mettle. If the man were to be believed, his life was in danger, and that meant he could trust no one—perhaps even this woman might be other than she seemed. 'Well, I do need a decent hat, so perhaps we should visit the haberdasher you mentioned.'

'Lock's are not merely haberdashers,' Hester repri-
manded him with a sparkling look. 'They are *the* hat
makers, Mr Clinton. No one who is anyone would dream
of going anywhere else.'

'Indeed?' A look of mockery came to his eyes. 'I have
plenty of good hats at home that did not come from that
particular establishment.'

'Indeed?' Hester looked at the battered example he had
taken off as they met. 'If that is so, one wonders why you
did not bring them with you?'

'Ah…' Jared smothered a laugh. She had him there. He
had spoken too hastily. 'Perhaps I should say that I had
plenty of hats once.'

'You were once in the position of being able to live
decently, I believe?' Hester said. 'Mr Birch gave us only
sketchy details, Mr Clinton—but we have been told that
you lost everything gambling?'

'Yes, most of what I had,' Jared agreed, keeping a
bland expression as he lied. 'I still have a small property
back home.'

'Yes, well, Grandfather isn't rich either,' Hester told
him. 'He has some property and the land. Unfortunately,
his sons and grandsons were mostly gamblers, including
my father.'

'Do you think it right that I should take the duke's money
for clothes?' Jared asked, his expression giving nothing
away. 'No point in pretending to be what I ain't—is there?'

'I am not at liberty to confide my grandfather's plans
for you,' Hester said with a frown. 'I do know that you
must be presentable if you are to succeed in the best
circles in English society.'

'I'm not sure I wish to succeed. In fact, I wasn't
planning to stay around long enough to meet your society
friends, Miss Sheldon.'

'Oh but you must,' Hester cried. 'If you don't… Grand-father is relying on you, sir. Surely you want your inheritance? It is not as much as it might have been, but it is still considerable and it might—' She stopped and shook her head. 'No, it isn't for me to say.'

'But you are privy to his plans, aren't you?'

Hester felt her cheeks becoming warm under his scrutiny. 'It would be quite wrong of me to disclose anything he may have told me.'

Jared sat down, crossing his long legs in front of him. He gave her a direct look. 'I have plenty of time, Miss Sheldon.'

'Really, we must go. I have taken the liberty of making an appointment for you to be fitted. It would be most rude of us to be late.'

'I don't think I should go anywhere until you tell me exactly what the old man is expecting of me.'

Hester looked at his stubborn face and sighed inwardly. If she had harboured any doubts that he was truly the heir, they fled. She had seen that look in her stepfather's eyes, and often in the duke himself.

'It is Grandfather's hope that you will marry to advantage. The family needs new money to restore it to its proper place in society.'

'Damn the old devil!' Jared's eyes gleamed with sudden anger. 'So that is why he summoned me and dragged you into this business! He wants me to marry an heiress.'

'Well, yes, I suppose that is what he wants—what the family needs,' Hester said reluctantly. 'You weren't brought up here and so you may not understand what your heritage means, but it is respect and family values—' She stopped as she saw his expression. 'What? Why are you so angry? It is no more than happens in many families of this kind.'

'Family values?' Jared said in an icy tone. 'Where were they when he cut my mother out of his life? She wrote to him when I was born and afterwards. Her letters were never answered—can you imagine how much that hurt her? Do not preach to me about the family, Miss Sheldon. As far as I am concerned, I have no family—at least none in this country.'

Hester stared at him, her face pale. 'Then why did you come? Why did you raise our hopes? If you had no intention of helping us restore the family fortunes, why not simply tell Birch that you wished to cut the connection?'

Jared got up. He had been wondering about that himself for the past several minutes. He went over to the window, staring out at the garden, his back rigid with anger as he considered his answer.

'Curiosity, I suppose. I wondered what kind of a man could cut his daughter out of his life simply because she ran away with the man she loved.'

'Grandfather loved her,' Hester said, and there was a little sob in her voice, because she knew how badly the duke would take this disappointment. 'I suppose his pride wouldn't let him answer her letters, but I know he still loves her.'

'Sure of that, are you?' Jared rounded on her, his eyes dark with anger, his mouth set in a thin line. 'What makes you such an expert? She certainly didn't know it, if you do.'

'Grandfather is proud,' Hester defended him, her face pale, her eyes carrying an unconscious appeal. 'Sometimes he says and does things that he doesn't mean—but that does not make him a bad man. He has always been loving and generous to me…' A single tear slipped from the corner of her eye, trickling down her cheek. She tasted its salt, but she made no attempt to brush it away or the others that silently followed. 'He is an old man, Mr Clinton. He doesn't have long to live. Please, I beg you, won't you at least humour him for a while? No one can force you to marry an heiress, but if you would just let Grandfather believe there is hope…for a while…'

Jared was standing over her now, his eyes blazing. He was furious that she could ask such a thing of him. What right had she or any of them to ask anything of him? She had none and he was determined to punish her, to punish them all for what they had done to his mother. Hardly knowing what he did, not thinking at all, he reached out, gripping her by her arms, gazing down at her. He pulled her to her feet. Looking into her eyes, he felt something stir inside him, and, without understanding why, he lowered his head, his mouth touching hers.

He hadn't meant to kiss her, had not realised how it would feel when he did, the fire that shot through him so unexpected that he reacted instinctively. His mouth possessed hers thoroughly, his tongue seeking access, forcing her to open to him by sheer willpower, slipping inside to explore her sweetness. She tasted like honey and wine, intoxicating. He felt his control slipping. He was inflamed by the taste and scent of her, the way her pliant body seemed to melt against him. She might have rejected him had she chosen, pushed him away, but she didn't, allowing the kiss to go on for as long as he chose, looking at him in a dazed manner as he finally drew away from her. Her eyes were wide, hazy with passion and startled, as though she had never been kissed—but of course she must have been.

'I should not have done that,' he said as sanity returned. 'I was angry, but my mother's unhappiness was not of your making.'

Hester touched a finger to her lips. She had made no

protest while he kissed her and she made none now. 'I am very sorry that your mother was unhappy, Mr Clinton. I think Grandfather loved her better than any other of his children, and I know that Papa often spoke of her. I am sure that he did not know her letters had been rejected.'

'As I said, it wasn't your fault—but I cannot forget what she suffered.'

'Was she not happy with her husband and you?'

'Oh, she was happy most of the time,' Jared said. 'She loved Pa and he loved her—but thinking of the past made her cry.'

'That does not mean she was unhappy,' Hester said. 'I cry sometimes when I think of people I love. Especially John. He was my brother and he died in a riding accident when he was sixteen.' Her eyes darkened with emotion. 'He was such a good rider. I have never understood how it happened.'

'You think it might not have been an accident?' Jared asked, his gaze narrowing as he saw the indecision in her face. 'You have your suspicions, I think?'

'Yes…though I have no idea who would want to kill John,' Hester admitted. 'He wasn't even the heir then. Papa was still alive.'

'I have been told that the Sheldon family is cursed,' Jared said. 'I think that is nonsense, don't you?'

'Yes…but John believed it,' Hester said and frowned. 'He told me the story once. It is very tragic and perhaps there was a curse laid on us many years ago, but I do not believe that it killed them all.'

'You mean your uncles and cousins? You aren't sure they died of natural causes either, are you?'

'I don't know…' Hester looked up at him. 'Who would want them dead?'

'Someone who could not inherit until they were?'

'What do you mean?' Her eyes widened. 'But you…no, I do not believe it.'

'But you cannot help wondering, can you?' Jared said, a glint in his eyes. 'Has it crossed your mind that I might have had them killed so that I could inherit?'

Hester stared at him, because something of the kind had been in her thoughts, but he was so angry…so proud. Her instinct told her that she ought to trust him; it would be unfair to suspect him of anything so evil.

'I do not know what to think,' she said. 'So many deaths… No! I cannot believe you capable of that, sir. I do know that you have tried to deceive us into thinking you something you are not…that awful accent…' She gave a choke of laughter. 'Did you really imagine it would work, Mr Clinton?'

Jared stared at her in stony silence for a moment and then he grinned. 'Well, damn my eyes if the little girl ain't rumbled me.'

'I do not think there is much I can teach you in the way of manners, for your mother will have done that when you were a boy,' Hester said. 'But I might be of use to you in other ways—we do have some odd customs here, you know. If you were prepared to give Grandfather a little of your time, I would be pleased to help in any way I could. And there are other things. I could teach you to dance, perhaps?'

'Maybe,' Jared said, smothering a desire to laugh. 'I dare say there are things I need to know about the family.'

'Anything you wish to know, of course.'

'Well, you could start by telling me who visited this house last evening.'

'Last evening?' Hester frowned. 'We were out for the evening, but someone did leave his calling card. His name is Mr Stephen Grant—he is a distant relation. Grandfather's great-nephew I suppose, once removed.'

'What exactly does that mean?'

'The duke had a half-brother—the son of his father's second wife, and Mr Grant is that half-brother's grandson.'

'I'm not sure how things work over here,' Jared said. 'As things stand, I am the duke's heir, right—but what happens if I die?'

'Well, I suppose Mr Grant would inherit everything. He is Grandfather's only other male relative.' Hester looked at the way his mouth had thinned. 'May I ask why?'

'You may ask, but for the moment I shall not answer,' Jared said. 'I'm not sure about anything.' His brow furrowed. 'When are we going down to the duke's estate?'

'As soon as you have your clothes,' Hester said. 'If you wish, of course?'

'As it happens, I don't think I have much choice,' Jared replied, all trace of the twang gone. His expression was serious, his eyes a deep blue-green. 'I have something to do here, Miss Sheldon. I am not sure where it will take me, and I am not sure of my motives for doing it—but for the moment I am happy to go along with things as you had planned.'

'You mean you will humour Grandfather for a while?'

'You could put it that way.'

Hester nodded. 'In that case, we could go and buy you a new hat—unless you do not think it necessary? And you will need clothes for the ball…dancing shoes, perhaps?'

'I am perfectly happy to buy a new hat in your company,' Jared said offering her his arm. 'I shall make my own arrangements about paying for it—but I expect you to keep that part of it to yourself.'

'All I ask is that you give us a chance to welcome you to your family, sir.'

'Is that really all you ask, Miss Sheldon?' Jared's smile was challenging. 'Don't you really expect me to marry an heiress so that I can repair the damage caused by the fire last year?'

'You know about that?' Hester's smooth brow furrowed. 'Mr Birch has exceeded his duty.'

'Mr Birch did not breathe a word other than as he was instructed,' Jared said. 'I have my own ways of finding out the truth, as someone else may discover to their peril before too long.'

Hester stared at him, feeling uneasy once more. This man ran very deep, she sensed it, sensed the underlying menace, the core of steel. She knew that there was much more to him than she had ever imagined—and she'd never dreamed he would have kissed her so wonderfully—but could she trust him?

Chapter Three

Hester said goodbye to Mr Clinton at the door of her godmother's house. She had spent a very pleasant morning at
the establishment of one of the finest gentlemen's hat
makers. The heir had purchased four hats: one for morning
wear, one for afternoon wear, one for evening and one for
riding. He had asked for the account to be sent to him at
his hotel and she had no idea how much had been spent,
though it must have cost him some guineas. It seemed that
he was not destitute, as Mr Birch had assumed, though
perhaps not as rich as they had once thought him.

He had been everything that was charming, showing
himself to have perfect manners as he escorted her about
the town, and Hester had been happy to introduce him to
three ladies and two gentlemen who stopped to speak to
them in the street. It had actually given her pleasure to introduce him as her grandfather's heir, using the title he
himself refused to accept.

'People will be curious about you,' she told him after
they had made their purchases and were walking home. 'I
think you will find that you receive many invitations after
Grandfather's ball—if you stay for that, of course.'

'You are fishing, Miss Sheldon,' Jared told her, his expression somewhere between amusement and annoyance. 'I shall stay for a few weeks, perhaps, longer than I had first thought—there, will that content you?'

'Yes, for the moment,' she said, crossing her fingers behind her back because she hoped that he could not read her mind. She knew how much the duke was hoping that he would make his home in England, and if there were some way to persuade him to stay, she would do her best to find it. She glanced in the window at some pretty bonnets as they passed a fashionable milliner's shop, but said nothing, though one in particular had taken her eye. 'When would it suit you to go down to the country, sir?'

'In the morning, if that would not spoil your own plans, Miss Sheldon?'

'My plans?' Hester frowned. 'I had planned to accompany you for reasons which I need not go into now—but you do not need my help, sir. I could stay here for a few days longer.'

'You would oblige me by keeping me company,' Jared told her. 'I prefer not to travel alone just at the moment.'

'You are not unwell, I hope?'

'I am perfectly well, though someone did their best to alter that situation last night as I left a gambling club, to which I was introduced by my hotel manager.'

Hester stopped walking and stared at him. 'Someone attacked you? Were you hurt? I do not understand—had you won a significant amount at the tables, enough to make it worthwhile robbing you?'

'You assume that the motive was robbery? Yes, perhaps—it might have been, of course,' he said.

'But what else can it have been?' Hester was puzzled. 'It could not be anything else.' Her expression was thoughtful. 'I know there have been deaths in the family that would bear further investigation, but how could anyone know you were here? I do not think that anyone other than Mr Birch, my mother, Grandfather and I even knew you had arrived until this morning, when I introduced you to some of my acquaintances.'

'Supposing someone did know,' Jared said, his eyes intent on her face. Either she was genuinely shocked or she was a very good actress. 'Do you think they may have wanted to kill me?'

'But who?' Hester shook her head. 'Why should anyone wish to... You do not think that Mr Stephen Grant...? No, I cannot think it. He is a man of the cloth and above worldly concerns.'

'He would inherit an estate and a title. Some people might think that worth committing murder for, might they not?'

'Not Mr Grant,' Hester replied in a tone of conviction. 'Besides, how would he have known you were here in London? You have never seen or spoken to him in your life. Surely the attack on you was random?'

'It may have been,' Jared said, deciding that it was too soon to trust her with more details. 'But you see why I would prefer not to travel alone just at the moment?'

'Yes, I do see,' she agreed. 'My godmother will send me home in her carriage. I shall have my maid and the grooms— and of course you will be welcome to travel with me.'

'I do not have any means of transport,' Jared told her. 'I could hire a horse, of course, but as I have no idea where to go...'

'No, of course you don't,' Hester said. 'What am I thinking of? Certainly I shall come with you. I thought you might have preferred to go alone, but I am happy to accompany you.'

It had been her plan in the first place, but Lady Ireland had begged her to stay longer, and it would have been pleasant, for with the heir staying at Shelbourne her grand-father would not need her as much. A visit to London was a rare treat for her, but in the circumstances she could do no other than agree—and perhaps it was for the best after all. She might find some means of persuading him to stay longer than he planned.

She took off her hat as she went into the hall, stopping to look through the pile of notes awaiting her and Lady Ireland. Picking them up, she took them through to the small salon at the rear of the house and gave them to her godmother. Lady Ireland glanced through them and then picked one out.

'This is for you, dearest.'

'Oh, I did not see it,' Hester said. 'It must have got caught in with yours. I think it is from Richard Knighton.' She broke the wax seal and frowned. 'Oh, this was written before I saw him last night. It must have been here when we returned last evening. It was just a note to say he looked forward to seeing us later.' She frowned as she slipped it into a pocket. 'Mr Clinton has asked me to go down with him to the country, ma'am. I had thought I might stay another day or two with you, but I cannot refuse.'

'Well, I dare say he feels it will be more comfortable at the duke's house with at least one person he knows,' Lady Ireland said. 'He may not be quite as awful as we feared, but I expect he does not go much into company—at least, not the kind your grandfather keeps.'

'Perhaps,' Hester said. Something was at the back of her mind, some small thing that she ought to remember, but she could not for the life of her recall what it was…

Hester was sitting in the parlour with her godmother when Mr Knighton was announced. He smiled as he entered, going first to Lady Ireland and kissing her hand.

She invited him to sit on the chair next to her and kept him busy with questions about his family until the tea tray was brought in.

'Your sister is well, Mr Knighton?'

'Maria is recovering from the birth of her third son,' he replied. 'I believe she is well in herself, though perhaps a little tired.'

'I should like to have seen her,' Hester told him. 'However, I leave town in the morning. Perhaps another time.'

'Mrs Tremayne would love to see you,' he assured her. 'She begged me to ask you to dinner tomorrow evening. She will be sorry that you are leaving so soon.'

'I fear I must,' Hester said. 'But I shall write to her in a few days, and perhaps we shall meet soon. She may wish to come to Grandfather's ball.'

'The duke plans a ball?' Richard Knighton frowned. 'I thought he was quite the recluse these days?'

'He has not entertained much since Papa…' Hester felt the familiar tightness in her chest, for she sincerely mourned her stepfather. 'However, as I told you last evening, the American heir has come to visit. It is for his sake that the duke intends to entertain his friends with a ball.'

'This American,' Richard said, frowning, 'what manner of a man is he?'

'I would say perfectly respectable, if not quite a gentleman,' Lady Ireland said before Hester could reply. 'He looks the part and his manners are polite—but his speech leaves something to be desired.' She glanced at Hester. 'Would you not agree, dearest?'

Hester hesitated. She had invited her mother's cousin to call with the intention of asking him to meet the heir and give her his opinion, but for some reason she was disinclined to speak freely.

'He does have some unfortunate expressions,' Hester said. 'I think him a little…deceptive.'

'You suspect that he is an impostor?'

'No, that is not what I meant,' Hester said thoughtfully. 'It is just that I am not certain he is what he seems to be—though there is no doubt that he is Amelia's son. There is a family resemblance, and his credentials have been checked. I believe Amelia wrote to her father several times after she was married.'

'No doubt she hoped to be forgiven. I dare say her son is rather pleased with himself. He could not have expected to inherit both a title and a large estate.'

'I am not sure that he wishes for either,' Hester replied. She did not know why, but something in Richard's tone displeased her. 'After all, there is very little money.'

'The house and land could be sold for a fair sum,' Richard said. 'The duke should be careful. He might do well to consult his lawyers, in order to be certain that the estate cannot simply be sold off after his death, and the money taken overseas.'

'There is an entail,' Hester said. 'If it had been otherwise…but as long as there is a direct heir, it cannot be broken without a huge payment.'

'If the American is the last in the line, I dare say he could do as he pleased with the estate.'

'But he is not the only heir,' Hester replied. 'I did not realise it until quite recently. Grandfather has another male relative—the grandson of his half-brother.'

'You have never mentioned the gentleman before?' Richard's eyebrows rose.

'Grandfather quarrelled with his half-brother many years ago. He had nothing to do with the family, but Mr Grant wrote to him a few months ago. He has visited us, and is a gentleman of the cloth.'

'That alters things,' Richard said. 'At least the American heir cannot sell the estate and take the money back to his home.'

'I think Grandfather would be very distressed if that happened,' Hester said and frowned. It had not occurred to her that something like that might be on the cards. 'No, I am certain he would not, even if…'

'Well, we must hope that it will not happen,' Richard said. 'It is most unfair that you cannot inherit, Hester. You have been a constant support to the duke for years. Such a sacrifice should be rewarded.'

'I do not consider it as such,' Hester replied. 'Grandfather has given me love, and as much as he could afford in the material way; it is my pleasure to do what I can for him. I know that he has often expressed a wish that I…but of course it could not be. Do not forget that, though I call the duke Grandfather, I am not truly of his blood—as you well know, sir.'

'I do not forget that your mother married for a second time after you were born,' Knighton told her. 'It is for your sake that I wish things were otherwise, Hester. You love Shelbourne so much, and when the duke dies you may have to leave.'

'I know that,' Hester said, unable to hide the pain his words had caused her.

Lady Ireland picked up her gold-handled lorgnette and stared at him through it, her manner a little frosty. 'As you may know, sir, I have no children of my own. I had a son, but he was killed in Spain…' For a moment her voice throbbed with emotion. 'But I do not speak of it. I love Hester as if she were a daughter, and she will always have a home with me, and when I die…' She smiled fondly at her goddaughter. 'Well, she will not be left penniless, let us put it that way.' Diamonds flashed on her hands as she moved them in some agitation, for she had seen that Hester was distressed and it moved her.

'Please, ma'am,' Hester said, 'you will not speak of such things. You are a fit, healthy woman and have years left to you.'

'Yes, indeed I do,' Lady Ireland said warmly. 'But it is well that you should know, Hester—and it may help to set Mr Knighton's mind at rest concerning your future.'

'As to that, ma'am, I am sure Miss Sheldon has many friends to care for her,' he said. 'But it is good to know that she has such a staunch one in you.' He smiled at her and then turned his gaze to Hester. 'I believe Miss Sheldon knows that I have a warm regard for her. I merely speak to set her mind at rest if she should be asked to leave her home.'

Hester felt her cheeks growing warm. She had thought of Mr Knighton as a man she could turn to for help, but had seen him as nothing more than a friend; now she suspected that his feelings might be deeper than she imagined. She found it embarrassing; though she liked him very well, she had not entertained the idea of anything more than friendship. In that moment she made up her mind that she would not confide her doubts concerning Mr Clinton in him.

She skilfully turned the conversation to a discussion about the Prince Regent's latest ball, and how hot it always was at the pavilion in Brighton.

'Mama took me there the year before Papa...' Her voice caught. 'Do you not think it beautiful in some strange way? I know it is fashionable to decry the prince's dreadful taste, but I found it rather endearing; he dotes on the place, you know.'

'You are generous to a fault,' Mr Knighton said and stood up. 'I think I have stayed long enough, ladies. I must leave you now for I have another appointment.'

'I shall come with you to the door,' Hester said and stood up. In the hall she offered her hand. 'It was so good of you to call, sir. I shall be sorry to miss your sister's dinner.'

'She will be sorry not to have seen you, Hester. You know that she is very fond of you—as I am, my dear friend.'

'Thank you, you are very kind,' Hester said as he held her hand for a moment too long. She withdrew it gently, unwilling to offend him, but not wishing to give the wrong impression. 'I know I can always rely on you if I need assistance.'

'I am glad that you do know it. I was under the impression that you wished to tell me something about the heir?' He flicked an invisible speck from the sleeve of his immaculate coat, his manner deliberately casual.

'It was only that he had visited us,' Hester replied untruthfully. 'He seems pleasant enough, though it is early days yet.'

'Remember that I shall stand your friend whatever happens,' he said, lingering for a moment as if he were undecided. 'I may call on the duke soon, and your dear mama. You will not be displeased by the visit?'

'No, of course not,' she replied. 'You must know that Mama and Grandfather are always pleased to see you— as I am, of course.'

He smiled and took his hat from the hall table. 'Until the next time, Hester.'

After he had gone, she stood for a moment in the hall, her expression thoughtful. His manner had seemed different that afternoon. Was she imagining it, or was he implying that he hoped for a closer relationship between them? Surely not! He was her mother's cousin by marriage and considerably older than Hester. She had never even considered… No, it was impossible! Her instincts were at fault here. Mr Knighton had never previously given her any reason to expect a proposal of marriage. She had misread the signs. She must dismiss the foolish idea at once.

Her godmother looked up as she returned to the small salon where she was seated. She was toying with a silver-gilt vinaigrette, which had a beautifully fretted interior to hold the scented sponge in place.

'My late husband bought me this,' Lady Ireland said, placing it back on the little table where several similar trinkets lay within her reach. 'I think Mr Knighton means to make you an offer, Hester—shall you accept him?'

'No! Pray do not say it,' Hester replied and frowned. 'Did you truly think it, ma'am?'

'He was most particular, and the way he looked at you seemed to indicate a preference, my dear. Have you not noticed a change in his manner toward you of late?'

'Well…' Being an honest girl, Hester could not deny it. 'I did wonder…but surely he could not be thinking of it? He is so much older and he is my mother's cousin.'

'The relationship is not close enough to preclude the possibility of a match, Hester. Though I do not as a rule approve of marriage between cousins, you are far enough removed for it to be thought allowable. However, I should be sorry if you married Mr Knighton.'

'Would you, ma'am?' Hester was surprised, for her godmother had often tried to persuade her to think of marriage. 'Why?'

'I dare say he is a decent gentleman, but I believe you could do better, my love—if you wished.'

'As you know, I have no intention of it,' Hester replied. 'If Mr Knighton asked, I should refuse him; I hope he will not, for it might sour our friendship.'

'Yes, that would be a pity,' her godmother said. 'Well,

I dare say he may think better of it. He must know that you are devoted to the duke and your mama.'

'Yes, I am certain he does,' Hester replied, but for some reason she felt an icy tingle at the nape of her neck. 'It would be most uncomfortable if he were to ask me, as I should certainly say no.'

'Perhaps he won't,' Lady Ireland said. 'I have been thinking that I should like to give you a little gift, Hester. Would you like the opal-and-diamond brooch that my husband gave me when we first married—or would you prefer the pearl bangle my mother gave me when I was sixteen?'

'You should not consider parting with either of them,' Hester told her. 'I have no need of gifts, ma'am.'

'You do not have much in the way of jewels,' Lady Ireland said. 'I think I shall give them both to you—and do not say no, for it would distress me. I like to give presents, and you are dearer to me than anyone these days.'

'You are so kind to me!' Hester went to kiss her. 'I am sure that I have done nothing to deserve such wonderful gifts.'

'Please do not be embarrassed. I had not meant to say anything, but Mr Knighton…well, he annoyed me. You are my heir, Hester. I have left small bequests to others, but you will inherit my estate. I am not outrageously rich, but you know that I have a very comfortable life—and you will too. I have said nothing about an allowance before this, for you live under the duke's roof, but if the worst should happen, I shall see to it that both your mother and you are comfortable.'

'You will make me cry,' Hester said, her eyes stinging at this further proof of her godmother's generosity. 'I can only thank you sincerely on behalf of my mother and myself.'

'You will say nothing to her,' Lady Ireland said. 'Indeed,

I should have said nothing to you for the moment, but Mr Knighton made me aware that you might be anxious.'

'Grandfather has already set up small trust funds for us both,' Hester said. 'He wished he might have given us more, but the entail prevents it and it is only what he has saved from his income that he may give freely. However, Papa left Mama a little money. In this instance, I mean my own father.'

'Yes…' Lady Ireland frowned. 'It surprises me that you were not left more, Hester. I would have thought Sir Peter would have made more provision for his only child.'

'If he did, I have heard nothing of it,' Hester said and shook her head. 'I do not think we shall starve, dearest Godmother. You must not worry about me.'

'Oh, I do not,' Lady Ireland said. 'I am certain you could marry if you chose, my love—and to someone far more deserving than Mr Knighton.'

Hester made no reply. She was surprised that her godmother should make her dislike of him so plain. She had never spoken of him in this manner before and it was a little strange that she should do so now.

'Well, we may be wrong in assuming that he intends to make me an offer, ma'am. I think I shall go upstairs and change as you have guests coming this evening, and I need to make certain that Anna has packed my trunk.'

'Yes, I shall go up myself after I have written a letter,' Lady Ireland said, smiling at her. 'Tell the duke that I shall be pleased to come and stay for his ball if he invites me.'

'Oh, I am certain he will,' Hester said and went out.

She was thoughtful as she went upstairs. She had never thought of it before, but it was a little odd that her father had not left her at least a small bequest. His fortune had not been large, of course, but it was surprising that he had left nothing to her. Not that it mattered. She was content as she was.

* * *

'Mr Clinton…' The lawyer got to his feet with alacrity and came round the large mahogany partner's desk, extending his hand. 'An unexpected pleasure. Should I have been expecting you?'

'Mr Roth, good to see you.' Jared shook his hand warmly. They had done business many times in the past and he knew he could trust his discretion. 'No, I didn't write because I was here on other business—but now I have something I want you to look into, if you will?'

'Yes, certainly, sir—a property, perhaps?'

'It is rather more complicated,' Jared said and sat down in the beautiful elbow chair provided for him. 'First of all I must explain something to you, and then you will understand why this needs discretion.'

'Oh, of course, sir. You know we are always very close-mouthed about matters of business.'

'You may not be aware that I am the Duke of Shelbourne's heir,' Jared said and saw astonishment in the other man's eyes. 'I do not wish to be addressed by my title, and it makes no difference to our business, sir. I tell you this only because I think it possible that my life and that of the old duke may be in some danger.'

'Good grief! Are you saying that you think someone wants to murder you? But surely…the inheritance is nothing to your own fortune?'

'My heir at the moment is my American cousin,' Jared said. 'My will provides for him and some other beneficiaries—but takes no account of the English connection. I am not sure what happens to that in the event of my death, though I understand there is another heir after me—a Mr Stephen Grant. I have been told he is a man of the cloth. Of course, there is also Miss Hester Sheldon. She is a cousin, too, but unable to inherit, I imagine, while there is a male relative alive?'

'Yes, that would be pretty much the size of it,' Jacob Roth agreed. 'I know the name, of course, sir—but little of the family. What is it you wish me to do for you?'

'I need a reliable agent to trace Mr Stephen Grant. I want to know what manner of man he is—whether he is in debt, what ambitions he has…'

'Yes, I see. He would be the natural suspect, I suppose.'

Jared nodded thoughtfully. 'There may be others who wish me dead for reasons unconnected with the duke's estate, of course. A wealthy man sometimes acquires enemies along the way without realising it. I can give your agent some details, which I have written here. I need an investigation as swiftly as you can arrange it. I also wish to know if there is anyone else who might have an interest in the estate—anyone distantly related.'

'Yes, of course.' His lawyer frowned. 'Have you taken steps to protect yourself, sir?'

'I think I am well able to handle this business for the moment,' Jared replied. 'If it is the other heir, he must be careful, for he would surely be the first to be suspected.'

'And Miss Sheldon?'

Jared frowned. 'I believe she is above suspicion, but I shall be wary until this matter is settled.'

'Have you considered that your relatives may be interested in your fortune, sir? I am aware that some of these old families consider themselves to be special, but many of them have not a tenth of your revenues, Mr Clinton.'

'I dare say they might,' Jared agreed. 'But they could not benefit from my death. This seems to be to do with the English family, and I believe it may have been going on for a while before I arrived.'

'That sounds ominous, sir.'

'Yes, it may be—though of course the others could have died from natural causes or in accidents, but there were three brothers and three other grandsons.'

Mr Roth pursed his lips in a soundless whistle. 'That would take dedicated malice if it were true, sir.'

'Yes, it would,' Jared agreed. 'When your agent has made his first report to me I may well furnish him with further work. It would be interesting to discover what is behind the family curse.'

'You think there may be some dark secret in the past?'

'It is one explanation,' Jared said and stood up. 'I have not included my property here in my American will, Mr Roth. I may have instructions for you concerning this another day.'

'You do not think you should see to it now, sir?'

'I shall write to you,' Jared said. 'I need time to consider in the light of recent events.'

'Yes, I understand.' Jacob Roth offered his hand. 'I shall beg you only to take care, sir—I am not sure whether congratulations are in order or not?'

'I think the jury is out on that one,' Jared said and grinned. 'I am going down to visit the duke in the morning. I may have more to say on the subject next time we meet.'

Jacob Roth nodded, watching as he went out. He sat down at his desk and took out a sheet of good quality vellum, dipping his quill in the ink. His client had asked for an agent to investigate his concerns, but it might be as well to have him watched over from a discreet distance. Clients like Jared Clinton didn't come along that often and he would not want him to suffer a premature death.

'It was nice to meet you, Mr Clinton,' Lady Ireland said the next morning as he and Hester took their farewell of her. 'Hester will look after you, I am sure. The duke is said to be a martinet for manners, but you will do well enough if you listen to my goddaughter. Her deportment and manners are universally admired.'

'You are very kind, ma'am. I sure appreciate it,' Jared said, a gleam of amusement in his eye. 'Damn my eyes, I never expected to mix with dukes and princes.'

'Well, I am not sure the Regent will attend Shelbourne's ball,' Lady Ireland said, her gaze narrowing as she looked at him. 'Are you amused about something, Mr Clinton?'

'No, ma'am, should I be?' Jared was all innocence as he pressed her hand. 'I hope to have the pleasure of meeting you again one day.'

'I shall attend the duke's ball, I dare say,' she replied and turned to Hester. 'Goodbye for now, my dear. I shall miss you.' They kissed and then she stood back. 'Have a good journey.'

Jared handed Hester into the carriage. She settled herself and glanced at him as he climbed in beside her. 'Why did you do that? You shouldn't tease her, you know.'

'Forgive me, I could not resist it,' Jared said. 'You were both so obviously expecting me to be some ignorant back-woods hillbilly. I thought I would give you what you wanted.'

'You gave Mr Birch that impression, deliberately I imagine. Why?' Hester searched his face, but his expression gave nothing away. 'I cannot understand why you wanted us to have a bad impression of you, sir.'

'Would you believe it if I said it was merely a jest?'

'I am not sure,' Hester replied. 'I can quite see that you might have thought it amusing. Did Mr Birch say something in his letter to make you angry?'

'I was told that a lady of impeccable manners would show me how to go on in English society.'

'And you were offended?' Hester nodded. 'Yes, I do see that that was offensive, Mr Clinton. It was badly put, but you see…there are certain rules that need to be followed. As an American, you might not have been aware of them.

I do not mean that you have no manners, of course not—just that we do things a little differently in some respects. It was simply meant to help you avoid embarrassment.'

'Is that so?' His brows rose, blue-green eyes narrowed and intent. 'Did it never occur to any of you that I had an English lady for a mother? Did you think I had been dragged up in the gutter? My mother may have fled with a man her family thought unsuitable, but she did not forget her birth or her manners. And, though you might not know it, the upper echelons of American society are as difficult to penetrate as your own, though perhaps for different reasons.'

'No, of course I did not think any such thing, at least at first! It was only after you met with Mr Birch…' Hester flushed. 'If you felt like this—why did you come?'

'Curiosity,' Jared offered. His expression gave her nothing. She blushed and looked away from his unblinking stare. 'Your lawyer was persuasive. Besides, I wanted to see the man who broke my mother's heart.'

'Oh, no, surely not? I mean, I know it was a dreadful quarrel, but surely she knew that Grandfather would forgive her in the end? She must have known she was his favourite child.'

Jared looked thoughtful. He had believed the reason his mother so often looked sad had been because of the quarrel with her father, but perhaps he had been mistaken. He knew his father had adored her, but Jack Clinton was a passionate man with a swift temper and perhaps they had quarrelled sometimes. Jared's anger abated a little but he was not prepared to give up his beliefs just yet. He would put this family to the test for a little longer.

'He made no attempt to repair the breach between them.'

'Have you come to quarrel with the duke?'

'I intend to tell him that he made her unhappy.'

'I wish you would not.'

'You do not think he deserves to be told?'

'He has been unwell for some time. He may not live long. I should be very distressed if you made him suffer for something that happened so long ago.'

'My mother was sad when she thought about her family. If he cared about her, why didn't he at least write to her? I know she disobliged him by running away with a gambling man, but it seems that my English uncles and cousins were not much better.'

'Perhaps that is why he did not wish her to marry a gambler.'

Her argument made more sense than he wished to admit. 'I can accept that he might have wished to protect her. She was young and at that time my father had few prospects, but he loved her. Whatever he did later was for her sake, and they were happy together. She never wanted for anything that he could give her.'

'If they were happy, why did she cry?'

'It was only when she thought of home and family. The rest of the time she was happy. Her death destroyed my father.'

'I am sorry.'

Jared shook his head, but the heat of his anger had cooled. 'It is all in the past. He has been dead for twenty years. I learned to live with the memories.'

Hester nodded. 'I can understand why you are bitter, but I beg you not to quarrel with Grandfather, Mr Clinton. It would hurt me if he died too soon because of his distress.'

'You drive a hard bargain, Miss Sheldon. You ask much of me, but you give little.'

'I believe you are a decent man, sir. Would it make you happy to drive another man to his grave in sorrow?'

Jared met her eyes and something in them gave him pause. He discovered that he would be reluctant to do anything that hurt this particular young woman.

'No, I do not suppose it would,' he admitted after a moment's silence. 'It would change nothing.' He arched his right eyebrow. 'What do you have to offer me if I give you the things you ask of me, Miss Sheldon?'

'My friendship,' Hester said and smiled suddenly; the smile transformed her face, giving her a kind of beauty. 'I do sincerely hope that we shall be friends, Mr Clinton. As for asking things of you, have you thought about what you might gain by obliging the duke? I have no idea how you live at home, but you are the heir to a beautiful old house and a considerable amount of land. You would need to marry an heiress to be able to live comfortably, because money is tight—but it would be so worthwhile. I thought it might be difficult before we met, but now that I have met you, I know that you could easily charm one of the many ladies you will meet once you have been introduced as Grandfather's heir.'

'Supposing I did agree,' Jared suggested, never taking his eyes from her face. 'What kind of a lady would you suggest? I am not sure that a very young girl would suit me.'

'Oh, no, I do not think it for a moment; you would frighten some of the innocents in society, Mr Clinton,' Hester replied. She wrinkled her smooth brow in thought. 'Most of them are young, of course—but there are other ladies...' She hesitated. 'Would it suit you to marry a wealthy widow, sir? I think you would find a woman to suit your taste if you were prepared to cast your net wider.'

A smile gathered at the corners of his mouth. 'I am intrigued, Miss Sheldon, but I defer to you. Tell me, do you have any particular ladies in mind?'

'Well...yes, I can think of two I think might suit you. Mrs Hines is four and twenty and has been a widow for six months. Her husband was killed fighting in Spain. She was already an heiress when she married and I imagine her husband left her something. She has blonde hair, blue eyes and is very pretty.'

'My taste is more for darker hair,' he replied urbanely.

'Then Lady Mary Jenkins might be just the lady you are looking for,' Hester said. 'She is two years older, but very lovely. She has a daughter and her husband Sir Hugh Jenkins has been dead for a year—which means there is nothing to stop you courting her. Six months is a little soon, though in some cases it is thought acceptable. Any less than that would be thought completely improper. She has money and I dare say she may look for a more prestigious title to give her consequence this time.'

'We have similar rules at home concerning the proper period of mourning,' Jared replied straight-faced. 'So you think I should try for Lady Jenkins? Would the fact that I am the duke's heir make me acceptable to her?'

'Well, yes, I am sure it would—if you are thinking in a purely business manner,' Hester replied, feeling oddly reluctant to agree. 'However, you have not met her and you may not wish to marry her. There are other ladies, of course—some of them older, some younger. I was trying to think of ladies I thought you might admire.'

'And what kind of lady would you imagine I might admire?'

'Well, I am sure she would have to be beautiful.'

'Attractive would do, provided she had a good complexion and her breath was not stale.' Jared folded his arms, a lazy smile touching his mouth as he stretched out and watched her.

'Yes, well, I am sure Lady Mary does not have bad breath.'

'And her figure?'

'She is not as slim as Mrs Hines.'

'I do not like overweight ladies.'

'I assure you she is not fat—just comely.'

'About your size would be my ideal.'

'Oh…' Hester's cheeks were warm. 'Well, we are of a similar size, though she may be a little more…comely.'

'Is she intelligent?'

'Oh, yes, very. I believe she likes poetry, music and art.'

'What about politics? Could she talk to me knowledgeably about what is going on in the world?'

'Is that a requirement?' Hester frowned. 'I do not think many ladies take an interest—some of the older ones may, of course.'

'Do you know anything of politics?'

'Yes, a little,' Hester said. She actually knew quite a lot, for she spent hours reading the newssheets to the duke, but that was beside the point.

'Then I should be able to find a lady who knows as much as you do, should I not?'

'Well, yes, perhaps,' Hester said, her gaze narrowing. 'Do you have any more particular requirements, sir?'

'Good teeth,' Jared said. 'Nice eyes and…' he glanced at her gloved hands '…clean nails.'

'I dare to suggest that all ladies have clean nails, sir.'

'I am glad to hear it.'

'Anything else?' Hester suspected that he was making fun of her and her eyes sparked.

'She should be able to ride well. I intend to breed horses if I stay.'

'Oh, nothing would delight Grandfather more,' Hester said. 'He was known for the quality of his bloodstock once.'

'So my mother told me. She rode as well as any woman I ever knew. It was a shock to us all when she fell and broke her neck. She died instantly.'

'I am so very sorry,' Hester said, feeling an ache in her chest because she could see that he still felt his mother's death keenly.

'So were we. It killed my father. He survived her for a few years, but he was only half the man he had been; he drank and lost a lot of his money—but gamblers usually do, I believe.'

'If he was mourning her, he might be excused, do you not think so? He must have loved her very much.'

'She was his whole world.'

'She was very lucky to find love like that—and very brave to do what she did. I do not know if I would have been as brave as your mother, sir.'

'I think you might. Tell me, do you ride, Miss Sheldon?'

'Yes. I believe I ride well. I have been told so by others—and I enjoy it very much.'

'Will you ride with me when we are settled at the estate?'

'Yes, if you wish it,' Hester said. She glanced at him, but the look in his eyes disturbed her. It was so very intense, penetrating, as if he could see into her thoughts. 'I believe we shall find something up to your weight, even though the stables are much reduced.'

'So,' he said after a short silence. 'Are we settled on Lady Mary?'

'Perhaps. At least, you should decide after you have met her.'

'Surely it matters little whether I like her or not? She has a fortune. You need a fortune to restore the house and put new heart into the estate.'

'Yes, but…' Hester looked into his unfathomable eyes. 'I would wish you to be happy with your choice, sir.'

'My happiness is of concern to you?' He arched his brows.

'Yes, of course.'

'Why?'

'Because…it just is, that's all.'

'You are a contrary creature, Miss Sheldon.'

'Am I?'

'Certainly you are. Let us review the list. I require a lady of about your height and stature, with dark hair. She should be attractive, intelligent, knowledgeable of the world of affairs, good humoured, nice teeth, nice eyes and sweet breath. I think you would fit my criteria rather well, Miss Sheldon. It is a pity that you do not have a fortune, is it not? Though perhaps as cousins we would be thought too close to marry?'

'Mr Clinton! You are mocking me. I have suspected it for the past several minutes, but now I am certain. As it happens, we are not blood related at all. I call the duke Grandfather, but he is only related by marriage. My mother had me by her first husband.'

'Then there is no reason we should not marry,' he said and grinned at her. 'Apart from the slight misfortune of your not being rich.'

'And one other rather important thing!'

'Yes?' He waited expectantly, a gleam in his bold eyes.

'I do not think I wish to marry, and even if I did, I should not marry you!'

'Would you not? You disappoint me, Miss Sheldon. I had quite made up my mind we should suit.'

'You are a wretched tease! Can you never be serious, sir? I am merely trying to point out the advantages of marrying for a fortune.'

'I do see that,' he said, a hint of wickedness in his voice. 'And I can see that you believe Lady Mary would be just right for me. Tell me, should I propose to her immediately or wait a few days?'

'You are provoking, sir. I should not dream of telling you what to do—and my advice was sought, remember?'

'Yes, you are right.' He looked at her, his lazy smile in place. 'Are you very angry with me, Miss Sheldon?'

'Yes, I am cross with you. It may sound mercenary to discuss marriage in such terms, but I can assure you it is the usual thing in families like ours—especially when there is a shortage of money.'

'I believe it is quite usual in other countries too, Miss Sheldon. The English did not invent the practice—even though you English seem to imagine your word is law on almost anything under the sun.'

'We English?' Hester glared at him. She knew that he was deliberately provoking her once more. 'You might care to remember that you are half-English, Mr Clinton.'

'Yes, but I had the advantage of being brought up in America. We are not so hidebound as you English. Our minds are more open to change—to taking chances and going for what we want from life.'

'I am not hidebound!' Hester said, losing her calm manner. 'I am perfectly capable of accepting new ideas, sir. If you did not wish for my advice, you should not have asked for it. Why did you?' Her eyes sparked with temper.

'For the pleasure of seeing you when your polite manners slipped a little,' Jared said. He had been sitting opposite her and he suddenly moved to sit beside her. She caught her breath as he reached out and pulled her into his arms. 'I like you very much when you forget to be the very proper Miss Sheldon.' He bent his head and kissed her soundly. Letting her go a few seconds later, he smiled as her eyes widened as if in surprise. 'That was your second kiss, I believe? You will bear some teaching, but…I think we should suit very well, Miss Sheldon.

You may teach me how to behave in English society, and I shall teach you how to kiss. I am sure that is a fair exchange.'

'Well, I am not,' Hester said, gathering her dignity. He was trying to provoke her into another display of temper. She would not oblige him. 'I shall not slap you for doing that, sir. It was not the action of a gentleman, taking advantage as you did, but I shall put it down to your unusual sense of humour and forgive you—this once. Should it happen again…'

'You would cut the acquaintance, I imagine?' Jared returned to the seat facing her. 'I agree that it was not the action of an English gentleman—but I never claimed to be that, Miss Sheldon. I am an American and wild in my ways, a bit of a savage. I thought your lawyer had warned you?'

'You are many things, sir,' she replied coolly, 'but not ignorant or untutored. I do not know quite what you are up to—but I am not going to fall out with you over a kiss.'

'Oh, how disappointing,' Jared said. 'I quite thought you would fly into a temper.'

'Would that have pleased you?'

'I don't know. You have eyes that reflect your mood, Miss Sheldon. When you are angry they are magnificent. I told you I like nice eyes.'

'You are incorrigible, sir. Please behave! I do not wish to have to force you to continue the journey on top of the carriage.'

'I see, I am in disgrace.' Jared leaned back, clearly unimpressed. 'Well, I shall not apologise, Miss Sheldon. I enjoyed the kiss—and I still think we should suit.'

'I do not have a fortune,' Hester said. 'I am almost seven and twenty and unlikely to marry anyone.'

'But I just told you…'

'You were mocking me. If you do not stop, I shall not speak to you for the rest of the journey.'

'Forgive me, Miss Sheldon. I'll marry Lady Mary to please you.'

'Ridiculous man!' She glared at him and then, seeing the gleam in his eyes, gave a reluctant laugh. 'Yes, you are a wicked tease, Mr Clinton. I do not think you have any intention of marrying Lady Mary—or any other heiress.'

'I am not so sure,' Jared told her. 'If you refuse me, I may be driven to it.'

'You cannot be serious?'

'Can I not? Well, perhaps it is a bit soon,' Jared said. 'I do not really know you—but I have decided that I do like you, Miss Sheldon. May I call you Hester? Is it too soon?'

'Much too soon,' she replied. 'But if you really wish to, I dare say I cannot prevent you.'

'No, but I shall not do it if it displeases you,' he said. 'I am sorry. I should not have kissed you just now. It was so tempting, but it was not right. Will you forgive me?'

'Yes, if you promise to behave in future.'

'I promise not to do it again for the remainder of the journey. I cannot promise that I shall never try to kiss you again.'

'You know that we could not marry,' Hester said. 'Please stop this foolishness and be sensible. Will you really stay here? Will you marry to oblige the family?'

'I shall make you a promise,' Jared said. 'If you find a lady I can love as much as my father loved my mother, I shall marry her—and if she has a fortune, so much the better.'

'You will look for a wealthy bride?'

'You will look for one for me,' Jared said and his expression was once again inscrutable. 'Present the right lady and I will marry her.'

'Oh…' Hester looked at him. He seemed to be serious for once. She did not know why she felt reluctant to agree, but he was clearly waiting for her answer. 'I shall try.'

'Good,' Jared said, settling back and closing his eyes.

Hester frowned. How annoying he was to declare his intention of going to sleep! They were just beginning to get to know one another and now he was refusing to talk to her. And after he had thrown her into confusion by kissing her in such a way that it made her pulses race. He really was too bad! She bit her bottom lip, feeling at odds with herself. She should be pleased that he had almost given his word to stay, and to marry an heiress if she could find the right one, but somehow she had an awful sinking sensation inside.

She began to review all the widows she knew in her mind, and the single girls who were heiresses to considerable fortunes. None of them seemed exactly right, and she found herself wishing that she had been an heiress herself so that Mr Clinton would not be obliged to marry for the sake of money.

What was she thinking? Hester pulled herself up sharply. How foolish she was to give even a moment's thought to his ridiculous assertion that they would suit very well. He had been mocking her. She was sure of it. They would not suit at all…at least, she had no wish to marry him. She had no wish to marry anyone.

Yet her eyes returned to his face as he sat with his eyes closed time and again. He had begun to grow on her, she found. At first she had thought his features harsh, but when you thought about it, he was rather attractive. Not handsome, but interesting, strong…a man you felt would support you in times of trouble.

This was foolish in the extreme. Even if they fell madly in love—which they had not and would not!—a marriage would be impossible. The estate needed money and it was Mr Clinton's duty to provide it.

Chapter Four

'Hester, my dearest child,' Lady Sheldon said and opened her arms to embrace her. 'You look very well. Did you have a pleasant trip?'

'Very pleasant, Mama,' Hester replied and embraced her mother, a pretty if delicate lady with a slightly anxious air. 'How have you been—and the duke?'

'We go on tolerably well, though you know my health is not always of the best, my love—and your grandfather misses you so much he growls like a bear when I try to be of help to him.'

'Poor Mama,' Hester said and laughed. 'It is just as well that I did not stay longer with my godmother.'

'I trust she is well.' Lady Sheldon looked past her daughter at the man standing watching them with evident interest, a gleam in his eyes. 'But we forget our manners, Hester. You have not yet introduced me to this gentleman.'

'Forgive me, Mr Clinton,' Hester said, turning to Jared, a faint flush in her cheeks. 'Sir, this is my mother—Lady Sheldon…Mama, this is Mr Clinton or perhaps, as Grandfather will insist, Viscount Sheldon.'

'My friends call me Jared, ma'am,' he said and took the

hand she extended, bowing over it as elegantly as any aristocrat at court. 'I am delighted to meet you at last.'

'Oh…' Lady Sheldon blushed, for she had not known quite what to expect. The lawyer's letter had seemed to hint that Amelia's son had gone to the bad, but this gentleman was perfectly presentable. His clothes had been cut by a master tailor, though not as exquisite as those worn by the pink of the *ton*, but the rather severe style looked well on him. She considered that he made his clothes rather than them making him, as was often the case with a tulip of fashion. 'You are very welcome, sir. The duke is looking forward to this visit.'

'We must hope that he is not disappointed, ma'am. I fear you may have hoped for a man of some fortune, and I am sorry I cannot offer a solution to your worries.'

'Hester has told you of the situation, I see…' Lady Sheldon looked at her daughter. She had been against Hester going alone to meet him in London, but the duke had said he trusted her daughter's judgement over any man's, and she had been obliged to give way. 'It is unfortunate that you see the house in its present state, sir. The fire made such a mess of one wing, and we have not yet been able to set the restoration in hand.'

Jared's eyes scanned the interior of the hall into which he had been led. Outside, the large, Queen Anne house was beautiful as the fire had made little difference to the thick grey stone walls, and, having been caught in time, had not reached the roof. It did not look as if it had touched the main section either, and here inside it was just a matter of years of neglect. The original ceiling had some beautiful friezes, but some of them had crumbled a little and would do better for careful repairing. The staircase leading up to the first floor was magnificent, the wooden balustrade ornately carved, but the carpet along the upper landing had seen better days. The furniture was of good quality, though old-fashioned and heavy. However, there was an ambience about the house that gave it a welcoming feel...the feel of a home for many generations, he imagined. His own apartments above the gambling casino lacked any such feeling, and his apartments in the various hotels he owned were all impersonal. He had preferred it that way since his father died.

'It is not quite what I expected, ma'am—but I can see that it would improve with a little money spent on it.'

'Sadly, this is not the worst of it,' Lady Sheldon told him with a wistful smile. 'Hester loves the house, you know. I find it too large myself. One day I shall take a small house in Bath for myself.' She shook her head. 'Tell me, sir, do you find it too ancient...too big for comfort?'

'I think it is too soon to pass judgement,' Jared told her. He was actually pleasantly surprised for he had been expecting something rather like the empty, echoing, ruined palaces he had seen when he visited Venice. The house was large enough for a growing family, with ample room for guests, but of a size to be easily maintainable for a man with a reasonable fortune.

'Yes, you are perfectly right.' Lady Sheldon sighed. 'I have wished that it might be possible to restore it for my daughter's sake—and the duke's, of course.'

'You do not need to be anxious for my sake,' Hester told her mother. 'You know I have promised I shall come with you to Bath, Mama.'

'Shall you, my love?' Lady Sheldon's slightly anxious air did not abate. 'We must see what happens when the time comes.' She glanced at the heir. 'I dare say you might not wish to live here. If we only had the money, the London house could be opened again. It is more modern than this place and my husband always preferred it.'

Jared smiled at her, but did not reply. He was assessing the situation here as he followed his hostess up the stairs. She led them to a door at the far end and then paused, turning to look at them with that anxious expression in her eyes.

'These are the duke's apartments, sir. He refuses to leave them, though he says he shall for the ball—and they were not much damaged by the fire, though I am sure the smell remains.' She dabbed a kerchief to her lips and the scent of lavender wafted on the air. 'I shall not come in with you, Hester. Your grandfather is eager to talk to you and his heir. I shall make sure your rooms are ready and your bags are being unpacked.'

'Would you mind asking the servants to leave my large trunk to me, ma'am?' Jared asked.

'Oh… Yes, of course, if you wish it,' Lady Sheldon said. 'Do you have the key with you?'

'Yes,' Jared said. 'The small bag may be unpacked as I shall need to change later.'

'I shall ask one of the maids to press your things,' she said and wrinkled her brow. 'I assure you the servants are to be trusted, sir.'

'I did not doubt it for an instant, but I prefer to unpack for myself.'

Lady Sheldon nodded and turned away. It was most odd, but perhaps being American he had his own way of doing things. She would not dream of interfering; after all, he was the long-expected heir.

Hester knocked at the door of her grandfather's apartments and was bidden to enter. They went into the comfortable sitting room, where a fire burned in the hearth despite the sun pouring in at the small windows. The duke sat in a high-backed wing chair near the fire. He had been getting out of bed for the past couple of days and was much recovered in health. His chair had been placed to face the window and it was possible to see a view of some trees, which were in full leaf and made a pleasant sight for a man who spent a great deal of his time tied to his chair these days.

'Grandfather,' she said and went over to him so that he did not have to turn his head to look at her. 'How are you, dearest?'

'Better for having you back,' he muttered. 'Well, have you got him here, girl? Will he do?'

'Oh, yes, I believe so,' Hester said. 'But he is here, sir. You may see for yourself.' She beckoned to Jared, who hesitated and then walked forward. 'Grandfather, this is Mr Jared Clinton—or, as he will now be known, Viscount Sheldon.'

'Good afternoon, sir,' Jared said, offering his hand to the elderly gentleman sitting in his chair. His hair was white and thin, but his eyes were as blue as ever—as blue as his daughter's and Jared's own at that moment. 'This is an unexpected pleasure. I did not imagine that I should ever be invited to my mother's childhood home.'

'Blame me for that, do you?' The duke's eyes met his in a challenge as they exchanged a brief handshake. 'Think I treated her badly?'

'I believe you had the right to be angry at first, but you might have relented later. Surely what she did was not so very terrible?'

'I dare say you may be right,' the duke said, his expression oddly like that of his grandson in that it gave nothing away, the blue eyes gleaming with suppressed emotion. 'I might have done in time if—'

'If she had not died?' Jared raised his brows. 'It was a tragedy for those who loved her.'

'You think I didn't?' the duke said, a sudden bleak look on his face. 'She broke my heart when she ran off with your father—he was a gambler and not her equal in any way.'

'I think he knew that,' Jared replied. 'But he loved her. He did everything to please her, gave her all the things she ought to have had by right—but I do not think he could ever quite make that sadness leave her eyes.'

'She wrote to me a few times…'

'You returned her letters.'

'I read them first,' the duke said. 'I wanted to know she was all right, but I couldn't forgive her. I'm a stubborn man. I've wished many times that I had kept the letters. After she died…' He shook his head. 'No fool like an old fool, sir. I regretted that I had not written to her, told her…I loved her. She could have come home if she had wished. She must have known I wouldn't turn her away.'

'Would you have accepted my father?' The two men glared at each other, a clash of wills as neither was ready to give way, and then the duke dropped his gaze.

'No, I probably wouldn't have welcomed him here. I never forgave him for taking my girl away from me.'

'She loved him and he loved her. Do you not think that the proper reason for marriage?'

'I married twice, neither of them for love, though I liked Amelia's mother the best of the two. She was a good-natured woman—but Amelia was my favourite.' He looked at Hester. 'I've got my girl now, but it was a long time before I recovered from losing Amelia.'

'I do not think she ever got over the hurt you inflicted in that quarrel before she left.'

'Told you, did she?' The duke put a hand to his eyes, shielding them as though he couldn't bear the younger man to see his pain, into his private thoughts. 'I have regretted the things I said a thousand times. If I could have taken them back, I would.'

'The spoken word is a dangerous weapon, sir. Use it unwisely and it may offer a fatal wound…and it can never be retracted once it is given.'

'You are not as forgiving as your mother,' the duke said, gazing up at him, eyes searching his face. 'In her last letter she told me she had forgiven me. She said that she loved me…' His voice broke and his hand trembled. 'If I had written to her then…but I was too stubborn—a fool!'

'Yes, you were.'

Jared's statement was brutal, unforgiving. The duke looked for some softness, but found none.

'Are you like your father? Was he as harsh as you?'

'My mother told me I reminded her of you, sir.'

'You like to punish,' the duke said. 'Yes, perhaps you are like me. I had hoped we might find some way we could deal together, but you hate me.'

'No…' Jared surprised himself as he spoke. 'I am angry, but I do not hate you. You hurt my mother. I saw her crying after some letters came and she talked about you—but she wasn't bitter. I shall not say that all is forgiven and forgotten, because it cannot be, but I see no reason why we should not deal honestly together, sir. Miss Sheldon has told me that you wish me to marry an heiress to restore the house and put some heart into the estate. As yet I cannot promise that I will do as you wish, but I shall stay for a while, and if Miss Sheldon finds me a suitable lady I will marry her.'

The duke stared at him in silence. 'You're an odd sort of fellow, sir. My lawyer did not think much of you, but you are not as bad as the picture he painted. We might be able to make something of you—what do you think, girl?' He shot a fierce look at Hester.

'Mr Clinton does not lack manners, sir. His clothes may need some refurbishment—'

'I thought you were to see to that in town?'

'We bought some hats, but I think—'

'I have sufficient clothes for my needs,' Jared said. 'I may not be quite the English dandy you would wish for, but I believe I am presentable?'

'Yes…I dare say you'll do, but you'll need something decent for the ball. Hester, I'll leave that to you. If you need money…'

'I believe I have enough for the moment,' Jared said in a voice that brooked no argument. 'I shall not disgrace you, your Grace.'

'Enough of that nonsense!' the duke said. 'We don't use titles within the family, unless speaking to servants or visitors. You will be known as Sheldon. I am Shelbourne— you see the distinction? Titles! There's a plethora of the wretched things, but they come in useful when you have a handful of sons. Sons are important to the family; they die too easily, Sheldon.'

'I am sorry that you have lost so many of your family, sir.' Jared frowned. 'Were they all accidents or is there some hereditary illness I should know about?'

'Some people say it is the curse,' the duke said and for a moment his eyes reflected amusement. 'The dowager Lady Sheldon believes in it, but it is stuff and nonsense. I'm nearly eighty and I haven't succumbed to any ill wishing.'

'Grandfather,' Hester remonstrated, 'Mama only wonders if it was because of the curse that John and my father died. I am sure she does not truly believe it.'

'May I be permitted to know how the tale came about, sir?'

'Hester will tell you, I dare say. Come, kiss my cheek, girl, and then take him away. He will want to see his room and then the rest of the house. Show him the portraits and tell him the story. I think it nonsense, but there's no doubt we've had too much tragedy in this family.'

'You're tired, dearest,' Hester said and took his hand, feeling it tremble within hers. 'You must rest now. We do not want you to be ill again or the ball will have to be postponed. You have been looking forward to that, I know.'

'I sometimes think none of it matters,' the old man said, looking at her, suddenly intent. 'If I have loved anyone, it has been you, girl. I wish this place was yours by right— but it would probably be a millstone round your neck. As it will be to you, Sheldon—unless you can find a way to make money and stick to it. My sons were gamblers, all of them, though Hester's stepfather was the best of them. It needs a miracle to bring this family back to its proper place, and I doubt it will be granted. We haven't exactly deserved it, any of us...' He lifted his gaze. 'You lived in a gaming house, I hear. Not much of a one either.'

'I had a run of bad luck,' Jared said, not blinking an eye as he lied. It would take small change to put things right here as far as he was concerned, but he wasn't ready to commit himself to this family yet—though one of them had got beneath his skin in a manner he had not expected. 'I managed to salvage something before we left New Orleans.'

'Keep you in boots, I dare say,' the duke said in a derisory manner. 'Well, you can't help your blood, I suppose. Your father was a gambler and your mother came from a long line of them. We have to think ourselves lucky that you are at least presentable. Do your duty by the family and you won't disappoint me.'

'My duty?' Jared stared at him, his expression unreadable. 'I wonder what that might be, sir? But I shan't tease you further. Miss Sheldon is glaring at me, and I am sorry if I have been too outspoken.'

'No, don't be,' the duke replied. 'If there is one thing I cannot stand, it is mealy-mouthed fools who wrap everything up in clean linen. Speak the truth whether it hurts or not and be damned to it, that has always been my motto.'

Jared inclined his head. It wasn't much of a recommendation in his estimation. The old man was unwell and lonely, that much was obvious. In other circumstances he might have felt sympathy for him, but he had brought his fate on himself. Jack Clinton would have brought Amelia back to England; he would have given up the life he had carved for himself amongst the wealthy citizens of New Orleans and started over if it had pleased his beloved wife. But her father had told her he never wished to see or speak to her again, and she had secretly broken her heart over it. Jared couldn't forgive that in an instant. He wasn't sure if he ever would, but he was going to give these people a chance, and they owed that to the quiet, attractive young woman who led him from her grandfather's apartments and then rounded on him fiercely.

'You promised me you wouldn't upset him.'

'It needed to be said. I shan't refer to it again unless he does.' His gaze narrowed. 'Did you expect me to fall on his neck and beg him to welcome me like the prodigal son?'

'No, of course not,' Hester said. She sighed as she realised he was right. He had spoken his piece, but he hadn't raged at the old man and he hadn't lied or pretended to be something he wasn't. 'But surely you could see that he is frail? I do not want him to die…' She smothered the sob that rose to her lips. 'I love him so much.'

'He loves you,' Jared said. 'Has he said it before—about wanting to break the entail and give this place to you?'

'Yes, many times,' Hester said and pulled a wry face.

'He knows it is impossible, of course. It would cost a lot of money and he doesn't have it.'

'Would you really want it?'

'Oh, yes, it is my home. The only one I remember. My real father died before I was born and Mama remarried a year later. My stepfather was like a father to me, and Grandfather is my grandfather. He always loved me as if he were my real grandfather and that is the way I think of him. I have no claim to any of it, don't imagine that I envy you or resent that—but I do care what happens to the house, the land and the people.'

'If you could, would you live here for the rest of your life?'

'Yes…perhaps…' Hester shook her head. 'It isn't going to happen. I have been running the house for some years. Mama always let me help because she has no head for it and after Papa died…well, I just took over. The servants come to me for instructions. When you marry, that will be your wife's right and I shall go away, though I hope you will invite me to visit occasionally.'

'You plan to live with your mother or your godmother?'

'I may move between them,' Hester said. 'I do not know. Mama does not care to travel. I might like to see something of Europe. I have always thought I should like to see Venice…'

'It is beautiful,' Jared agreed. 'But so is Rome, and there are other places equally as beautiful. I like Paris because it has a charm all its own.'

'You have travelled extensively?' Her eyes narrowed. 'You have been to England before?'

'To London, yes, but this is my first trip to the south of the country, Miss Sheldon. I was in England something over a year ago. I do not remember exactly, but I had business in Paris, and I stopped over in London until the weather became more favourable.'

'I am not sure what to think of you, sir,' she told him frankly. 'You say things…and then you seem to contradict them. What business in Paris, may I ask?'

'At this time, no,' he said. His eyes met hers and he gave nothing. 'If you would show me my room, I should like to refresh myself—and then perhaps you will give me that tour of the house?'

'Yes, of course. Grandfather told me to make you acquainted with the old tale.' Her eyes dwelled on his face, but she could not penetrate his thoughts. 'Who are you exactly, Mr Clinton? I know you are Amelia Sheldon's son—and you have admitted that you are a gambler—but who are you? I think you run much deeper than you are prepared to admit.'

'I have been accused of keeping a close mouth,' Jared said with a slight smile. 'I know others find it annoying that I do not confide all my business to them in an instant. I find it is dangerous to disclose all until one knows the person to whom one is making the disclosure. If I told you my secrets, it might even be dangerous for you, Miss Sheldon.'

A shiver ran down her spine. 'Are you a dangerous man, Mr Clinton? Should I be wary of you?'

'You?' He smiled at her then. 'You have no need to fear me, and neither does your mother or the duke—but others may fear me, Miss Sheldon. They would do well to do so, for I do not forgive easily.'

'I think you have secrets.'

'Doesn't everyone?' he asked. 'Do not look so anxious, my dear Miss Sheldon. I give you my word that I shall not harm you or those you love—will you accept it?'

Hester met his gaze for a moment and then inclined her head. 'Yes, I shall accept your word, sir. Come, I shall show you your rooms. They once belonged to your mother and the duke has kept them just as they were. I think you will like them.'

Hester availed herself of the chance to change out of her travelling gown, which was sadly creased after so many hours on the road. She took a pale yellow silk evening gown from her armoire and changed in to it without summoning a maid to help her, fastening her glossy dark hair into a knot at the back of her head. She looked at herself in the mirror for a moment or two and then teased a tendril of hair here and there so that the severe effect was softened.

'Vanity, thy name is Hester,' she said and laughed at herself. She knew that she had dressed in one of her best things in Mr Clinton's honour, which was very foolish of her, but made her feel much better. She fastened the pretty gold bangle set with pearls that her godmother had given her about her right wrist, dabbed a little perfume on her wrists and behind her ears and then went along the hall to the east wing, where Mr Clinton's apartments were situated. She knocked at the door, but, getting no answer, turned the handle and peeped inside. 'Mr Clinton—are you ready?'

There was still no answer, so she closed the door and went down the landing, down a short flight of stairs to the main reception rooms at the front of the house. Seeing one of the footmen, she called to him, asking if he had seen Viscount Sheldon.

'Yes, Miss Sheldon,' he said. 'He asked me where he would find the duke's library, so I took him there myself.'

'Thank you, Renyolds,' she said. 'I dare say I shall find him there.'

She was a little surprised that Mr Clinton should have chosen to go wandering about a house he did not know alone, but at least he had asked a footman instead of getting lost, which would be easy to do since there were a great many rooms. She found him in the library, which was at the back of the main section of the house and looked out towards the park and a lake.

'I thought you would wait for me, sir.'

Hester was surprised as he turned to her for she saw that he was wearing evening dress that was equal in cut and quality to anything her father had worn, but of a more severe style. There was nothing of the dandy about this American. He wore black with a white shirt, but no jewellery of any kind, not even a signet ring, which was a little odd since it was an item most men found invaluable, and a plain neckcloth.

'You look very…well, sir.'

'Thank you. May I return the compliment, Miss Sheldon. I might even say that you look quite lovely.'

'I look well enough. I am not beautiful, Mr Clinton.'

'Did I say beautiful? Lovely means something else—at least to me.'

'Oh…thank you. We should not quarrel over small things. Would you like to see the portrait gallery? It will be easier to explain our history there.'

'Then by all means, let us go.' He offered her his arm and Hester took it, feeling a little flutter about her heart not unlike the sensation she had felt when he kissed her in the carriage on their way here.

'I was looking for records that might explain a little of the family history,' he told her. 'My mother spoke of the library as being one of her favourite places. I understand she often went there when she wished to be alone.'

'Did she?' Hester looked at him. 'I do too. Grandfather prefers his own apartments these days, though I think he used the library for business when he was able to move around the house at will. He has to be carried downstairs now, and that is why he prefers his own chambers.'

'Yes, I understand his reluctance,' Jared said. 'He needs a chair that can be easily moved. Two footmen could quite easily carry it and him downstairs between them.'

'You mean a bathchair, I suppose. I am not sure he would agree.'

'The right chair would solve many of his problems,' Jared said. 'Leave it to me. I may be able to sort something out.'

'Would you? It would be more dignified for him than being carried in someone's arms every time.'

'Yes, I would have thought so.' Jared paused to admire the long room ahead of them. 'The picture gallery, I presume.'

'Yes. We are all here. My mother and stepfather and me, though I suppose I should not be, really... Where would you like to begin? Oh, your mother's portrait, I imagine?'

'Is there one?'

'More than one,' Hester replied with a smile. 'Some of them were done when she was a child. She is with her brothers here...and this is her with her first pony...and this is the last when she was sixteen.'

Jared looked at the group of family portraits. He smiled at the pictures of his mother as a young girl with her brothers, and stood for a while staring at her last portrait as an unmarried girl.

'May I see your mother and stepfather—and you?'

'We are just here.' Hester led him a little further into the gallery. 'I was sixteen when this was painted...and this was done last year.'

'Why did you start wearing your hair in that severe style? It looks pretty loose.' His eyes moved over her. 'The artists have hardly done you justice.'

'I prefer that they do not flatter,' Hester replied. 'I am as you see me, sir—and now, if we move a little further, we come to the older portraits. The large picture is of the

Marquis of Shelbourne. He is your great-great-great-grandfather. The dukedom did not come to the family until the year 1690 when the ninth Marquis of Shelbourne's son did great service to the crown, and, already being very wealthy, was given the honour in lieu of monetary reward.'

'What was this great service?'

'I believe he married a royal favourite who was with child and averted a scandal, but it is in the family archives—most things are if you search. This gentleman here is the second Duke of Shelbourne and your great-grandfather—and the curse began in his time.'

'What did he do to bring it down on the family? Presumably he did something awful?'

'There are many stories, but it had to do with one of the second duke's sons. My brother once told me the story, but he had it wrong because he thought the duke's eldest son was murdered. What actually happened according to the journals I have read was that he seduced the daughter of a country gentleman; they were a good country family, though not aristocracy, and the girl's father was outraged when he discovered that she was with child. He arrived here in a rage and demanded that the culprit marry his daughter, but the duke refused to see him. The duke's eldest son, who was of course Grandfather's elder brother, died a few days later of a putrid fever, but he was not murdered. The girl's father was angry at being turned away and it is said that he took something of great value—a gold chalice set with rubies and sapphires that was thought to have come from ancient Egypt and to have magical powers; supposedly while the chalice remained in the family they would prosper. The ancient Egyptians were believed to be powerful magicians, of course.'

'Do you believe in such things?'

'I'm not sure,' Hester said. 'No, I do not think I do—

but apparently the duke did and he fell into a terrible rage when he discovered it was missing. He sent some of his servants to fetch the man back and recover his property, but the man was killed resisting the duke's men and died cursing the family. He said that the duke's issue would all die violent deaths and that they would never recover their former glory unless they could find the chalice…which he had hidden in such a way that they never did.'

'An interesting tale, but hardly believable,' Jared said. 'I expected something more chilling.'

'That was not the end of it,' Hester said. 'The gentleman's daughter was left to fend for herself and, being ashamed of what she had caused, she left her home and wandered until the babe was due. It was then that she turned up at the duke's door and gave birth, dying straight after. Her child was left on the steps of the house in a shawl as the servants did not dare to take it in.'

'Tragic, but predictable.'

'No, but what happened after that was perhaps worse. The duke returned home from a day's hunting with his dogs and he gave the child to one of the servants, telling her to get rid of it. A few days later she told him it had died. Apparently, he flew into a rage, blaming her for neglect. And then he went out on his horse and broke his neck trying to jump a fence he usually took easily. Someone said that a grey shape appeared out of nowhere and spooked his horse.'

'Ah, now I see it,' Jared nodded. 'You have a grey lady who appears when a member of the family is about to die?'

'Well, there are tales of certain members of the family seeing a grey shape. I do not know if she is a lady or…' Hester shook her head, her eyes suddenly bleak. 'My half-brother was an excellent horseman and yet he fell from his horse to his death.'

'Forgive me, I had forgotten you mentioned that once before.' Jared saw the pain it had caused her to speak of her brother's accident. 'You do not think the grey lady appeared to him, surely?'

'No, I doubt that very much,' Hester told him. 'But I have wondered if something spooked his horse.'

'A fox or something else…someone else?' Jared's eyes narrowed. 'Have you thought that someone wanted him dead?'

'I do not know. I suppose I have wondered, but at the time my stepfather was alive. It must simply have been an accident, I think…don't you?'

'It would seem that way, and yet it is almost too much of a coincidence that so many of your family have died young, from accidents or fatal illnesses.'

'Two of my step-uncles died of a weakness in the chest, as my stepfather did at the end, though he had a long illness…but my brother was healthy. He did not appear to suffer from any hereditary weakness.'

Jared nodded. 'There were two other grandsons—how did they die?'

'One of them was killed when his carriage overturned and he was thrown into the road. They say he was driving too fast and under the influence of strong wine; there is talk of him having taken a bet that he could beat another man's record. The other one died in a duel. He was provoked into it, they say, and the other man fled abroad… but he was a gambler and he lost so much money that, had he lived, I think nothing would have remained to the family.' She raised her troubled gaze to his. 'I do not believe in the curse, sir—but there is no doubt that this has been an unlucky family.'

'Yes, undoubtedly.' He frowned, wondering whether to tell her what had happened to him a few nights previously.

It seemed probable that someone had paid to have him killed, though his informant might have been lying to save his own skin. Yet there was no connection that he could see, no clear indication that someone had deliberately set out to get rid of everyone who stood between him and the dukedom. And therefore no need to upset her by telling her something that might distress her. 'It is a tragic story, Miss Sheldon, and your family has suffered tragedy too often— but it seems to me that most died of natural causes or through their own folly. Your brother's death remains a mystery. I cannot tell you what happened to scare his horse. It was simply a tragedy.'

'Yes, of course you are right,' Hester agreed. 'I know that it is foolish to dwell on these things. Nothing will bring John back, and my stepfather was ill for a long time. He caught a chill, which lingered and eventually turned to pneumonia; there was no mystery concerning his death, for Mama and I nursed him ourselves.'

Jared nodded. It did seem unlikely that anyone could have been gradually killing off members of the duke's family, though one or two of the accidents might bear investigation. Some of the deaths might be too far in the past to discover the truth, but he would ask his agent to see what he could discover about the duel and that carriage accident. If both men had been provoked deliberately…

Jared decided to keep an open mind. If the attack on his person turned out to be nothing more than a rogue seizing his opportunity, he would forget the whole idea, but if not…it meant that someone might have to answer for more than one death.

'I should put all thought of the curse from my mind if I were you, Miss Sheldon,' he said and smiled at her. 'I do not think your troubles are being caused by an Egyptian chalice that went missing a long time ago.'

'No, of course not,' she said. 'I told you it was a foolish tale, and now we should join Mama, for she will be thinking you have got lost and we do not want to keep Cook waiting.'

Hester took the pins from her hair and shook it loose, looking at herself in the mirror for a moment as she started to brush it. She had been wearing her hair loose in the portrait the duke had commissioned when she was sixteen, but she had put it back out of the way when she was helping to nurse her stepfather and she had never bothered with it since. Her own appearance had seemed unimportant during the time of her mourning.

Oh, what did it matter? Hester got to her feet. She would be silly to let herself dream simply because she was beginning to like the heir rather a lot—perhaps too much. He had flirted with her outrageously in the carriage, saying things he really ought not, and kissing her.

She allowed herself to smile. She had fought the temptation to think about that kiss all evening, as there was no doubt that the more she saw of Mr Clinton the more she liked him. Oh, she ought to think of him as the Viscount Sheldon, of course, for her grandfather would insist on the title for his heir, but somehow she could not think of him as anything but the Mr Clinton who had played such an outrageous joke on her at their first meeting.

She perfectly understood his reasons now that she knew him better. It was obvious that his mother had meant a great deal to him, and he was angry at the way she had been treated—and at the implications in the lawyer's letter. No wonder he had been offended at the idea that she would teach him how to behave in society. He did not behave as an English gentleman would, perhaps. He was outspoken and he did not try to wrap things up in clean linen, but then neither did the duke; they were more alike than either of them realised. However, Mr Clinton's manners needed no direction; he was, in fact, refreshing, like a breath of air blowing through the stale corridors of convention. His normal accent was different, but acceptable, and there were sometimes words he used that had different meanings in England, but as yet he had said nothing out of place in Lady Sheldon's hearing. Indeed, as they spoke for a few minutes before retiring, she had told her daughter that she thought he was utterly charming.

'Mr Birch's letter was completely misleading,' she told Hester. 'I dare say he is a gambler and he may have been down on his luck, but then your papa gambled—not as recklessly as your Uncle Thomas, but more than I felt right in the circumstances. The heir may be a gambler, but he is charming.'

'I do not think we should hold the gambling against him, Mama. It is unfortunate that Mr Clinton lost his money, but it may not have been as much as Grandfather had heard. These tales become exaggerated in the telling.'

'Yes, of course, dearest. Besides, it really is of no concern to us. While the duke lives he will only receive an allowance and after that...'

'I should not like to think that the estate might need to be sold,' Hester said. 'But it will not be our affair, Mama.'

'He said something rather remarkable to me earlier,' her mother said, a little sigh on her lips. 'He said that this house would always be a home for us if we wished it and that we must not think of leaving unless we wished—even after the duke... I thought that very handsome of him, Hester.'

'Indeed, it was kind, but it would not be comfortable once he is married, Mama. You have been used to being the mistress here.'

'As to that, I rather think that you are more the mistress of this house than I could ever be,' her mother told her. 'You know that it is beyond me. I never expected to live here. Your stepfather was never supposed to inherit. He had his own small estate, which is mine, of course, though it would have been John's if…' Her sigh deepened. 'But we shall not dwell on these things. I have no wish to live there or here as it happens. I have told you that I shall retire to Bath when the time comes. I think I shall ask the Viscount to look at my estate for me. He will tell me what to do about it, for I am not sure that my bailiffs are managing it as well as they ought.'

'Do you think you should trouble him, Mama?'

'Oh, I do not think he would find it a trouble,' Lady Sheldon replied. 'I think him rather astute in matters of business. We were talking when you went up to say good-night to your grandfather earlier this evening, and he seems a sensible man to me. When I mentioned my small estate, he promised he would see what could be done to make it less of a worry to me.'

'That was kind of him.' Hester frowned. 'What makes you think him astute in such matters?'

'Oh, he spoke of land management, and of the cost of re-storing the house, which he seems to think may not be as horrendous as we imagine. He says he intends to have a builder in to see what it would take to restore the fire damage.'

'Does he have Grandfather's permission?'

'I dare say he would need it to set the work in hand, but he told me he would speak to the duke about it tomorrow.'

'I am not sure we could afford it.'

'Well, I have no idea about these things,' Lady Sheldon said. 'And he did tell me that it was only a preliminary ex-amination to discover what needed doing.'

'Yes, but…' Hester had not questioned her mother further. Mr Clinton had said nothing to her of these matters, but she would ask him about it the next day. 'Goodnight, Mama.'

'Goodnight, dearest.' Her mother kissed her cheek. 'I am glad to have you home—and the viscount likes you, my love.'

'Did he say so?'

'No, but one can always tell.'

Hester frowned as her mother drifted away down the hall and went into her own room, intrigued by these new developments. It looked as if the heir had decided he might stay. She was still thoughtful as she finished brushing her hair and got up to go to bed. She paused to glance out of the window into the garden. There was a crescent moon and the sky was quite light, shedding its silvery glow on trees, bushes and lawns. She saw something in the shrubbery. Was it a man standing there, gazing up at the house? She could not be certain as she had seen only a shadow and when she looked harder, she could no longer pick it out; it had disappeared, perhaps a figment of her imagination.

Had their visitor gone into the garden to smoke a cigar? She knew that he did smoke them, for sometimes a faint scent of it hung about him, but it was not strong and she rather liked it. However, he had not smoked that evening, and he had not excused himself in order to do so. Perhaps he had waited until the ladies had retired. And yet…the figure had not been his, if she had seen a man at all. Mr Clinton would not loiter in the shrubbery and stare up at her room. She felt it instinctively and shivered suddenly. If it hadn't been him, who was it? Not a servant. She was sure of that, for the silhouette she felt she had seen was of a gentleman, staring intently at the house—at her window.

'No, you are imagining things,' Hester told herself, and yet she fastened her window securely and drew the curtains before getting into bed and blowing out her candle. 'It was merely a trick of the moonlight.'

Outside in the garden, the man continued to stare at the house after Hester's candle had gone out. He frowned as he waited in the shadows. He had not expected her to look out and he wondered if she had seen him. If she had, she might wonder what he was doing here—but he believed he had reacted quickly enough. Even if she had caught a glimpse of someone, it was unlikely to have been enough for her to recognise him.

He did not want her to be aware of his presence just yet. He had not had time to decide what to do about recent developments; he must wait and watch before making his next move.

Chapter Five

Hester woke early and dressed in her riding habit, going down to the stables, as was her custom when in the country. She enjoyed a good canter before breakfast; it blew away the cobwebs of sleep and made her feel full of energy and hungry. The head groom came forward to meet her, greeting her with a smile. She was popular with everyone and always had a word for those who served her.

'Good morning, Jones,' she said. 'I hope your son is better now?'

'Yes, miss,' the groom said. 'The doctor said it's just teething problems and gave Mrs Jones something to rub on his gums.'

'I am glad to hear it,' she said and slipped her hand in her pocket. 'I brought some sweets for your eldest boy, to thank him for the lovely flowers he picked for me before I went away.'

'Thank you, miss, Tommy will enjoy those,' he said and slipped her offering into his coat pocket. 'Will Poppy do for you this morning, miss—the Viscount took Fire Dancer out for a gallop. I did mention that you sometimes rode him, but he seemed to think the horse would suit him.'

'Yes, I was going to ask for Poppy anyway,' Hester said. 'Fire Dancer must be a little fresh, for he hasn't been out much since he had that colic—is he properly over it?'

'Oh, yes, miss, and Lord Sheldon has good hands. I don't think you need worry.'

'No, I shan't,' Hester agreed. She allowed him to give her a hand up as one of the younger grooms brought out her mare. Fire Dancer had been her stepfather's favourite mount and Hester knew the stallion did not get as much exercise as he needed, because he would not tolerate anyone but Mr Jones or herself in the saddle. However, she had a feeling that the new viscount knew his way around horses, and if the head groom had allowed him to take out Fire Dancer, he must agree. She looked at Jones. 'Stand back, lad. I am ready.'

'You won't take a groom with you, miss?'

'I do not think it necessary,' Hester said. 'I shall not leave the estate and I doubt Poppy will throw me; she doesn't have it in her nature.'

She set off at a canter, leaving the yard and racing across an open stretch of undulating grassland towards the lake. It was her favourite ride, because there were stretches of open land that were perfect for letting the horse have its head if she felt the urge to gallop. However, this morning she was perfectly content to canter, relishing the feeling of freedom and the gentle sting of the wind in her face. The duke had had some landscaping done when he was younger and beyond the lake there was a pleasant wood, which looked picturesque in the early morning sunshine. It was as she approached the near side of the lake that she saw the man on a horse at the far side. She knew at once that it was the heir and she was considering whether she should ride that way to join him when she heard the shot. It seemed to come from the trees and its immediate effect was to spook Fire Dancer.

Hester watched in horror as she saw the way the stallion shied and bucked, finally rearing up as it shrilled its terror. Oh, Jared would be killed! It would be like losing her brother all over again! The shock could kill her grandfather and she would find it unbearable.

At first all she could feel was dismay because she was not near enough to be of any assistance, but then as she watched the tussle between man and horse, she was lost in admiration. She began to realise that the new viscount was certainly not a novice when it came to controlling temperamental horses. Indeed, he showed an impressive display of coolness. He held his seat despite Fire Dancer's attempts to dislodge him, and after a few minutes the horse began to settle, until at last he was merely tossing his head and snorting, his front hooves pawing the ground. When he had him quiet, Jared slid from his back and went round to his head, holding him firmly by the bridle and soothing him; he appeared to be talking to Fire Dancer and then he did something that seemed a little strange. Was he kissing the horse? Hester's gaze narrowed... No, he seemed to be breathing into its nostrils and talking. Whatever it was, it had a calming effect. A few moments later, he had remounted. Hester waved and rode around the perimeter towards him. Jared came to meet her. As she got closer, she saw that his expression was grim.

'Oh, well done, sir. You managed him brilliantly. Did I hear a shot just before Fire Dancer tried to throw you?'

'It came from the direction of the woods,' Jared said. 'I felt the ball whistle past my cheek. A fraction closer and I should have been hit.'

Hester stared at him in shock. 'No! I had no idea. I thought it must have been a poacher in the woods.' Her eyes narrowed in dismay as his words sank in. 'You don't think it was deliberate?' She read the answer in his face.

He did think it had been a deliberate attempt on his life. 'But why... Who would want to kill you? Hardly anyone knows you are here.'

They sat close together, gentling the horses, Hester trying to come to terms with what he had just told her. If the shot had been meant for him, someone who did know he was staying here must have fired it.

'It isn't the first time,' Jared said. 'A clumsy attempt to rob and kill me was made in London as I left a gambling club. I didn't tell you, because I wasn't sure that it was anything more than a chance attack, even though the rogue told me he had been paid to do it. I thought he might have been lying to save his own neck, but now I must think again. It seems someone wants me dead.'

Hester's face was very pale. She felt a little sick and her stomach was churning. 'Because you are the heir?'

'I am keeping an open mind for the moment,' he said. He seemed so calm and she followed his example. Clearly he did not intend to make a fuss over his brush with death. 'What you told me about your brother—I believed it was quite possibly just a simple accident—but what would you have thought had I fallen and broken my neck and the horse went off in a wild gallop and possibly injured itself?'

'I might have wondered if you had found Fire Dancer too much for you to handle, though I ride him myself and he is well behaved as a rule.' Her manner was as controlled as his own, though her throat felt tight and she wanted to scream her rage aloud. How dare someone do this outrageous thing?

'But the horse was new to me and you could not know if I was up to handling him, therefore there would have been doubt—which would be a clever way of disposing of me without arousing too much suspicion, I think.'

'Yes...' Hester looked at him intently. It seemed so fantastic to speak of these things, but she must hold her nerve, as it was obvious that he expected her to remain calm. 'It does seem plausible, even likely…but who would want you dead?'

'I have no idea. Unless the gentleman you spoke of in London…Mr Stephen Grant.'

'He would inherit,' Hester agreed. 'Yes, I know the suspicion must fall on him, but I do not think…' She shook her head. 'I would not have thought it possible that he would even consider it, Mr Clinton, but I heard the shot myself and I saw what happened. It was a miracle you were not thrown at the very least.'

'Why do you consider Mr Grant above suspicion? Is it because he is a man of the cloth?'

'In part,' Hester agreed. They were walking the horses side by side; to a casual onlooker it must seem that nothing untoward had happened. 'But I do not think him an ambitious man…somehow he would not fit the part as you do.'

'You think I fit the duke's shoes?' Jared's brows rose. 'Good grief! You surprise me, Miss Sheldon.'

'I surprise myself,' she said and laughed softly. Some of the tension had drained away in the face of his coolness. She found herself thinking that he would be capable of handling anything. 'At first I thought I should not like you in my grandfather's place, sir, but I have discovered that you have many attributes that would bring distinction to the part.'

'Do tell me, for I cannot see it myself!'

She saw the mischief in his face and blushed. 'You shall not tease me, Mr Clinton! I refuse to be drawn further. You impressed Mama, for she thinks you astute in matters of business, and you must know that such a skill is desperately needed at Shelbourne.'

'I was told that the English aristocracy thought it bad form to discuss money?'

'Yes, in certain matters it is,' Hester agreed. 'It would be thought vulgar to brag about what one had paid for one's possessions, and it is not done to haggle with tradesmen.'

'But perfectly acceptable not to pay them?'

'No, of course not,' Hester said and saw the scepticism in his eyes. 'Well, yes, I know that gentlemen often leave their tailor's bills unpaid when things are difficult.'

'But a gambling debt is a matter of honour?'

'Yes, certainly. Do you not agree?'

'A gambling debt must be paid, but I think the tailor is equally deserving of payment, perhaps more so since he has given his time and his goods.'

'Yes, of course, but one simply doesn't talk about it.'

'Not if one is a gentleman,' Jared said and grinned at her. 'Personally, I do not like to pay over the odds. I always get an estimate for work before I set it in hand—as I shall tell your grandfather when I see him this morning. If the house is to be restored, we need a price before we begin.'

'You are right, of course, but…' Hester shook her head in disbelief. 'Why are we even discussing it? You have just been shot at! We should be trying to think who might have done it. Do you have enemies—anyone who bears a grudge against you?'

'We have ruled out the second heir, so who else is there?'

'We haven't exactly ruled out Mr Grant,' Hester said. 'He is next in line and it is possible that he may think of what he would inherit if you died—but you said the shot came close to hitting you. If it had, your death would have been murder and the suspicion would then fall on him.'

'Yes, that is a valid point,' Jared said. 'He would be unlikely to show his hand so openly—unless he is a rotten shot and meant only to spook the horse.'

'I believe he told us he enjoyed shooting for sport,' Hester said. 'I cannot say for sure, but I would have thought he was possibly quite a good shot.'

'Then perhaps I do have an enemy,' Jared said. 'I may have made enemies in the past, though I am not aware of any that would try to kill me—and why now? These things only started when I came to England as the duke's heir.'

'Mr Grant is the only beneficiary of your death, sir,' Hester said thoughtfully. 'Unless you think that I…' She raised her gaze. 'You heard Grandfather say that he would leave everything to me if he could, and you know that I love this place.'

'It could not have been you who shot at me—and I do not think you the kind of person who would hire an assassin,' Jared said. 'Either I have an unknown enemy or it must be Mr Grant.'

'If you were wealthy yourself…who would benefit from your death, sir? I know you no longer have a fortune, but you said you had something.'

'I have a cousin,' Jared said. 'At this moment he would inherit most of my possessions…but Red is a rich man. He isn't interested in anything I have.'

'Didn't you lose your casino in New Orleans to your cousin?'

'In a manner of speaking,' Jared replied. He toyed with the idea of revealing the truth to her, that in fact he had given the gambling house to his cousin before he left, but he held the words back. 'Believe me, it isn't Red—he is still in New Orleans.'

'You can't be sure of that—and he could have paid someone to kill you, to make it look as though it had something to do with your English inheritance.'

Jared frowned. There was something in what she said, but he knew Red too well to give her suggestion more than a passing thought. He shrugged his shoulders.

'Anything is possible, but I would be inclined to rule that one out.'

'I'm just trying to help.' She wrinkled her brow. 'This family has suffered enough tragedies, Mr Clinton—I would rather it didn't happen again. I do not want to weep at your grave.'

'Would you?' His blue eyes were narrowed, intent on her face. 'Miss Sheldon—or may I call you Hester?'

'Yes, if you wish,' she replied. 'I think we are beginning to know each other, sir. I do not object to the use of my name in private. And, yes, I should weep if you died.'

'Then I shall not, at least for some years.'

'It is not amusing!' Her eyes flashed at him as she saw the gleam of humour in his eyes. 'You do understand that I said you may call me by my name in private?'

'Yes, of course I shall be discreet,' he said. 'In return I ask that you be discreet about what you saw this morning. I would prefer that no one knew about the shooting incident—and I believe we should keep our suspicions to ourselves about it perhaps being an attempt at murder.'

'Is that wise? Do you not think we should inform the duke—and make some inquiry into the possibility of an intruder on our land?'

'I think you may safely leave all of the latter to me,' Jared said. 'I assure you that I am more than capable of handling this—and the distress might make your grandfather unwell again if he were burdened with it.'

'Yes, that is very true,' Hester agreed, a little surprised that he should show such consideration. 'But you must take some precautions, sir. If this evil man were to succeed in his aim, it would destroy us all.'

'I am flattered that you should think so,' Jared replied. 'However, I believe that you would hold the family together, Hester. I think you a very capable young woman.'

Hester pulled a face. 'How dull that sounds, but I shall take it as a compliment, Mr Clinton—or perhaps I should start to call you Viscount Sheldon since it is your title?'

'Why do you not call me cousin—or Jared in private?' A smile quirked the corners of his mouth. 'Or is that too much to ask? You must tell me, for I am not rightly sure what you quaint English folks would think proper.'

'Cousin Jared!' Hester gave him a fulminating look. 'Please do not think you can fool me again. I admit that I was unsure at our first meeting, but I no longer believe you to be either uneducated or ill mannered enough to need any tuition from me.'

'Do you not? That is a shame. I had thought we would begin our lessons after breakfast. How shall I persuade you to spend time with me if it is not to teach me how I should go on in English society?'

'Incorrigible! You need no excuse, cousin. I shall naturally defer to you in estate matters. There is a great deal for you to learn about the way things have been run here. Since Grandfather's last illness, his people have come to me for their instructions. I have always asked for Grandfather's advice in the important matters, but I have tried to spare him all the small problems. Now that you are here, I shall come to you. Indeed, you must meet Mr Roberts today. He is Grandfather's agent and takes care of business matters, then there is Johnson—he is the bailiff and I am sure he would be happy to discuss land issues with you.'

'Ah...' Jared's eyes gleamed. 'I told you, I thought you capable, Hester. You are a remarkable young woman.'

'I am nearly seven and twenty and I have lived here most of my life. Everyone knows me here, and it has come to me naturally. You may find it harder, though if Mama is right you have experience of business yourself.'

'You look much younger,' he replied but his expression

was serious. 'I prefer that you continue to do just as you have been for the moment, Hester—though you may ask me if you think I can help you. I do not want to be seen as interfering. Besides, I have not decided to stay for good and it is better that you should remain in charge.'

'Oh...' She was oddly disappointed. 'I thought...when you showed an interest in the house...I hoped you might be prepared to stay and do your duty to the family.'

'I do not consider it my duty to live here unless I choose,' he replied. 'However, I may be prepared to marry a lady who meets my criteria—and I may do something for the estate. I believe it may not be beyond my means to restore the fire damage without resorting to a marriage of convenience.'

They were approaching the stables. Hester reined in and stared at him, trying to penetrate his mind, but failing.

'I have some idea of what it might cost. Mr Grant told me he thought it might run into some thousands of guineas.'

'Did he, indeed? Had he any thought of obliging you with the money?'

'No...at least, he said that he would advise me if I wanted to employ the right builders.'

'Indeed? Tell me, did you ask for his advice or was it given of his own accord?'

'He said that in his opinion it might exceed five thousand pounds.'

'Not a gentleman, then, since he was prepared to discuss money,' Jared said wryly. 'I should ignore what he told you, Hester. Leave that side of it to me, if you please.'

It was on the tip of her tongue to ask if he could afford to spend something in the region of five thousand pounds restoring a house he was not sure he wished to reside in, but she held the words back. It would be too personal, offensive—and she did not wish to be accused of vulgarity.

'Very wise,' he remarked as he got down and came to her assistance. 'For I should not answer if you did ask—and it avoids embarrassment.'

Hester gave him a baleful look as he set her on her feet, his hands lingering about her waist a second longer than necessary. Tossing her head, she walked away in a purposeful manner, leaving him to deliver their horses up to the waiting grooms. He might not be the ignorant hillbilly he had tried to make her believe him at the start, but he was still an extremely irritating man!

As Hester went swiftly into the house, she met her mother coming downstairs. She was immediately aware of Lady Sheldon's air of unease.

'Is something wrong, Mama?'

'We have a visitor, Hester. Mr Grant has invited himself to stay. He says he intended to call on you in town, but when he presented himself he was told you had left.'

'Oh, yes, I should perhaps have written to him. It slipped my mind.'

'Well, it made him anxious on your behalf and he came posting here immediately to reassure himself that you were not unwell.'

'He had only to ask my godmother,' Hester said and frowned. 'Surely there was no need to come in person. It is not as if we know each other well. We have met only a few times.'

'He seems to think that you may need him,' Lady Sheldon said. 'He did not come right out and say it, but he hinted that Mr Clinton might not be a trustworthy person.'

'Oh, how dare he?' Hester exclaimed, forgetting that she was cross with the heir herself.

'I reminded him that Mr Clinton's proper title is Viscount Sheldon,' Lady Sheldon said softly. 'I do not think he is best pleased. He claims to have come to offer us his protection, Hester—but I think we need protection from him!'

Hester looked at her sharply. 'What do you mean?'

'Only that he is so pompous,' her mother said. 'Do not look so startled, Hester dear. I dare say he means well.'

'Yes, perhaps,' Hester said. 'When did he arrive and where is he?'

'A few minutes ago, and he is having breakfast in the parlour.'

'Then I shall wait for a while,' Hester said. 'I shall go up and change, Mama. Please excuse me—and do not worry.'

She ran up the stairs and along the landing to her own rooms. It was a nuisance that Mr Grant had arrived so unexpectedly, especially as she could not help wondering if perhaps it had been he who had taken a pot shot at Cousin Jared.

Hester deliberately took her time changing into a practical morning gown. It was a pale grey with a demure neckline and had a pretty lace collar as its only ornament, in keeping with her advanced years, she decided. Since the heir saw her as capable, she would present him with the image his word conjured up in her mind. She arrived at the breakfast room just as Mr Grant was leaving. He smiled as he saw her.

'My dear Miss Hester, how pleased I am to see you looking so well. I was anxious when Lady Ireland told me the situation and I came at once to see if I could be of help. And I think it is a very good thing I did, for it must be a difficult situation for you all. Have no fear, I shall protect you to the limit of my ability.'

'I was not aware that I was in need of protection. However, we must always be glad to see you, sir,' Hester replied a little untruthfully. 'Perhaps we should talk later?

I went riding earlier and I should like to break my fast. As you have already eaten…'

'Yes, of course. I have been summoned to the duke's apartments and must wait on him immediately, but I shall certainly hope to see you later.'

Hester watched him walk away. He was not an unattractive man, being of medium build and height, his features pleasant but not handsome, at least to her eyes. His hair was a light brown, cut very short and thinning a little at the crown, his eyes a hazel green. His clothes were very plain, dark as suited his calling, but his boots, she noticed, were as fine as any dandy's and shone with a brilliant gloss.

Hester was thoughtful as she went into the breakfast room. She was the only one and she helped herself to some muffins and honey, and a cup of tea, which might have been hotter. However, she did not wish to summon the maid to make more, so she sipped it as she ate in solitary state. As she was leaving, she saw Jared come into the house. He was still wearing his riding clothes. She stopped to speak to him.

'Have you had your breakfast? Mr Grant has arrived— did you know?'

'The answer to both questions is yes,' he replied. 'As it happens, I had my breakfast with Mr Grant while you were upstairs.'

'Oh…' Hester frowned. 'What did you think of him? It seems a little odd that he should arrive this morning.'

'A short time after someone took a shot at me?' Jared nodded. 'I do not think we should make too much of that as yet, Hester. He seemed a decent enough chap, told me he hoped I would not cause the family any more grief for they have suffered enough.'

'He did not!' Hester was shocked. 'Oh, how dare he say that to you? It is not his place. We hardly know him, for he did not visit us until after Papa died—and…he spoke out of turn, sir.'

'I thought you were to call me cousin?'

She saw the gleam of humour in his eyes and was immediately suspicious. 'What did you say to him?'

'Now why do you suspect me of something?' Jared asked, a smile quirking the corners of his mouth. 'What should I have said to him?'

'He seemed to imagine he had arrived just in time to save us from you. Mama was very cross for she does not like him—and she does like you.'

'I am much obliged to her, and the feeling is mutual,' Jared said. 'I assured Mr Grant that I valued his advice and would try not to shame the family any more than I could help…though I must rely on you to set me right as I did not know how to go on in English society.'

'Oh, you!' She shook her head at him, because the sudden gleam in his eyes told her all he had neglected to say. 'You put on that awful twang, didn't you—and you acted as if you had come out of the backwoods.'

'Well, he seemed to expect it,' Jared said. 'Darn it, cousin, I didn't want to disappoint the man.'

'No wonder he was worried about us,' she said ruefully. 'If he insists on staying here to protect us from you, I shall blame you!'

'But I think we need him to stay—here, where we can watch him,' Jared said. 'If he does plan to get rid of me, it will give him plenty of opportunity, and the sooner he makes his move the better—if indeed it was Mr Grant who shot at me.'

'Does the evidence not point to him?'

'Yes, very much so, but that makes me inclined to doubt it.' Jared arched his brows. 'You really must not worry about me, Hester. I am capable of dealing with it, you know. One gets used to these things when one lives and works with hardened gamblers.'

'Did you truly own a gambling casino in New Orleans? I am never sure whether you are making things up or telling the truth.'

'Yes, but not the rundown hell your lawyer found me in,' he replied. 'I had recently bought that with the intention of pulling it down to build warehouses.'

'Oh…' Hester wrinkled her brow. 'What did you want those for, cousin?'

'Oh, for certain goods I wished to store there from time to time.'

'Were you a smuggler of goods to avoid tax?'

Jared's laughter was warm and delightful. 'I think you have a vivid imagination, Hester. I have a small import business in New Orleans. It was quite separate from the casino and remains in my possession.' It was actually rather larger than he had told her, but even this snippet of information seemed to have astonished her. 'I thought you might think it vulgar—I understand being in trade is not quite the thing.'

Hester pulled a wry face. 'My dear cousin, when your estate is on the edge of ruin, any source of money is more than welcome. Besides, importing isn't truly being in trade—and no one needs to know.'

'Are you a snob, Hester?'

She flushed. 'I don't know—am I? I was merely thinking of your image. Being a newcomer, you cannot afford to attract speculation—at least, no more than necessary.'

'I think perhaps you are a little bit snobbish,' he said, tipping his head to one side, a gleam of mockery in his eyes. 'But I don't mind it. I expect you've been taught to think that way.'

Hester smothered a laugh. 'Yes, I dare say I have. I do

not mind it for myself, cousin. I am glad that you are not as short of money as we were led to believe. It did seem odd that you had lost everything.' She gave him a considering look. 'Is there a lot more you aren't telling me, Jared?'

'Perhaps, but nothing that need worry you. Do not imagine that I have dark secrets that will jump out and shame the family. I am even considered respectable by some.'

'Nevertheless, you do have secrets you are not prepared to share,' she said. 'Tell me to mind my own business if you wish—but are you actually still in possession of a considerable fortune?'

'Mind your own business, my very astute, adorable Miss Sheldon,' Jared said. 'I have told you everything I intend to tell you for the moment—and it might be dangerous for you to know more.'

'Perhaps…' Her gaze narrowed as she studied his face, his expression revealing nothing. 'At least you did not give me a set-down, and perhaps I deserved it, for it was an impertinent question. Very well. I shall not pry into your secrets—but I hope you will tell me one day.'

'I may do that,' Jared said. 'The duke wishes to talk to me later this morning. Do you think I could speak to Mr Roberts first? I should like to become acquainted with him, as I think he may give me some good advice.'

'Yes, of course. He has his offices here in part of the house. I shall take you to him, and then I must speak to the housekeeper before I go up to Grandfather.'

'How efficient you are,' Jared said, his harsh features softening into a smile. 'I like you so much, Cousin Hester.'

'Oh…thank you,' she said, a little taken back by his directness. 'As it happens, I like you too, Cousin Jared.'

'We must see about those dancing lessons soon,' he

murmured, the warmth in his eyes setting up a very strange fluttery sensation deep in her stomach. 'Yes, I think it would be most pleasurable to learn to dance with you, Hester.'

'Lessons that I dare say you have no need of,' Hester said. 'But if you wish it...one afternoon in the long gallery.'

'I shall look forward to it,' he promised with such a look that her heart caught.

Her cheeks were warm as she avoided meeting his gaze. She had the feeling that he was flirting with her, but she tried to dismiss it as unlikely. If it were true, it must mean that he was bored and she was the only female available to him, apart from Lady Sheldon. She had noticed that he was unfailingly courteous and kind to her mother, which was one of the reasons that she had begun to like him very much. Perhaps too much for her own comfort, she thought. She must remember that Jared was intended for an heiress, and therefore a marriage between them was out of the question—even though he had teased her about it.

He had told her they would suit, and she was becoming more and more certain in her own mind that he was perfectly right.

After she left Jared to become acquainted with Mr Roberts, Hester went to the flower room, which was used only for the purpose of filling vases with flowers the gardeners delivered daily to the house. She spent a pleasant hour arranging various vases, and took one filled with her grandfather's favourite tulips up to his room. She knocked and was invited to enter. The duke was holding a book and seemed to be at ease with himself, for as he laid it aside she saw that it was a volume of poetry.

'How are you this morning, dearest?'

'Very much better now that you are home. This house

comes to life when you come back from wherever you've been.'

'You flatter me, Grandfather. What are you after today?' She set the vase close enough to him that he could see the beautiful blooms easily, and then bent to kiss his withered cheek. 'Is there something I can do for you?'

'Yes, you can promise me you will not marry that pompous idiot who came to see me earlier and had the audacity to tell me that he believed you would make him a good wife.'

'Mr Clinton said that to you?'

'Damn it, no,' the duke said, looking wrathful. 'I don't say you could do better than him, Hester, but he is at least a reasonable chap—one of us, and he'll have this place. I meant that fool who imagines he is God's ambassador on earth.'

Hester was bewildered. 'Surely you cannot mean Mr Grant, Grandfather? He did not ask you if he could address me?' She saw the truth in her grandfather's eyes. 'How dare he? I had no idea and I should never have permitted it.'

The duke looked relieved. 'Thank goodness you are a sensible girl, Hester. I know I have been unfair to you, keeping you here when you ought to have had your chance— but you're still young enough to find a better man than Grant.'

'He is a gentleman, sir.'

'Well, I know that, but he's a pompous fool. I never liked his grandfather and I cannot like him. I know nothing of his mother because I never met the woman above a few times—and he is too old for you.'

'I doubt he is much beyond five and thirty.'

'He talks as if he were older,' the duke growled. 'You won't listen to him, Hester? I couldn't stand having him here and I do not wish to lose you just yet. You'll have plenty of time when I'm gone.'

'Please do not speak of leaving us,' Hester begged. 'I love you and I do not wish to lose you. Besides, Mr Grant would not suit me.'

Her grandfather smiled, reassured. 'Well, how is he shaping up then—the American heir? I rather like the cut of his jib. Blunt and to the point at times, but he's like her, Hester—he's like my Amelia.'

'Yes, I have seen her portrait, and I agree.'

'I meant in nature. She was quick to fire up and we quarrelled too often, but I loved her—and, damn it, I think she loved me.'

'I am sure she did,' Hester said. 'I think her son is more than you might have expected, sir.'

'Bit of a dark horse, is he?' The duke nodded, looking pleased. 'Just what I thought myself. Did you know he is going to invite a builder to look at the fire damage? He said we need to get estimates before we set the work in hand—does that sound like a gambler to you, Hester?'

'No, it does not,' she said. 'I asked him if he truly had a gambling house in New Orleans and he said he did. Not that rundown place by the waterfront that Mr Birch told us of, but something better.'

'Playing a deep game, ain't he?'

'Yes, I think so.'

The duke's eyes narrowed thoughtfully. 'You'll get it out of him if anyone can. I think he likes you, Hester. He would be mad not to—but it's the way he speaks of you. He respects you.'

'I am glad to hear it, sir, but I do not think he will tell any of us anything until he is ready.'

'Do you think he still has some money?'

'Yes, a certain amount—I do not know whether it could be called a fortune.'

'Has our luck changed?' the duke said. He frowned at

her. 'I've wondered at times if the curse really was hanging over us, Hester—but this man…he could be the saving of this family if he chose.'

'Yes, I think you may be right,' Hester agreed. 'But will he choose to stay? I am not sure that we can hold him. I think the title means little to him, and at the moment he sees the house only as something that needs money spent on it. He doesn't love it as we do.'

'Give him time, girl,' the duke said. 'Something brought him here. He didn't have to come, and we can't keep him unless he wants to stay—so we have to hope that he comes to understand what being a part of a family like this really means.'

'I think he came because of his mother,' Hester said. 'He wanted to see her childhood home…and you.'

'He blamed me for making her unhappy. I dare say it was my fault if she was. I wished I could change it when she died, Hester—but it was too late.'

'I think he will come to understand that in time,' Hester said, looking thoughtful. 'We must hope that he likes us as a family…likes us enough to stay.'

'He likes you,' the duke said. 'As for the rest of us…' He shrugged his shoulders. 'Well, we shall just have to wait and see.'

Jared had found his way back to the library. He knew that many of the answers he sought had to be here in this room, the room his mother had liked to escape to at times. It was a long room, covered on three walls by beautiful mahogany bookcases, which were filled with leather-bound books. A cursory investigation had shown him that some of them related to the family history and were in the form of heavy family bibles or journals. Mr Roberts had informed him that the family had always recorded births and marriages in their bibles, but anything else would be found in the various journals.

Mr Roberts had told him a lot about the state of the family fortune, which was perhaps worse than he had imagined. Without help, the duke would soon have to sell either land or family treasures. Jared glanced around at the various pieces of porcelain that adorned small tables and stood on the deep windowsills. His practised eye knew the worth of all of them as he was a connoisseur of fine things, and had imported them into New Orleans to satisfy the tastes of its wealthy citizens for some years. Many of the items in his own suite at the hotel he owned there contained the finest pieces, often taken from the homes of aristocratic families forced to sell.

It would be humiliating for Hester if her beloved grand-father were made to sell things that had been in the family for centuries. He couldn't let that happen to her. He had come to England prepared to dislike his mother's family, to tell them exactly what he thought of them, and what they could do with their titles and their pride. He had held back because of a spirited young woman…and, yes, because of something he had seen in an old man's eyes.

Jared gave a harsh laugh. Red would say he had gone soft; he would say that he was letting himself be used by people who didn't deserve his help—and perhaps he would be right. The duke certainly hadn't behaved as he should towards his daughter, but he seemed genuinely to have regretted it. Besides, Jared had discovered that there would be no pleasure for him in venting his spite on these people.

To him the house was old, attractive in its way, but not as comfortable as some he owned. It had history, and in this room he could feel himself being seduced by it, knew that if he gave in he could easily be sucked into the world that was his by birthright…but was he prepared to go that far?

He had everything he wanted elsewhere. A life that suited him, wealth, friends, his empire of property and commerce that he enjoyed—and the freedom to come and go as he pleased. If he became Viscount Sheldon and in time the Duke of Shelbourne, he would lose that freedom. His brief talk with Roberts had shown him that, once accepted, it was a burden he could not put down. An estate like this wasn't just land and an old house that might be beautiful if he cared to spend a small fortune on it—it was people too.

Roberts had told him about cottages that needed repair, children who had no school to go to and men who would be thrown out of work if the estate were split up and sold. He frowned, because he knew he could not simply toss all that to one side. As the heir he owed it to the people who depended on his family to at least see if their lives could be made better.

But if he did that, would he be able to cut free? Did he want to if he could?

'Ah, my very dear Hester,' Mr Grant said as she came down from visiting the duke. 'I was just admiring the flowers and Lady Sheldon told me it was one of your duties. How talented you are, to be sure.'

Hester held her temper and her tongue. 'You are very kind to say so, sir,' she said, leading the way into one of the small rooms that led off to the right and were connected. Each of them had a pair of beautiful doors, which had been magnificent in their day, though the gilding had chipped in places and was looking decidedly sad. The room itself was furnished elegantly, though the upholstery had faded slightly and the curtains at the windows had seen better days. Hester had not always noticed it, but there was an air of neglect about some of the rooms that were used for family purposes.

She wished that she might be alone, for she had letters to write. The duke had asked her if she would send out invitations for the ball, which he wanted to hold in two weeks' time. She sat down at the desk near the window and took out a small pile of notepaper that carried the Shelbourne crest.

'Am I disturbing you?' Mr Grant asked as he chose a chair nearby and sat down, his gaze fixed on her. 'You are such a competent female, Hester. I have observed how you manage everything here to perfection, and I am persuaded that you will make some fortunate gentleman an excellent wife.'

The complacent look on his face told her that he was imagining himself in the role of that gentleman and believed his proposal must meet with success. She wished that the duke had forbidden him to speak to her, but unfortunately he had not done so, though he had begged her not to listen.

'You are welcome to stay if you wish, sir, but I have a pile of invitations to write. The duke is giving a ball in two weeks and there is no time to lose.'

'Perhaps I may be of assistance to you? I could seal the letters as you write.'

'Thank you for the offer, but I prefer to do them myself. Perhaps you might like to read a book or something?'

'I am disturbing you. Forgive me.' He got to his feet. 'I shall leave you in peace, Hester. It might be best if I had a little talk with the viscount.'

'Yes, please do so if you wish,' Hester replied, dipping her pen in the ink. She bent her head over the first invitation, mentally apologising to Jared for landing him with his pompous relative. Becoming aware that Mr Grant was still hovering, she looked up. 'Was there something more?'

'I wish to speak to you in private about something…
personal…but I can see this is not a good moment…'

'No, sir, it is not,' Hester told him firmly. 'I really must
get on—perhaps another day?'

'Yes, of course. Another time.'

She was aware of the slightly offended tone of his voice.
It was obvious that he meant to speak despite being dis-
couraged by the duke.

'I couldn't forbid him, Hester,' her grandfather had told
her. 'But I told him that I did not think you wished to hear
a proposal of marriage from anyone.'

'I wish you had forbidden him,' Hester had replied.
'But I understand that you could not. I shall try to dissuade
him from speaking at all, but if he does…I must refuse
him.'

The duke had been pleased with her answer, but that did
not stop her feeling apprehensive about the interview with
Mr Grant. She could not imagine why he had decided that
she would suit him—they hardly knew one another and
she had done nothing to encourage a proposal of marriage.
Giving her head a little shake, she bent her head to her
work once more. The duke's list of guests was rather long,
and though she suspected some of them might be unable
to attend, she must follow his wishes and invite all of his
old friends. Her mother had added a few names to the list,
and Hester herself had added the names of some young
ladies she happened to know. If everyone accepted, they
would have almost a hundred guests and at least thirty of
them would be invited to stay for a day or two.

It would make a lot of work for the servants, and would
probably mean getting extra help in from the village, so
the sooner she sent out the invitations the better.

Chapter Six

'I have been looking for you everywhere,' Mr Grant said in an accusing tone as he saw Jared enter the hall that afternoon. 'No one told me that you had gone out.'

'I was not aware that I had to leave word of my intentions for you, sir,' Jared replied. He had just accompanied Mr Roberts on a brief tour of the estate and was feeling grim about the prospects for its people unless something was done swiftly to stop the rot. 'I believe it is time for that quaint English custom of taking tea? We had best not keep Miss Sheldon waiting—but if you wish, I can spare you a few minutes afterwards.'

'I beg your pardon?' Mr Grant looked as if he could not quite believe his ears. 'Are you aware of the position I hold in this family, sir?'

'I suppose you're the one who gets this place if I have a fatal accident and die—after the old man is finished, of course.' Jared deliberately slipped into his practised twang.

Mr Grant stared at him in horror. 'I find that deeply offensive, sir. I am the grandson of the duke's brother and as such I am entitled to respect from you.'

'If you want respect from me, you have to earn it,' Jared

said, not a trace of the twang in his clipped tones now; his gaze was steady, cold, giving nothing. 'I have just come from looking at cottages not fit for beasts to live in—women with young children having to cope with a leaking roof and walls so damp you can see the mould. Tell me what you were planning to do about this before I came along and you may have something worth saying.'

'I do not understand you, sir. What has the condition of these cottages to do with me? Naturally, I deplore the situation, but it is quite common amongst the poor.'

'Then as a potential heir you should be ashamed of yourself,' Jared said, clearly angry. 'I don't hold with slavery; its abolition cannot come soon enough for me, but I know people who would be ashamed to let their slaves live in conditions as desperate as those I've seen today.'

'I know nothing about these things…' Mr Grant stuttered, stunned by this uncalled-for attack. 'In my parish I do what I can to alleviate the plight of the poor.'

'Excuse me, I need to speak to Miss Sheldon.'

Jared walked off, leaving his offended relative to stare after him in dismay. He headed for the larger salon at the back of the house, expecting that he would find Hester and her mother about to take tea. He knew that he should not have lost his temper, but he was disgusted by what he had been shown that afternoon. What right had this family to gamble away a fortune when the people they should care for were forced to live in conditions he would not tolerate for his horses? As he entered the large parlour, he saw that Hester was alone. A large silver tray had been brought in and there was a stand with an array of tiny cakes, biscuits and scones. The comfortable scene made him even more aware of the poverty he had just witnessed and the anger welled up in him.

'Miss Sheldon?'

Hester glanced up as he stood on the threshold. She was immediately aware of his rage and rose to her feet. 'Is something wrong, cousin?'

'You're damned right there is!' he said. At that moment he looked and sounded more like his grandfather than he had any idea of. 'Did you know—did you know about those cottages? The conditions those people have to live in…have you seen the way Mrs Blinch has to bring up her child in that ruin of a place? It's no wonder the babe is never free of colds.'

'You have been to Mr Blinch's cottage?' Hester was taken aback by his attack.

'And to a few more, though that was the worst. I am surprised at you, Hester. I would have thought you would do something about it.'

'You are accusing me of neglect?' Hester was startled and then offended. She had not called on the Blinch family since her return from London, but it was her habit to take gifts of food and clothing to many of the poor in the village. 'We do not actually own their cottage. Mr Blinch works for us, it is true, but the cottage is his own—Grandfather sold some of the cottages to the tenants years ago. Mr Blinch wanted to own his cottage and Grandfather agreed.'

'From what I understand, the cottages you do own aren't much better—and as the main landlord in the district you could have done something for the family, even if it was only to move them into something better.'

'We do what we can, but money is tight. We repair the cottages in turn—and it is really Mr Blinch's responsibility to repair his own roof.'

'You sold them the damned place, and he works for your family. Mrs Blinch said they offered the property back to your grandfather in return for repairs that would make it habitable.'

'I did not know of this,' Hester said. 'I am not sure Grandfather does either. But we do try our best. It just isn't possible to do all the work necessary. You visited the village, but there are other cottages on the estate where repairs have been made.'

Jared's eyes narrowed. 'You knew about these things and yet you were only concerned about restoring the fire damage here—and you are preparing to give a ball for friends. Don't tell me that doesn't cost money.'

'We have accounts for wine and foodstuffs.' Hester flushed beneath his scornful gaze. 'They will be paid in time.'

'They certainly will. Roberts will bring them to my attention, I dare say.'

'If you are here,' Hester said with a flare of defiance.

'Oh, I shall be around long enough for that,' Jared told her. 'I might have ignored what was going on if I hadn't seen it, but this place is sinking into the mire. If someone doesn't do something, you will all go under.'

'I know the situation leaves much to be desired...' Hester had never seen him like this and it made feel uncomfortable. It was as if he were blaming her for all the ills that had befallen the estate and the people that worked for the family. She had done her best with what little resources she had, and she felt hurt and humiliated that he should speak to her in such a fashion.

'Too damned right it does! I wouldn't keep my horse in a ruin like that cottage,' Jared said. 'I've given orders for it to be pulled down and rebuilt.'

'You've done what?' Hester was taken aback. 'What are the family supposed to do in the meantime?'

'I've arranged for them to move into the dower house until the new cottage is prepared for them, and I've instructed Roberts to have the doctor call on them by tomorrow morning at the latest. His bill will be sent to me here.'

'I am not sure that Grandfather would approve of your acting in such a high-handed way, sir.'

'If he wants my money for this house, he will swallow it,' Jared said grimly. 'If you will excuse me, I am not fit for a lady's sitting room. I have things to do. I shall see you this evening.' He turned and pushed his way past Mr Grant, who was staring into the room in stunned silence, and disappeared from view.

'Well, really,' Mr Grant said, walking into the room as Hester sat down again. 'I must apologise to you for such a show of bad manners, Hester. I think he must have lost his mind, speaking to you in such a way.'

'He was angry,' Hester said, her hand trembling slightly as she poured the tea. Tears were stinging behind her eyes, but she was too proud to give way in front of Mr Grant. 'I know the cottage is terrible, and some of the others are not much better, but there simply wasn't any money to spare. We had to attend to our tenants as and when we could manage it.'

'The blame cannot fall on you,' Mr Grant said. 'To subject the ears of a delicate lady to a tirade of that nature is not the behaviour of a gentleman.'

'I have the responsibility for what goes on here. When my father died, Grandfather became ill and could see no one other than my mother and me for months. I have done what I could, but…' She shook her head, refusing to let the viscount's accusations upset her. 'Tea, Mr Grant?'

'Thank you, milk but no sugar,' he said, giving her a look of such sympathy that it made her cross, which helped to restore her natural balance. 'It is unfair that you should have carried such burdens. No lady should have to concern herself with business matters.'

'I assure you that I do not consider it a burden,' Hester said, smothering a sigh. 'It has disturbed me that we could not do more repairs, but…' She shook her head. Had it been selfish of her to care more for Shelbourne House than the villagers' cottages? She was not immune to their distress, but the house was very dear to her heart.

'Miss Sheldon—my very dear Hester…' Mr Grant had got to his feet and then, as she stared at him in bewilderment, he rather awkwardly went down on one knee. 'You must know that it would give me great pleasure to take you away from all this…to make you my wife. I am not a rich man, but I have sufficient for our needs and you would want for nothing that a delicate lady requires. You would never again have to bother your pretty head over money or estate matters.'

'Sir! Mr Grant, I beg you will please get up,' Hester said. She stared at him in dismay. If it was not enough that she had just endured a lecture from Jared, now she was being forced to deal with something she would rather not. 'Mother…' She gave a sigh of relief as Lady Sheldon walked in. 'How is Grandfather?'

'Oh, the same as ever,' Lady Sheldon said, looking at her daughter and then the rather flustered-looking Mr Grant. 'Do forgive me if I have interrupted something?'

'Oh, no,' Hester said and glanced at her embarrassed suitor. 'We shall speak again another time, sir. Forgive me, but I am a little upset for the moment.'

'Oh…yes, of course,' he said. 'Excuse me.' He went hurriedly from the room, leaving mother and daughter together.

'Oh, dear,' Lady Sheldon said, looking rueful. 'I did interrupt something, didn't I?'

'Yes, thankfully,' Hester told her wryly. 'He tried to gain my attention earlier and again just now. It is very awkward,

Mama, for I do not wish to receive a proposal of marriage from him.'

'I should think not,' her mother said. 'Your grandfather could not stand him living here and we cannot do without you, Hester.'

'I think you will find the situation is changing,' Hester replied, looking thoughtful. 'The viscount just harangued me for not doing something about Blinch's cottage. He has ordered it pulled down and intends to rebuild—and he has had the family moved to the dower house until their new cottage is ready.'

'Yes, so Mr Roberts told me. He was very pleased about things. He says that the viscount is a revelation…whatever that means.'

'I am sure he is doing the right thing—but he blames me for neglecting the Blinch family and not having their house repaired.'

'It was not truly your business to do so, my dear. I know they live in terrible conditions, but Blinch might have taken a hammer and nails to the roof himself.'

'It was in bad condition when they bought it, and I dare say Mr Blinch has enough to do. He works for us and he keeps pigs on that piece of land he owns. I suppose he did not realise that cottages need repairing often when he asked to purchase it.'

'Yes, I dare say. I suppose he imagined it would be advantageous to own his home, but ownership brings responsibility.'

'That is what Cousin Jared was implying,' Hester said. 'He thinks we are bad landlords and intends to show us how things should be done.'

'I have observed that he is a determined gentleman,' Lady Sheldon said and smiled at her daughter. 'Be content that he is prepared to do something for the estate, Hester.

If he lifts the weight from your shoulders, it cannot be a bad thing. You have enough to do with the house and servants, I imagine.'

'It is only a matter of time before he starts to tell me what I am doing wrong here!'

'No, I do not think it,' her mother said. She gave Hester a knowing look. 'Surely, this is what you hoped for, my dear? You could not have expected that things would remain the same. Indeed, they could not. I had visions of the house being sold over our heads. I shall sleep very much better now that the viscount is in charge here.'

'Yes, well, of course, it is his place to handle the estate matters,' Hester agreed with a frown. 'But he was angry with me, Mama. I have not seen him that angry before.'

'I do not think it was truly you that aroused his anger,' Lady Sheldon told her. 'And I am certain that once he has calmed down, he will realise that none of this was your fault. You did not gamble the family fortune away, and you have done your best to hold us together this long.'

'I do not think he sees it that way,' Hester said and shook her head. 'I shall not think about it, Mama. I am far more distressed by the knowledge that I have yet to allow Mr Grant to speak. I shall refuse, of course, but I do not think anything will stop him from asking.'

The truth was that she was far less upset by the knowledge that she would have to bear with Mr Grant's proposal than the attack on her by the viscount. She had thought they were becoming friends. How could he think so badly of her?

Jared had already begun to calm down and to realise that he had been unfair to Hester. His disgust at the way a family like this had squandered their wealth and allowed their land and property to fall into neglect had made him so angry that he had poured it all into her ears. She had been struggling to keep the family above water for months, and she had done what she could for a few tenants. He frowned as he changed out of his riding breeches and stripped down so that he could wash the stink of the stables from his body. Anyone seeing him now would be aware of the strength of the man, his muscles toned and hardened, his skin slightly tanned by the sun. He looked powerful and confident, a man in his prime.

Jared's fury eased as he dressed. It wasn't Hester's fault things had come to this pass. It had taken years of careless management and reckless gambling to bring a once-proud family to this. He knew that he had been wrong to blame her as she had undoubtedly done what she could and it was not she who had brought the Shelbourne family to this precarious state.

He had intended to walk away once he'd set work in hand at the house, to cut and run before he was sucked in, held by tenuous bonds that were growing tighter with every hour he spent here. He groaned as he began to pull on clean linen and the clothes one of the servants had set out for the evening. A young footman was waiting on him, and he was pleased by the man's choice. Frederick would make an excellent gentleman's gentleman, and he would need one if he decided to make his home here in England. At home he had often dressed carelessly, enjoying the freedom to work with his hands or ride out where he pleased without bothering about what he wore. It would be different if he stayed here, became the man this family needed.

Was he really considering it? Jared frowned at himself in the shield-shaped mahogany dressing-mirror. The furnishings in his apartment were adequate, but he would want to make changes. He could send for his furniture from his home in New Orleans, instruct Red to sell everything there, because he doubted that he would live there again—though he would keep some of his property in France.

Was he mad? Jared stopped in the act of brushing his hair. Why should he contemplate spending a fortune on this house? Why should he sink thousands of dollars into the estate of the man who had not even bothered to find out anything about his American grandson until he had no other choice?

Because his mother would have wanted him to rescue her family from the pit they had worked themselves into! The answer came to him like a blinding flash. It was the reason he had been drawn here against his will. He had fought it, but the serious eyes of a young woman had made him accompany her down here, and the feeling that this house, this life, was his future had been growing on him ever since.

Jared swore softly. It seemed that he was caught whether he liked it or not, and it might be as well to tell his relatives that their worries were over. He could afford to turn this estate around without even noticing it, and he would—but he could still leave when it was done, still go back to his old life.

What did he really have waiting for him in New Orleans? Friends, his cousin, property…but he could have most of those things here. He might have something more if he hadn't blown his chances with Hester earlier.

Would she forgive him? Jared pondered his future. He would need a helpmate in this place, a woman who could put up with him as he was, because he wasn't likely to change. Jared had a temper. He was used to having his own way in most things. The woman he married would have to accept that, if she could. He had asked Hester to find him a bride; at the time he had been jesting, but now he saw that the right wife would be necessary if he were to make a life here. He would just have to see if things worked out as he hoped.

Hester changed into a pale grey evening gown. Most of her gowns were grey, because she had been in mourning, and she had only a few in colours. This gown was not one of her best. She asked her maid to dress her hair in the old severe style and she wore no jewellery when she went downstairs that evening. She was determined to show the viscount that she was not prepared to flatter him by making an effort with her appearance. He had taken the estate affairs into his own hands and she could only be grateful for that, but she would draw back a little. It would not do to become vulnerable where he was concerned. If she allowed herself to like him too much, she might be hurt.

Jared was already in the drawing room when Hester entered. Lady Sheldon was there also, and they seemed to be talking together. Mr Grant had withdrawn from them and was staring out of the window, clearly preferring his own company. Lady Sheldon looked at Hester and smiled.

'Cousin Jared has something to say to you, dearest. He tells me that he owes you an apology.'

'I was rude to you when I came back this afternoon,' Jared said, looking at her seriously. 'Forgive me. I should not have blamed you for the condition of those cottages. Lady Sheldon has told me that you have always done what you could for the villagers.'

'You are forgiven,' Hester replied. She lifted her head proudly and gave him a regal stare, aloof, reserved but polite. 'I understood that you were angry, and I am relieved that you have done something to help.'

'I was just telling Lady Sheldon that I think we should

tear down all the cottages one by one and rebuild. Spending good money on repairs is a waste of time when we can build modern cottages with some indoor sanitation and walls that do not run with water.'

'It would cost a great deal of money,' Hester said, wrinkling her brow. 'Are you prepared to invest so much here?'

'Yes, I believe I have no choice,' Jared said. 'If I am to live here as the heir—and, in time, the duke—I must be satisfied that things are as I should want them.'

Hester stared. His announcement was all that she had prayed for, but somehow she was not prepared for it. It would make her life so different, so much easier in some ways—and so difficult in others.

'Yes, of course,' she managed. 'I am…delighted that you have decided to make this house your home.'

'As to that, I dare say I shall spend some of my time in London,' he said, 'Though when I am there I shall make sure that things go on smoothly here.'

'I see…' Hester breathed more easily. If he were not always here, she might be able to bear it when he was in residence, at least for a while. 'Have you told Grandfather yet?'

'No, but I intend to do so this evening, after dinner,' Jared said. He frowned at the reserve in her that had not been there before. 'I trust that my plans for the village meet with your approval?'

'Of course—but it is your decision, sir.'

'Are you angry with me, Hester?'

'No—why should I be? You have apologised and that is enough.'

'I think she ought to be angry if she is not,' Mr Grant said, coming out of his lurk at the far side of the room. 'You were abominably rude to her earlier, sir.'

'Yes, I was,' Jared admitted. He would have said more, but felt it inappropriate at that moment. 'Hester has been kind enough to accept my apology.'

'It is fortunate for you that she is good-natured,' Mr Grant said and glared at him. 'If someone spoke to my wife in that way, he would answer to me.'

'Please, Mr Grant, say no more,' Hester begged. 'It is forgotten.'

'You must be aware of my regard for you, Hester. I have never been more shocked in my life—to hear this…person speak to a lady in that way…and the lady I admire above all others!'

'Really, it does not matter,' Hester replied. 'Viscount Sheldon had his reasons to be angry and I do not dispute them. Besides, if he is to put money into the estate, he has a right to do as he pleases.'

'Put money into the estate?' Mr Grant scoffed. 'I doubt that he has any to speak of.'

'In that you are mistaken, sir,' Jared replied easily. 'I was intending to tell you privately, Lady Sheldon, but let me assure you that your financial worries are over. I have decided that I shall spend what is necessary to turn this estate around. When I first came here I was not certain that I wished to use my money for that purpose, but I have made my decision. The new cottages are but a part of it. Tomorrow I shall speak to a builder recommended to me by Mr Roberts, and we shall set all the work that needs doing here in hand. Though, of course, we may need to employ more than one master builder and I dare say the work will be ongoing for some time—though I hope to repair the fire damage in time for the ball.'

'A likely tale!' Mr Grant pulled a face and turned away as someone came into the room. 'Thank God, dinner is ready!' he remarked in a voice of doom.

'I am sorry, my lady,' the butler said. 'Cook is not quite ready for you just yet—but there is a visitor…'

'A visitor—at this hour?' Lady Sheldon was surprised. 'Who can that be?'

'I hope I am not putting you out,' a man said from the doorway. The butler stood aside and he walked in. 'Lady Sheldon, Miss Sheldon…I sent you a letter to tell you that I was on my way, but it appears that you have not received it. I am so sorry to appear unannounced, as it were.'

'Mr Knighton—Richard!' Lady Sheldon went forward to meet her cousin, hands outstretched. She smiled at him as he kissed her on both cheeks. 'How delightful to see you, my dear cousin. Please come and meet someone. I do not think you have met the duke's heir—Viscount Sheldon, this is my cousin Mr Richard Knighton.'

'Delighted to meet you, sir,' Mr Knighton said, extending his hand. 'Hester mentioned you to me, but to meet you is a great honour. May I welcome you to your new home. I hope that you are finding your feet, sir. It must have come as something of a shock to see this place.'

'I was pleasantly surprised. It is large, but I had expected a much older house. This is not so very old as country houses go, I believe.' Jared took his hand and shook it. The newcomer seemed a pleasant, well-spoken gentleman and his appearance could not have been more timely.

'The main building is perhaps something over a hundred years, though the wings were added later,' Mr Knighton replied. 'As you say, it might have been worse—those Elizabethan mansions can be impossible to heat, so they tell me. My own house in Hampshire is very much smaller, but also more modern. If I were you, I should pull this place down when you have the opportunity and build something more modern.' He saw Hester's expression and smiled. 'Yes, I know you love it, Hester, but you cannot expect the viscount to feel as you do.'

'As a matter of fact, I believe it could—and shall—be beautiful,' Jared said. 'Most of the neglect is superficial and a master builder will soon rectify it. With some finer furniture and new curtains, it would be much improved.' He saw Hester's eyes widen and smiled. 'It will take time, Miss Sheldon, but I think I can see the way to make it a much nicer place for all of us to live in.'

'It will be yours to do as you wish one day.'

'I mean to refurbish my own apartments first,' Jared told her. 'I intend to have my personal things shipped over from America.'

'Then you do intend to stay?' Mr Knighton said, his gaze narrowing. 'I had thought it unlikely, but I am delighted for Hester's sake—and my cousin's.' His gaze moved across the room, discovering, as if for the first time, that another gentleman was present. 'Sir—I believe it is Mr Grant, is it not? We met once before in London, I think.'

'Sir.' Mr Grant inclined his head stiffly. 'Miss Sheldon introduced us, if you remember. It was here, not London.'

'Of course. How foolish of me to have forgotten. It is pleasant to see you again, sir.' He crossed the room to shake hands just as the housekeeper came in to announce that dinner was served.

'Ma'am, will you take my arm?' Jared offered it to Lady Sheldon, who took it willingly, giving him a warm smile. 'Shall we lead the way?'

'Yes, certainly,' she said. 'I think you should take the chair at the head of the table, sir. Indeed, I have asked that it be set for you. Yesterday we left it empty as it is rightly your grandfather's place, but he does not dine with us these days.'

'If it is your wish,' Jared acceded. He glanced at Hester,

seeing that she had accepted Mr Knighton's offer to take her in. Mr Grant was looking decidedly annoyed over it. He was certainly sulking about something and would bear watching. 'I hope you are satisfied with the arrangements I am making, ma'am?'

'I shall defer to you in all matters of business,' she said. 'I have never had a head for it, sir. Poor Hester has had to do it all since her father died and the duke became ill— but you will take the burden from her shoulders.'

'I am hoping that she will continue to advise me,' Jared replied in a voice that he knew would carry to Hester. 'I have much to learn and your daughter knows everyone. In household matters she will continue as usual, I hope?'

'Oh, you may rely on her good will,' Lady Sheldon replied. 'She has the good of the estate at heart, sir—as I am sure you know?'

'Yes, of course, I never doubted it.'

Hester cast him a suspicious glance as she waited for her chair to be adjusted by her escort. Jared was doing the same for her mother, and he smiled at her as he made his way to the head of the table and took his seat.

The servants had begun to serve, starting with Lady Sheldon. However, they took the wine to Jared to approve, which he did after asking what vintage it was. Hester was fascinated to see his expression when he tasted it, because she could see that he did not particularly approve, though he did not dismiss it out of hand. She signalled to the butler.

'Yes, Miss Sheldon?' he inquired, bending his head to listen to her softly spoken words.

'The better wines please, Mr Harris. We have guests…'

The butler nodded and went away. She knew that he had been reserving what few good bottles they still had for the duke's use, but there was no longer the need. She had no doubt that the new viscount would make his own arrangements about stocking the cellars.

A few moments later, the glass at Jared's side was replaced with another and a different wine offered in its place. He looked across the table at Hester, raising his brows. She gave him a cool nod, but felt a secret satisfaction as he tasted it and smiled his approval. He lifted his glass to toast her as the wine was served to everyone. Hester met his gaze, but gave nothing away. She was torn between conflicting emotions.

His decision to stay was both amazing and satisfying, because she knew that now he had made up his mind to invest in the estate he would do it well. The new cottages were a sign that he meant to leave nothing to chance. It was a stroke of fortune that she could not regret—and yet there was a small hurt inside her still. If he really liked her, thought anything of her, he would surely not have accused her of being uncaring.

His attack had brought her close to tears, something that happened very rarely these days. She was not sure why this should be and found that he occupied her thoughts throughout dinner.

She had begun to like him more than was sensible, and his outburst had been a sharp reminder. She knew nothing about this man. He might be anyone—anything, for a matter of birth was nothing. Jared had admitted to having had a gambling club—what else was there in his past that she did not know?

She had assumed that the attempt on his life must be something to do with his having become the duke's heir, but why should it be? It could quite easily have something to do with another part of his life. Besides, she was almost seven and twenty, well past the first flush of youth. Now that he had accepted what he was, he would be inundated by invitations—and there would be endless match-making mamas with beautiful young daughters in tow. He was an attractive man and he clearly had a fortune at his finger-tips, despite his early attempts to hide it. Once news of that got out, he would be able to take his pick of all the eligible ladies in London.

It was hardly likely that he would look at Hester for his wife. He had once said laughingly that they would suit, but he had been mocking her—pretending to go along with the need for a rich wife. Yes, he had been laughing at her all the time. Perhaps she had deserved it for attempting to judge him from the lawyer's reports, but how could she have guessed the truth?

He had punished her for thinking him an uneducated hillbilly and she suspected that he had not intended to rescue the estate when he first came down to Shel-bourne. Something had convinced him that it was his duty to restore the family pride, but she could not fool herself into thinking it was because of her. He had shown compassion for the poor and needy, and she re-spected his integrity. If she had liked him before he had shown his compassion, she liked him all the more now—but he had also demonstrated that he had a temper and could be harsh. On consideration, she decided that she did not like him the less for it, but she was not certain that she could bear to live in this house once he found himself a bride.

Lifting her head once more, she glanced towards Jared and found his eyes on her. His expression was so intent that she blushed and turned away to talk to Mr Knighton, who was sitting next to her.

'Lady Ireland tells me she shall come down at the weekend,' he told her. 'I dare say you will be busy now that you have decided on the date for your ball.'

'How did you know that?' Hester asked. 'I only wrote the invitations this morning.'

'I did not know. I assumed it,' he replied easily. 'Did you not tell me that you were intending to have a ball quite soon?'

'Yes, of course I did,' Hester said. 'I have an invitation for you. You will come, I hope?'

'I was rather hoping I might stay until after the ball?'

'Oh…yes, of course. I see no reason why not,' Hester said, a little surprised that he should ask. 'I know Mama will be pleased to have you.'

'And you, I hope?' he asked, smiling at her.

Hester recalled that she had felt he meant to propose to her in London and her heart sank. It was bad enough that Mr Grant should be determined on making her a proposal. To have to turn down two suitors would be so much worse.

For Hester, the remainder of the evening was something between a source of irritation and a source of mirth. It seemed that Mr Knighton had taken a dislike to Mr Grant, and the feeling was reciprocated. They both paid a great deal of attention to Hester, which she found unwelcome, but the expression in their eyes as they looked at each other was mildly amusing. She could not help suspecting that she was the reason behind their dislike of one another, and while she found the idea amusing that the two of them were behaving like dogs guarding a bone, she did not like to think that either of them was serious about courting her. Indeed, she could not understand it, because she was not an heiress and, now that the viscount had decided to accept his duties to the estate, there was no possibility of it ever being hers.

It was years since she had thought of marriage. She had received one proposal as a young girl, but had not liked her suitor, who was much older. Since then things had changed and she had put any girlish dreams she might have had behind her. To have not one, but two gentleman displaying their feelings was astonishing. She did wonder if she were making too much of their hints, but the signs were there and kept her restless for part of the night, though in the end she slept soundly.

The following morning when she went out for her usual ride, she found that Jared was still in the stable yard. She wasn't sure that he was waiting for her, but at a signal from him one of the grooms brought out her horse already saddled.

'I thought we might ride together—if neither of your beaux has made a prior arrangement?'

He had noticed it too, which meant she had not imagined the rather foolish posturing of her suitors the previous evening.

'I would have refused them had they asked,' Hester told him at once. 'I enjoy my morning ride and I do not wish it to be spoiled.'

'Shall you think it spoiled if I accompany you?'

'No, as I do not imagine you are looking for the chance to make me an offer, Cousin Jared, and that is what I particularly wish to avoid.'

'You do not find pleasure in being courted by two eligible gentlemen?' Jared asked, apparently innocent, but with a gleam of mockery in his eyes.

'No, I do not,' Hester replied. 'I cannot imagine what has got into their heads! I have no fortune and I am not a beauty. I cannot see why they suddenly wish to marry me.'

'You may not be what society calls a "beauty"—if that is the correct term? But you must know that you are attractive, intelligent and lovely.'

Hester felt herself blushing under his scrutiny. 'Well, I do not think I have improved greatly in the last eight years and no one has asked me to marry them in all that time— so why should they now?'

'Has no one asked? What fools these English gentlemen must be,' Jared said, but still with that mocking look that she distrusted. 'Perhaps it is my arrival that has made them realise what they might lose?'

Hester accepted his help to mount, but refused to be drawn by his teasing. She glanced at him as he mounted his own horse. 'What made you decide that you wished to stay?'

'Do you wish for the truth?'

'Yes, of course.'

'I do not like being shot at, for one thing. If it was meant to frighten me away, to perhaps make me give up my claims to this place, it was miscalculated. My second reason is more complicated. I find that I have some attachment to this place—these people. I suppose it was realising that if I did nothing a lot of people besides the family would suffer.'

Hester glanced at him as they walked their horses from the yard. She was a little offended by his plain speaking for clearly he had planned to leave the family to sink or swim alone, but the plight of the people who depended on the estate for their living had swayed him.

'You are compassionate, sir. I cannot fault that, though I would hope you also have loyalty to the family. You are, after all, one of us, whether you like it or not.'

'Perhaps…' His eyes seemed to dwell on her face in a manner that made her look away. 'I have little sympathy for a family who threw away all the advantages that birth and wealth had given them—but you have not had the advantage of wealth, I think?'

'I have never been denied anything I wished for,' Hester

assured him swiftly. 'I may not be an heiress, but I consider myself fortunate.'

'Yes, I thought so,' Jared said. 'Shall we let these horses have their fun? I'll race you as far as the lake, but we shall not go beyond—though I doubt another attempt will be made on my life while you are with me.'

Hester acquiesced and they both gave their horses free rein, galloping side by side over the turf. It had been dry and bright of late and the ground was hard beneath their horses' hooves. She was a little anxious as they came near the lake, but nothing happened and they gradually slowed their horses, ambling back towards the house by another route. Apart from that first conversation they had hardly spoken until just before they returned to the stables.

'Do you want me to send the pair of them packing?' Jared asked, giving her a penetrating look. 'I shall do it if they are annoying you too much, Hester,'

'Oh, no, you must not,' she said quickly. 'Mr Knighton is Mama's cousin by marriage—her only relative outside the Shelbourne family really. And Mr Grant...if Grandfather is prepared to accept his visits, then I must.'

'I thought you would say that,' Jared said, dismounting and coming to lift her down. His hands encircled her waist and he lifted her easily. She was aware of the power and strength of him as they stood close together for a few moments. Something in his look made her swallow hard, her heart seeming to pound against her ribs. He was so very masculine, so powerful! She had never met another man who made her feel this way. 'But if you change your mind, just tell me.'

'I am more worried about your safety,' Hester confessed. 'If that shot was a deliberate attempt on your life, it must mean someone wants you out of the way.'

'I am aware of the problem, therefore the element of

surprise has gone,' Jared replied, his mouth thinning to a hard line. 'I assure you that I am not as careless about this as you might think. I have set matters in hand, and I may have to go off to meet someone another day. Perhaps after I have my meeting we may know a little more about the situation.'

'Oh…' Hester's heart caught. 'Will you be away long?'

'Perhaps only a few hours, perhaps a day or so. Not long. I shall be here for the ball, and I have builders to see before that. Why do you ask?'

'No reason in particular. I suppose I am getting used to having you around, cousin.' Ridiculously, she was thinking that she would miss him!

'Well, that is nice to know,' he drawled. 'I appreciate that, ma'am. It's right nice to be appreciated.'

'Oh, you…insufferable man!' Hester retorted and walked away. He was impossible. He delighted in teasing her and she never knew whether to take what he said seriously or not! She was fermenting inside as she went up to the house. Her life had been so ordered, so sensible before he arrived, and now she hardly knew whether she was coming or going. It was all his fault for arousing feelings, sensations that she had never experienced or expected to experience. Before that kiss she had been willing to settle for what she had but since then…impossible, foolish thoughts kept coming into her mind. One of them was that she would rather like to be kissed that way again.

'Ah, there you are, Hester,' Mr Knighton said, coming to greet her as she entered the hall. 'You have been riding. Had I known, I should have come with you—you never know who might be about. I have heard tales of a high-wayman working in this area. I understand he is ruthless and will shoot anyone who dares to defy him.'

'Oh, I doubt such a rogue would be on our land,' Hester

replied, giving him a sharp look. 'He must know that the duke's keepers would shoot or capture him if he was seen doing something he ought not on our estate.'

'If they are not in league with him,' Mr Knighton said. 'I dare say he has friends who tell him about the routes wealthy visitors are taking—inside knowledge is always helpful to a man of that nature.'

'Yes, I suppose it must be,' Hester said, but knew that she had never considered it. 'Servants, I expect…if they bear their employers a grudge. It would not happen here.'

'You think not? You are very confident of your servants, Hester.'

'Yes, I am, of course. Most of them have been with the duke all their lives. I cannot imagine they would do anything to disoblige him.'

'They may not be so happy at the thought of their new master.' Mr Knighton frowned. 'Do you find him acceptable, Hester? Grant says he has a shocking way of speaking at times—though I cannot say I particularly noticed it last night.'

'He has a wicked sense of humour,' Hester replied drily. 'He sometimes likes to tease. I assure you he has all the manners of a gentleman—and something more. He is strong and one feels as if one may rely on him.'

'That sounds as if you like him.' Mr Knighton raised his brows. 'In London I thought you did not particularly care for him?'

'He is something of an acquired taste,' Hester said carelessly. It was a throwaway line because she did not like being quizzed in this manner. 'At first I thought we should not get on, but now…I like him. Yes, I do like him and I think he will be good for the estate.'

'Then I am satisfied,' Mr Knighton said. 'I was anxious that you might feel you were being usurped, your authority taken away by someone who is only here because of the tragedy that has overtaken your family.' He smiled at her with a warmth that made her distinctly uncomfortable. 'You must know that your comfort…your happiness…is of paramount importance to me.'

'You are very kind to say so,' Hester replied. 'Mama always says that we can rely on you, sir—and now, if you will excuse me, I must go up and change.'

'It is your birthday a week after the ball, is it not?'

'Yes…why do you ask?' Hester hesitated and looked at him in surprise.

'Oh, it was just something I was thinking…' He looked a little odd. 'I wondered what you might like as a birthday gift?'

'I do not expect anything, but any trinket would be acceptable, sir.'

'I must think of something special for such an important day.'

'Important? I hardly think so. When I was eighteen I thought such things important, these days I do not consider them so.'

'But it is a special day.' He frowned at her. 'Is it possible that you have not been told, Hester?'

'Been told what?'

'You will, I believe, be seven and twenty this year?'

'Yes, I fear so. It makes me feel very much like an old maid and I do not take it kindly that you should remind me of it,' Hester said, laughing because she spoke in jest.

'Your age means nothing except in one regard.'

'Which is?'

'I am reluctant to say since your mother has not seen fit to tell you—but perhaps you should know. I am sure Grant knows of it and that is why he has begun to pay you attention.'

'I should be glad if you could explain that, for it is a mystery to me.'

'Your lawyer should be contacting you soon, Hester. Your father's great-aunt died two days after he did and her will states that if he should die before her, her estate comes to his heir or heirs, which is you, because there was only one child—but not until the day of your twenty-seventh birthday. I do not know the extent of your inheritance, but I imagine it must be perhaps twenty thousand pounds.'

'Twenty thousand pounds…that is a small fortune,' Hester said, staring at him in amazement. 'Are you certain of your facts, sir? I had no idea that anything had been left to me.'

'It would have come to your father had he lived another three days and then your mother would have inherited half of it, but the terms of the will are quite clear. As things stand, the money is yours. Lady Sheldon asked me to look into it at the time.'

Hester was shocked. 'I cannot understand why no one has told me anything.'

'Perhaps your mother thought it might make you vulnerable to fortune hunters, Hester. I had imagined she would have told you before this—and, as I said, I believe that Grant has got wind of it.'

Hester frowned. His suggestion that Mr Grant wished to marry her because she had twenty thousand pounds coming to her in a few weeks was less than flattering, but it might well be true. She had been puzzled by his sudden interest in offering for her.

'I wish that I had been told,' Hester said, frowning. 'Had I known, I might have borrowed against it to put things right here before this.'

'Perhaps your mother did not tell you for that reason,' Mr Knighton replied. 'I hope you are not angry with me for telling you?'

'I am grateful for it, sir,' Hester said. 'I shall ask Mama why she did not tell me—and now, if you will excuse me, I must go up and change.'

She was not aware of his eyes following her as she ran lightly up the stairs. Instead of going immediately to her own room, she went to her mother's private apartments, knocking and entering. As she had expected, her mother was sitting propped up against the pillows, sipping the dark, rather bitter chocolate drink that had been brought up for her by her maid.

'Hester, darling,' Lady Sheldon said, glancing up at her. 'You look as if you have been out in the fresh air.' She frowned as she saw her daughter's expression. 'Is something wrong, dearest?'

'Mama—why did you not tell me that I am to inherit money on my next birthday?'

'Oh, has the letter arrived?' Lady Sheldon questioned.

'No, not as far as I know. Mr Knighton told me. He wanted to warn me because he thinks Mr Grant knows and is after my money.'

'How very disobliging of him,' Lady Sheldon said. 'I meant to tell you some time ago, but the duke asked me to wait. He thought that if you knew about the money you would borrow against it to pay the estate debts and he was determined you should not—at least while he lives. Had he been able to leave it to you, as he would like, it would have been a different matter.'

'But you must have known that I should discover it soon?'

'Well, it does make you independent, dearest. I suppose I was afraid you might decide that you wished to set up your own establishment…or marry.' Her expression was one of guilt. 'It was selfish of me, Hester, but I should hate to live here if you went away…and I could not desert the duke, you know.'

'Oh, Mama…' Hester sighed. 'As if I should leave you and Grandfather in the lurch simply because I am to come into some money. I should certainly liked to have used some of it before this had I known. I am sure the lawyer might have arranged a loan or something.'

'Then I suppose I ought to have told you. Forgive me, Hester?' Lady Sheldon looked guilty, for she knew herself at fault.

'There is nothing to forgive, Mama, but it was something of a shock when Mr Knighton told me.'

'I dare say he may be right, you know, about Mr Grant. He has a small estate, and is comfortably off, I believe, but twenty thousand pounds would be very tempting to a man of moderate wealth—and you are a good catch for any man, with or without the money.'

'I think I may receive a proposal from Mr Knighton, Mama. I believe he told me because he wanted to scupper Mr Grant's chances.'

'Did he have any in the first place?'

'No, none at all,' Hester said and suddenly laughed as she saw the funny side of her situation. 'Do you think I shall receive other offers once it is generally known that I have twenty thousand pounds?'

'It will not be known, dearest. It would be vulgar to speak of it. If someone you liked made an offer, you would disclose it then, but otherwise I do not think we need to mention it.'

'Well, Mr Grant must have discovered it somehow. I hope it will not make life uncomfortable for us. I shall, of course, settle some of it on you once I have it, Mama.'

'Now that is something I shall not allow,' her mother told her. 'I am quite comfortable living here, dearest, and now that the viscount has told me that I am welcome to stay even after the duke… Well, I have no need to worry. I can visit Bath as often as I please and return here when I wish. My income will be sufficient for my needs. You must promise me you will not spend yours on the estate, Hester.'

'I should certainly have done so before Cousin Jared came, but it is not necessary now—and I do not think he would permit it.'

'No, I dare say he would not. Cousin Jared, as you call him, is a very determined gentleman. Quite different from what we were led to believe. I have every confidence in him, Hester.'

'Yes…' Hester frowned. 'It was very kind of my father's great-aunt to think of me.'

'It would have gone to your father, your real father, of course, had he lived,' her mother told her. 'Lady Mountblain was very fond of your father—and she had no children of her own, or none that survived their childhood. It happens all too often, dearest. If you manage to rear one or two healthy children, you must think yourself fortunate.'

'I do not think I shall marry.'

'You might. Not to Mr Grant, of course. I could not approve that, but you might find someone else you like.'

Something in her mother's eyes told Hester what she was thinking, but she refused to let herself dwell on such pipe dreams. She knew that at her age, and even with twenty thousand pounds, it was unlikely she would find a suitor—at least, one she could really like. Though her inheritance would make her acceptable to many gentlemen with pockets to let if it were public knowledge. She must hope that no one would know of it, for being hunted for her twenty thousand pounds was the last thing she wanted!

Hester left her mother's room. The shock of discovering that she was an heiress had begun to wear off a little, and she realised that she did already have the means to set up an establishment of her own somewhere if she cared to—and she might wish to do just that if Viscount Sheldon were to bring his bride to this house.

Hester discovered that thought was almost too painful to be borne. She put it from her mind as she went down the hall to her own room. At least the mystery of her sudden popularity had been cleared up. A little smile played over her soft, rather sensual mouth as she thought about telling Cousin Jared. She was certain he would see the funny side of it, and she needed to explain that she had known nothing of it. If she had known, she would never have allowed things to continue to slide here at Shelbourne. It was important to her that he should know that and she changed quickly, wanting to find him and tell him of her discovery before he learned it from someone else. However, when she went down and inquired after the viscount, she was told that he had gone out and was not expected back for the rest of the day.

Feeling restless, Hester took herself off to the flower room where she commenced filling vases with beautiful blooms. It was a job she normally enjoyed, but that afternoon her mind kept straying from the task. She was impatient to tell Cousin Jared her news, and she had no idea that by the time he returned something would have happened to put it right out of her mind.

Chapter Seven

'Are you certain of your facts?' Jared asked. His expression was hard as he looked at the face of the man he had employed to investigate the circumstances surrounding the attack on him in London. 'You are sure that you've seen this man lurking in the shrubbery at Shelbourne?'

'Yes, sir. I still don't know his name, but I followed you here the way you told me, and I caught sight of him once on the road, but then I think he saw me and I lost him. But I kept following you, making sure the young lady didn't spot me—and I was in the grounds that night…the first night you came down, me lord. I am certain I saw him. Staring up at the house he was. I watched him the way you told me, and he didn't see me this time. He just stood there looking up at the windows until the young lady looked out. After that he left sharpish. I don't think he wanted 'er to see him.'

Jared looked thoughtful. 'That means she would probably recognise him. It all fits with—' He broke off, for he was still not certain he could trust this man. 'And have you seen him again?' His instinct was telling him the answer, but he waited for the man to continue.

'Yes, sir. It seems as if he's a guest at the house because I've seen him talking to the young lady. It's a bit queer, ain't it, me lord?'

'Yes, it is rather strange. Unless…and then of course it all makes perfect sense…' Jared nodded, keeping his thoughts to himself. 'Can you describe this man to me in detail?'

'Yes, my lord,' the man replied and proceeded to do so in such a graphic way that Jared was left in no doubt of the man's identity. Only his motive remained in question— that was still a mystery.

'You have done well.' Jared drew a handful of gold coins from his pocket. 'This is what I promised you. You may return to London now and go back to your business… whatever that may be.'

'Don't you want me to keep watching him, me lord?'

'What I do not want is for him to realise that he is being watched,' Jared said. 'He might decide to put off his plans to eliminate me and I prefer that he make his move sooner rather than later. If he saw you hanging around, he might guess that I had recruited you to my side.'

'I could tell him that I was merely trying to earn the money he paid me,' Tyler said. 'I've took a fancy to workin' for you, me lord. I might be able to help you in lots a ways.'

'Well, if you wish to work for me, you may continue to do so,' Jared said. 'But I want you to stay away from him. There is something else you may do for me. Listen carefully, because it is important.'

Hester was working at her household accounts in her grandfather's library when she heard a commotion. She laid her pen down and looked up as the door opened and one of the footmen came in.

'Yes, Briggs?' she said, getting to her feet because he looked concerned. 'Was there something you wanted?'

'It's Mr Knighton,' he said. 'It's bad news, Miss Sheldon. He was out riding and someone shot at him. The shot went wide, but he fell from his horse and he has injured his arm. I've had him helped up to his room, miss, and I was wondering if I should send for the doctor. His horse came back to the stables. One of the grooms went looking and found him lying up near the lake. He was unconscious, but he came round as Ned reached him, complaining of pain in his shoulder and arm.'

'Mr Knighton was shot at—and he fell from his horse?' Hester was shocked. It had so nearly happened to Jared! 'Yes, yes, of course you must send for the doctor. This is terrible—to think that he was attacked on our land.'

Hester followed the footman from the room, her mind whirling in confusion. Two men had been shot at in a matter of days. This was something that could no longer be ignored! She had been almost convinced that the shot that might have killed Viscount Sheldon had been fired because he was the duke's heir—but why should anyone fire at Mr Knighton, who was merely a guest in the house?

Her first thought had been to see how Mr Knighton was, but it would have been most improper for her to go to his room. She went instead to find her mother, who was sitting in her favourite parlour at the front of the house.

Lady Sheldon was working at her embroidery and she glanced up with a frown as her daughter entered. 'These silks do not match, Hester. It is most annoying, for I ordered the same colour and this yellow is brighter. It will look odd, do you not think so?'

'I do not know, Mama, but you must forget it for the moment—Mr Knighton has had an accident while out riding. He fell from his horse.'

'How dreadful,' Lady Sheldon said, getting to her feet at once. 'Is he badly hurt?'

'I have been told that he complains of pain in his shoulder and arm,' Hester said. 'The doctor has been sent for and he was helped to his room. It would not be right for me to visit him there, but perhaps you would care to see if he has all he needs?'

'Yes, of course. I shall do all I can to make him comfortable,' Lady Sheldon said. 'It is most unfortunate. I have never liked horses…nasty unreliable creatures, if you ask me.'

'I do not think it was the horse at fault,' Hester said. 'I believe there was a gunshot nearby—perhaps a poacher in the woods.'

'A poacher? Mercy on us!' Lady Sheldon looked even more shocked. 'The keepers are not doing their duty properly. Your grandfather should know about this!'

'I think it best to wait and tell Cousin Jared,' Hester said. 'We do not wish to worry Grandfather over this, Mama.'

'I dare say you are right,' Lady Sheldon agreed. 'You must speak to him as soon as he returns. I shall go up to Mr Knighton at once.'

Hester watched as her mother left the room. She picked up the embroidery Lady Sheldon had abandoned and looked at the silks. She saw at once that the shade of yellow in the needle was much darker than the one previously used and pulled it out, searching in her mother's very untidy workbox until she found the correct colour. She was just about to rethread the needle when the door opened. Glancing round, she saw that Jared was standing there, watching her.

'Embroidery, Hester? I did not think you had time for such things.'

She threaded the needle and put it back on top of her mother's work, frowning as she looked at him. 'Mama could not find the colour she wanted. She has this minute gone up to see what she can do for Mr Knighton until the doctor comes.'

'Is Mr Knighton unwell?'

'He was shot at while out riding by the lake and fell, injuring his shoulder and arm.' Hester looked at him anxiously. 'I am afraid that he may have been right, though I did not believe him when he told me this morning.'

'What did you not believe?' Jared's brows arched.

'He said that there is a highwayman operating in the district.'

'Did he, indeed? Why did he tell you that, may I inquire?'

'He was concerned because he thought I had been out riding alone, and he said he would have come with me to protect me.'

'It seems that he was in need of protection himself,' Jared said. 'But I believe his advice was sound, Hester. I would prefer that you took a groom with you when you go out riding.'

'You cannot think that I would be in any danger?' She stared at him in surprise. 'I have lived here for most of my life, cousin, and I have walked and ridden wherever I please without coming to harm.'

'I understand that,' Jared replied, 'but for the moment it seems that there is a dangerous character at large. I do not wish you to come to harm.'

'Well, I suppose…' Hester bit her lip. She had remembered her surprising news and was about to speak of it when her mother came back into the room.

'I am so glad you are back,' Lady Sheldon said, clearly distressed. 'This is a terrible business. Mr Knighton says that he believes whoever shot at him intended to kill him and it was only good fortune that made him lean forward just as the rogue fired.'

'He does not think it an accident—perhaps a poacher?' Jared asked, shaking his head as Hester looked at him.

'I do not know what to think,' Lady Sheldon said. 'Mr Knighton told me that he believes there is a dangerous highwayman at large in the district. It has given me the shivers. Hester, dearest, you must stay inside the house until this creature has been caught.'

'Mama…'

'I think she must be sure to take a groom when out riding, unless I accompany her,' Jared said. 'But I should not worry too much, ma'am. I think it more likely to have been a poacher. I cannot believe a highwayman would shoot at your guests for no reason—unless Mr Knighton was robbed?'

'He did not mention being robbed,' Lady Sheldon said, looking relieved. 'Do you really think a poacher may have misfired?'

'I think it more likely,' Jared said. 'However, I shall speak to Mr Roberts. We shall employ more men, for I do not wish anyone to come to harm, especially Hester—or you, ma'am.' He smiled at her warmly. 'Please try not to worry too much, Lady Sheldon. I can promise you that no harm will come to your daughter if anything I can do will prevent it.'

'It is such a relief to me to have a gentleman here that I may rely on,' Lady Sheldon said. 'Hester, please go up to the duke. He may have heard of this business and he will want to speak to you.'

'I shall go up and reassure him,' Hester said. 'Excuse me, cousin. I shall see you later.'

'Yes, of course,' Jared replied. 'I have things to see to myself—but we shall talk again later this evening. After dinner, perhaps?' He smiled at her, a teasing look in his eyes. 'You have not yet given me my dancing lessons.'

'You are teasing me, of course.'

'Perhaps, but I do need to speak to you alone.'

'Yes, of course, after dinner,' Hester said. She wanted to talk to him now, because her thoughts were confused and she needed to ask him what he was truly thinking about this business. It was bad enough that he had been fired at, but now Mr Knighton had also been on the receiving end of a shocking attack. Who was behind it all—and what was the reason for what was happening here? But he had things to do and her grandfather might be in need of reassurance. 'I shall look forward to it, sir.'

She went quickly from the room and up the stairs to her grandfather's apartments. Her knock was answered immediately and she went in, finding him sitting in a chair, a rug over his knees and a glass of cordial on the table beside him. He gestured towards it. 'Take that rubbish away, girl, and bring me a glass of wine if you will.'

'The cordial might do you more good,' Hester said, but obeyed his instruction, bringing him a glass of his favourite Madeira.

'I've had the doctor in here, thought I might need something to restore my nerves, damned fool!' he said. 'He tells me he was called out to see Knighton—the man fell from his horse apparently. Something about a shot being fired at him, might have been serious…but it's merely a badly bruised shoulder, so I'm told.'

'Cousin Jared thinks it may simply be a poacher misfiring,' Hester told him calmly. 'He intends to set more men to keep a guard and discover who the culprit is, Grandfather. It is nothing to worry about.'

'Good thing he was here. He'll sort it,' the duke grunted. 'He's a capable chap, I'll say that for him. Calling him cousin now, are you?'

'He did not wish me to call him by his title.'

'Humph! I suppose he thinks it pretentious, but he'll get used to it. He has a lot to learn about us, Hester, even if my girl did teach him to be a gentleman. We do things differently and he needs to learn that if he wants to keep his feet on the ground.'

'I think he is learning very quickly,' Hester said. 'Mama relies on him completely. She feels very much safer now that he is here, I believe.'

'Your mama is a ninny, to put not too fine a point on it, Hester. Charming and sweet-natured, I'll give her that, but as much sense as a peagoose.'

'Grandfather! That is not kind of you,' Hester reproved. 'Mama is perfectly sensible—if a little nervous at times. After what she has suffered it is understandable. She lost my father, my brother and Papa. I think she could not stand it if anything happened to me.'

'Why should anything happen to you? Ninny!' He frowned at her. 'Why should anyone want to harm you? You aren't keeping something from me?'

'No, sir—but I understand that you and Mama have kept something from me. I think it was a little unfair not to tell me I would inherit twenty thousand pounds when I was twenty-seven.'

'You would have insisted on spending the money on the estate,' he growled. 'I couldn't let you do that, girl. Told your mother not to say—but I suppose she told you?'

'No, it was Mr Knighton. He thought I already knew.' Hester looked thoughtful. 'He gave me to understand that he believes Mr Grant also knew about the inheritance.'

'You think Grant asked for you because of the money?' The duke glared at her. 'Stuff and nonsense! He knows a good thing when he sees it, that's all—the money would be a bonus. Besides, Grant ain't short of a shilling or two. He told me that he was in a position to offer you everything that you had been accustomed to and more—pompous idiot! As if you would marry him!'

'I would not marry him if he were the richest man in England!'

'Well, he ain't that, but my heir may be. I received a report from Mr Birch this morning. Apparently, he made a few more inquiries and he thinks the viscount was having a little fun at his expense—says he may be rolling in the readies.'

'Yes, well, I know Cousin Jared has more money than he led us to believe,' Hester replied. 'We are fortunate that he seems inclined to spend some of it restoring the estate, Grandfather.'

'Yes. I don't suppose I could have expected it in the circumstances. I didn't treat his mother as I ought.'

'I believe he understands that you regret what happened.'

'Humph…well, it seems we've been fortunate.' He gave her a calculating look. 'If you married him, you would have your place here for the rest of your life, Hester. It's where you belong.'

'Thank you, dearest Grandfather,' Hester said and smiled. 'But I rather think he might have some say in the matter.'

'A girl like you could marry anyone. If we'd been fair to you, you would have married long ago. I wanted to keep you here and so did your mother.'

'I wanted to stay here, so you need not feel guilty—but I ought to have been told about my inheritance.'

'My fault. She would have told you before this, but I asked her to wait.'

'Well, I know now and I am not planning to leave you in the lurch. Once Cousin Jared has everything under control, I may decide to spend some of my time elsewhere.' She saw his frown. 'It will only be for a visit now and then, so do not look like that, Grandfather. I shall not desert you.'

'I'm an old fool, and a selfish one,' he told her with a

rueful look. 'I don't deserve you—but I couldn't face life if you left us for too long.'

'Do not distress yourself. I have no intention of leaving just at the moment. I have received a few acceptances for the ball this morning, from our nearest neighbours. I dare say I shall receive more soon.'

'It's time we opened this house to visitors. I shall come down for the ball, Hester—and I think I might start coming down for dinner again soon, though not tonight.'

'I know we should all like that,' Hester said and kissed his cheek. 'If you feel well enough, dearest?'

'I'm as right as I shall ever be,' he growled. 'Run along now and get changed yourself. And don't worry about poachers or pompous idiots who fancy their chances. If Grant gives you trouble, send him to me.'

'Yes, sir, I'll do that,' Hester said, laughing to herself as she went out.

She walked along the landing, turning the corner to the main part of the house, and then stopped as she saw Mr Grant coming towards her.

'Miss Sheldon—Hester…' he said, making it impossible for her to go on by blocking her passage along the hall. 'What is this I hear about Knighton? Took a tumble from his horse, they say.'

'I believe his horse may have been startled by a shot,' Hester said. 'He thinks there may be a dangerous highwayman in the area—but the viscount says it is more likely to be a poacher.'

'Are you sure it wasn't him?' Mr Grant said. 'Where was he when the shot was fired? He is a bit of a dark horse, if you ask me. Wouldn't trust him myself.'

'I think that is a wicked thing to say.' Hester was immediately angry. 'Why would Cousin Jared want to cause Mr Knighton to have a fall?'

Grant shrugged his shoulders. 'Can't say—unless Knighton is on to him. He was here in England when the fire started. Did he tell you that, Hester? He could quite easily have come down here and started it himself before going back to London.'

'That is ridiculous! Why would he wish to do such a thing?'

'He is next in line after the duke,' Grant said, looking disgruntled. 'He wanted to get his hands on the estate, if you ask me.'

'Jared would never stoop to anything that low!' Hester spoke sharply, her temper aroused. 'I think you should be careful what you say, sir—that is slander of the worst kind.'

'Well, the man is a liar,' Mr Grant said. 'Coming here and pretending to be something he isn't.'

'He has a sense of humour, which is something you seem to lack, sir.'

'It seems to me that I am not welcome here,' Grant replied. 'It might be as well if I were to take myself off in the morning.'

Hester was tempted to answer that as it deserved, but held her tongue. 'It is your decision, sir. I am sorry if you feel unwelcome, but...you must know that you are welcome to stay on if you wish.'

'Give me a reason to stay, Hester! Tell me that you will marry me.'

'Mr Grant! I am flattered that you should wish to marry me, but I am afraid that my answer is no.'

'Is that final?' he demanded, clearly angry. 'I suppose Knighton asked you. I knew he meant to when he warned me off.'

'If Mr Knighton spoke to you about this subject, he had no right,' Hester said. 'Even the duke would not do that, sir. I am nearly seven and twenty and my own mistress. If I wished to marry, I should make my own decision.'

'It isn't for the money,' Grant said, looking petulant. 'I like you and I thought you would make me a good wife. You seemed the right sort of girl to be a vicar's wife—but you've changed. I think the money has gone to your head.'

'I knew nothing of my inheritance until today,' Hester replied with dignity. 'I assure you that it has made no difference to the way I feel about anything.'

'Well, be careful of Knighton,' he said with a bitter twist of his mouth. 'And of Viscount Sheldon. I would not trust either of them too much if I were you. I have some business at home in Cambridgeshire, so I shall leave in the morning, but I shall return for the ball.'

'I shall be happy to see you, sir,' Hester replied, maintaining her dignity with difficulty. 'But I must tell you that I do trust Viscount Sheldon as much as any man I know.'

She inclined her head and walked past, going up a flight of stairs at the end of the hall to her own rooms. Inside she was feeling furious that he should have made such wicked insinuations against the viscount. To suggest that he might have set the fire so that he could inherit sooner was malicious and evil—and his obvious jealousy of both Mr Knighton and Jared was plain. Ever since she had learned of the attack on Mr Knighton she had been trying not to let her suspicions cloud her mind, but now she could no longer deny them.

She believed that Mr Grant had tried to kill them both. His attack on Jared was clearly to rid himself of his only rival for the title and…he must have attempted to get rid of Mr Knighton because he considered him a rival for Hester's hand. The duke had thought Grant unlikely to have fired the shot that had caused Mr Knighton's accident, and perhaps he had not done it himself—but she was convinced that he was responsible.

She could hardly wait to change into her evening gown and go in search of Jared. The sooner she alerted him to what she had learned, the better!

It was frustrating to find that Mr Grant was already in the drawing room when she came down that evening. He was standing by the window, looking out at the gardens, leaving Lady Sheldon to talk with Jared alone. Hester's mother was smiling, clearly finding pleasure in the heir's company. When Mr Grant turned his face he wore a sullen expression, his eyes narrowing with dislike as he stared at the viscount.

'Hester, dearest,' Lady Sheldon said, 'Mr Knighton has decided that he will take his dinner in his room this evening. His shoulder is too sore to bear a coat. He hopes to be well enough to dine with us tomorrow—and Mr Grant tells me he has business elsewhere, but shall return for the ball.'

'Lady Ireland will be with us tomorrow,' Hester said. 'We shall have at least ten couples staying with us for the ball, Mama, and some will arrive towards the middle of next week.'

'It will be so pleasant to have mixed company in the house again,' Lady Sheldon said. 'And your godmother is always a welcome guest.'

'I am not certain that Lady Ireland approves of me,' Jared said, a twinkle in his eyes as he looked at Hester.

'Oh, I am sure she will once she really knows you,' Lady Sheldon said serenely. 'We are particular friends, you know. She must like you when she knows how kind you have been to us.'

'Well, I must hope so.'

'I am certain I am right.' Lady Sheldon glanced at the gentleman watching them with a scowl of displeasure.

'Mr Grant, will you take me in, please? My lord, please give your arm to Hester.'

Jared came to her as the others preceded them. He offered her his arm. 'Hester, something is bothering you. Is it this business with Knighton?'

'Yes, and no. I must speak with you alone later.'

'After we have dined, as we agreed. I shall not linger over the port with Grant.'

'Be careful of him,' Hester said. 'It would not be wise to offend him.'

'I am aware that the gentleman does not like me.'

'I think it may be more,' Hester said, 'but now is not the moment, sir.'

'Later,' he said and pulled out a chair for her. His hand brushed her neck as he helped to adjust her chair when she sat down and a delicious little shiver ran down her spine. She was very much aware of him at that moment, and her heart caught as she turned her head to look at him. His smile was intimate, making her pulses race. Her lips parted on a sigh—she wished that they might be alone now, at this very moment. However, being the sensible girl she was, she gave him a polite nod and he left her to take his seat at the head of the table.

It was a ridiculously long table for the four of them, far too formal to allow intimate conversation, and so the talk had been general, concerning various small scandals that had been reported in the society columns of a London newspaper. Hester was glad when she was able to follow her mother into the parlour they favoured for the evening, because it had a good fireplace that did not smoke and was comfortable in both summer and winter.

'I shall be quite pleased when Mr Grant leaves us,' Lady Sheldon told her daughter with a confidential air. 'I do find his company a little tedious, but of course we must not show him any discourtesy. He is the next in line and…' She shook her head. 'That is all over. I believe we shall be lucky now that the viscount is here.'

'Of course we shall, Mama,' Hester replied and turned away, so her mother would not see that she was anxious. Lady Sheldon was far too nervous to cope with the idea that someone might be trying to murder Jared.

The tea tray had been brought in and Hester had only just handed a cup to her mother when Jared arrived, closely followed by Mr Grant. Obviously, neither of them had wished to spend time alone with the other. Mr Grant said that he would take a cup of tea, but Jared refused, standing by the window, staring out into the darkness until Hester had finished serving.

'I think I should like a little air,' he said, turning to look at Hester. 'Would you care for a stroll on the terrace, Hester?'

'Yes, very much,' she said, getting up at once. 'I have been suffering with a headache and it will make me feel better.'

'Hester, dearest,' her mother said. 'Why did you not tell me? I hope you are not ill'?'

'No, of course not,' she said. 'All I need is a little air, Mama, and I shall be better.'

'You may trust me to take care of her, ma'am,' Jared said.

'Yes, of course I do,' Lady Sheldon said. 'Enjoy your walk, my dears.'

Hester could not resist glancing at Mr Grant, but the look of sheer jealousy and spite made her shiver as she preceded Jared from the room. She led him from a side door into a small, secret, walled garden, which was filled with the scent of jasmine and late spring flowers.

'Oh, how lovely it smells out here,' she said as Jared came to stand at her side as she reached the sundial in the centre of the garden. 'This is one of my favourite places, particularly at night.'

'I think I can smell jasmine—or is it honeysuckle?'

'Possibly both,' Hester said. 'It is so sheltered here that they flower again and again throughout the spring and summer.' A little sigh escaped her as she looked up at him. 'I wanted to warn you—I believe Mr Grant was behind the attempt on your life and that of Mr Knighton.'

'Do you, indeed?' Jared looked down at her anxious face. 'You were inclined to doubt it earlier. May I ask what has made you change your mind?'

Hester hesitated for a moment, then, 'I think he made the attempt on you because he wishes to have the title for himself—and he is jealous of Mr Knighton because I have refused his offer of marriage and he imagines that I might prefer my mother's cousin.'

'And do you?'

'I think I like Mr Knighton more than Mr Grant, but I have no wish to marry him.'

'But Mr Grant thinks you may?'

'I understand that Mr Knighton warned Mr Grant off and that has made him think it, I suppose. Mr Knighton was concerned that Mr Grant wished to marry me only for my inheritance.'

Jared raised his brows. 'Your inheritance? Forgive me. I did not know that you were an heiress.'

'Neither did I until this morning,' Hester said. 'If I had, I should never have allowed things to become as bad as they are here. Grandfather knew that I would insist on borrowing against the money to pay for repairs we needed— to the cottages and the house—and he insisted my mother did not tell me. Mr Knighton told me this morning that I am to inherit twenty thousand pounds on my twenty-seventh birthday in three weeks' time.'

'Are you really almost seven and twenty?' Jared's eyes teased her. 'I would have thought no more than three and twenty at most.'

'You flatter me, cousin,' Hester said and shook her head at him. 'But do you not see how serious this situation is?'

'For the moment I can only think how lovely you look by moonlight,' Jared replied in husky tones. He reached out for her, his hands holding her firmly but without hurting her as he drew her towards him. He gazed down at her for a moment as her eyes widened, her lips parting on a little breath of surprise, and then he bent his head, his mouth caressing hers in the softest of kisses. Hester felt the heady sensations surging through her at the touch of his lips, moaning and swaying towards him as she lost control.

Feeling her response, Jared deepened the kiss, his tongue probing her mouth and, when she opened it, entering to tease and taste her. His hand moved down the arch of her back, cupping her softly rounded buttocks and pressing her closer so that she was aware of the throbbing heat of his manhood through the fine silk of her gown. She felt as if she were melting into his body, becoming a part of him, her whole being blissfully light.

'Jared...' Hester gazed up at him as he released her at last. She felt weak with desire, overcome with a longing for something she had never experienced before in her life. 'I...oh, I do not know what to say.'

'Say nothing for the moment,' he told her with a smile. He ran his thumb over her mouth. 'You have a beautiful mouth, my dearest Hester—it begs for kisses. You were made for love and loving, and I am amazed that no one has snapped you up long before this.'

'I have never met anyone I wanted to kiss me until…'
She faltered, shy and uncertain, her eyes searching his
face. 'You did like kissing me as much as I liked being
kissed?'

Jared chuckled deep in his throat. 'My precious darling!
Do you imagine I kiss every woman I meet like that?'

'Perhaps. I have no idea. I hardly know you, cousin.'

'I know you,' he replied in a voice that was like thick
melted honey invading her, flooding through her veins,
making her stomach clench with what she understood
must be desire. 'I want to make love to you, Hester.' He
saw her flinch and smiled. 'I know this is new to you, my
love. I am in no hurry, so do not fear me. You will learn to
want me as I want you—but before we can indulge ourselves, we must clear up this unpleasant business.'

'Mr Grant hinted that you were in England at the time
of the fire. He insinuated that you might have come
down here and set fire to the house in the hope of
becoming the new duke.'

'What was your reply?' Jared's gaze intensified.

'I told him that it was a gross slander,' Hester said.
'You would never do anything that low!'

'I thank you for your faith in me,' Jared replied, the lazy
smile that made her heart catch touching his mouth. 'It is
true that I may have been in London for a night or two
before I went to Paris on business, but I did not come here
and I did not set fire to this house.'

'Of course you didn't! It was a wicked thing to say. He
is jealous of you, Jared.'

'Perhaps he knows that I want you for myself.'

'Jared…' She looked at him uncertainly. 'I do not think
it is that…but he certainly dislikes you.'

'Yes, he has made that clear enough,' Jared replied, his
expression serious now. 'He has motive and he may be im-

plicated in the attempt on my life in London, but...' He
shook his head. 'I am not sure that Mr Grant is a murderer—or even a failed murderer, Hester.'

'But if it is not him...' She looked up at him, feeling
uncertain. 'At first I did not think him capable, but now...'

'I know the evidence points to him being the culprit,'
Jared said. 'Perhaps that is the reason I am not certain.'

'What do you mean?'

He shook his head. 'I am not sure myself. I am going
to London tomorrow afternoon, after I have spoken to the
builders and set some work in hand. I may be able to tell
you more when I return.'

'You are going away.' She stared at him in dismay, her
immediate reaction concern for his sake. 'You will take
care, Jared? You will come back soon?'

'Of course I shall come back. Do you imagine that kiss
meant nothing to me?' He smiled at her, his eyes mocking
her. 'I know that you are not yet wholly mine, Hester, but
I intend that you shall be. I would come back if it were
merely that—but there is work to be done here and I have
given my word. Do you not yet trust me?'

'Yes, of course I trust you.' She drew a sighing breath,
her head against his breast. It felt so good to be close to
him. 'I am afraid.'

'That something will happen to me?'

'Yes, of course—but Mr Knighton was attacked too.'
She looked up at him, her eyes wide, dark with concern.

Jared lifted her chin with the tip of one finger. 'Do not
be anxious, my love. I shall return safely—and Mr Grant
is leaving in the morning. I believe you will find that
there will be no more accidents, at least until he returns
for the ball.' His hand moved in her hair, the fingers long
and shapely, but a man's hand, a hand that had been used
to work.

'Then you do think he is responsible?'

Jared thought for a few seconds before he answered. 'What I have at the moment is a handful of pieces that, put together, would make up perhaps half the picture we need. I cannot be certain of anything until I have more pieces, and I hope to find them in London.'

Hester looked into his eyes. She had begun to read him a little, to be able to guess at what was in his mind, but at this moment his expression gave nothing away. 'You know more than you are telling me, do you not?'

'Perhaps…but I can prove nothing, Hester. Until we have proof, we cannot accuse anyone.'

'No, that is true,' she said, her eyes scanning his face. 'Promise me you will be safe! Promise me you won't die!'

'I have no intention of letting this person—or persons unknown—take my life. Will that content you, Hester?'

'It must for the moment, because you will not tell me until you are sure—and you would never allow anyone to dictate to you.'

'You begin to understand me, my dearest, so sensible Hester.'

'Do not tease me! I know that I am sensible and dull and I cannot see why you wanted to kiss—'

She got no further for he pulled her into his arms, kissing her this time with such a hungry intensity that she felt as if she would have swooned and fallen had he not held her clamped to his body. When he drew back, she saw the light of mockery in his eyes.

'I tease, but I do not ridicule you, Hester. You are everything I want in a woman, and I intend that you shall be mine very soon.' His fingers caressed her face, sending shivers of delight mixed with fear down her spine. 'And now, my Hester, I believe we must go in or even your obliging mama will begin to think I have abducted you.'

Hester gave a shaky laugh. His words both thrilled and terrified her. She could not think he intended marriage as his words were those a man might say to his mistress, and no other gentleman had ever intentionally made her aware of his physical need the way Jared had. She could still feel the burn of his manhood as it pressed against her, and she was in no doubt of his need. He wanted her in his arms, in his bed—and God help her!—she wanted him too.

Hester hoped that she had recovered her composure when she returned to the salon. Her mother was talking to Mr Grant and struggling to be as polite and friendly as she felt it her duty to be to the second in line behind the present duke. When she saw Hester, closely followed by the viscount, she looked relieved and stood up.

'I think I shall retire now, Hester. Shall you come up now?'

'Yes, I believe I shall, Mama,' Hester said. 'Goodnight, Mr Grant. I wish you a safe journey and I hope you will return for the ball.'

'You may be certain that I shall return, Miss Sheldon.'

'Goodnight, Cousin Jared. I may see you in the morning?'

'Perhaps,' Jared said and turned to the other gentleman with a friendly smile. 'Would you care for a game of billiards, Grant?'

'Thank you, no,' Mr Grant said. 'I have an early start and I think I shall retire now.'

'As you please.' Jared met Hester's eyes across the room. 'Goodnight, Lady Sheldon.'

Hester followed her mother from the room. They walked up the stairs together. At the top Lady Sheldon turned to her daughter, a look of curiosity in her eyes.

'Why did you say that you might see the viscount in the morning, my dear?'

'He has to return to London, but he has an appointment in the morning and will not leave until the afternoon.'

'Ah, I see…' Lady Sheldon looked at her inquiringly. 'And what else did you talk about on your walk, my dear?'

'We talked about many things,' Hester said, a faint blush in her cheeks. 'Nothing important, Mama.'

'I see…' Lady Sheldon smiled oddly. 'Well, I dare say you will tell me when you are ready. Goodnight, Hester.'

Hester watched her mother walk away before turning towards her own room. Inside, she leaned against the door, a smile on her lips. Had her mother seen something new in her? She felt different! Laughing, she ran to look at herself in the shield-shaped dressing-mirror. Her eyes were brighter and she did look different. She felt as if she had been walking in a dream all her life and now, suddenly, she was wide awake for the first time. Jared's kisses had roused the latent sensuality in her, making her aware that she was a woman. Until now she had never truly thought about what it would be like to lie naked in a man's arms, but now she was seeing it, feeling it.

'Ohhh…' She turned away from her mirror, hugging herself as she went to sit on the edge of her bed. She was tingling all over, a melting feeling deep down inside her. She wanted to relive those few precious moments in the garden when Jared had held her, kissed her.

But she was such a fool! He had not spoken of marriage, of love or respect—merely of wanting. His kisses had spoken of desire, of physical need—and her untouched virgin body had responded with a hungry need of her own. She understood now what she had been waiting for all these years. No other man had ever spoken to that part of her; it had remained dormant, sleeping, but now it was awake and creating a need in her that burned so fiercely that she feared it. Hester had no doubt that what she felt for Jared was love—not the gentle love she felt for her mother and grandfather, but a hungry burning that threatened to consume her.

'What am I to do?' she whispered as she began to undress, not bothering to send for her maid. 'I want him so, love him so…supposing he was merely flirting with me…amusing himself…'

The renegade thought wormed through her, wounding her, frightening her, because she knew that she had surrendered herself to him completely that night. If he wanted her, he had only to reach out and take her.

Everything she had ever believed was shattered by the knowledge that Jared had the power to destroy her control, to lead where he would and compel her to follow. If he did not intend marriage, she would be his mistress…but, no, how could she even consider such a thing? She had always been sensible, respectable, in control of her thoughts and feelings. He had swept that away as he kissed her. Had he come to her at this moment she would have gone to him, holding nothing back, even though it would ruin her…but Hester knew that come the morning she would begin to doubt. She would begin to remember why it was impossible to cast away the world for love.

She would recover her strength while he was away. When he came back she would find the strength to resist his lovemaking…because if she didn't, she would be lost.

In another part of the house, a man paced the floor of his bedchamber, the jealous anger coursing through his veins like a bitter poison. The little harlot had betrayed him, going so readily to another man's arms! He had seen her kissing that upstart from America and he had guessed that the man wanted her—might even marry her.

That would upset all his plans! He had been so certain

of her that he had not hurried, making his moves carefully and slowly, waiting for the right moment. The fire had been an impulse, but it had worked better than he'd first imagined, as it had brought the heir here. The old duke would not last long and he was a patient man; he would have been content to wait had it not been for certain other factors that had come to light.

But he would not be thwarted at the last. He knew what was owed him, what ought by rights to be his, and he had first begun to plan for the future when he'd seen the late Viscount Sheldon's son die in an accident. It had been an accident, but it was the last of many—so many men had stood in his way back then, but now there were only two. When they were out of the way things would go as he hoped, as he'd planned for some years now.

And then he would have the revenge he had craved for as long as he could recall. It had begun in his childhood with his father's stories and he had carried the anger inside him for the long years between. The key to his success was Hester. If she married him, then the debt would be paid. If not…his eyes glinted with malice as he thought of what he might do if she was steadfast in her refusal. She had become proud and wilful of late and if she denied him what he had worked for so long, she would pay the price at the end.

Chapter Eight

Hester did not see Jared privately the next morning. He was busy with the builders he had called in, and he did not ask her to accompany him on the tour of the damaged wing. She felt that he might think she was interfering if she asked to be allowed to listen to their conversation concerning the work, and so she stayed away, though she longed to know what they were discussing. However, Jared had promised that they would not be disappointed and she knew she must trust him to keep his word.

Feeling at a loss, she took the gig and drove down to the village, accompanied by one of the grooms. She would normally have gone alone, but in the circumstances she decided it would be foolish to take such a risk. Her visit took most of the morning, because she had brought food, clothing and some medicines from Lady Sheldon's still-room. She was welcomed with smiling faces, because everyone wanted to talk about the new viscount and tell her how grateful they were for what he was doing. Hester understood that he was generally popular and they were all eager to praise him.

* * *

It was a little past noon when she returned home and she went straight to the dining room. Her mother was there and so was Mr Knighton, who had managed to struggle into a coat, but still had his left arm in a sling.

'I am glad to see you up again, sir,' Hester told him. 'I hope you are feeling better this morning?'

'Yes, much better, thank you,' he told her with a warm smile. 'I fear too much fuss was made over a very small incident, Hester. I took a tumble from a horse, nothing more.'

'But I understood there was a shot that frightened your horse?'

'Yes, but it must simply have been a poacher in the woods—do you not think so?'

'I thought you believed a dangerous highwayman was in the area?'

'Yes, I did hear something—but why would he shoot at me? I had little of value about my person. Unless he imagined I was someone else.'

'You think he might have thought you were Viscount Sheldon?'

'Perhaps.' Mr Knighton frowned. 'I wanted to speak to him about it, to warn him of the danger he may be in, but he left a few minutes ago for London, so I understand.'

'Jared has left already?' Hester was unable to hide her disappointment. 'I had hoped to see him before he left.'

'He asked for you, dearest,' Lady Sheldon said. 'I told him that you had gone to the village to take food and clothing to villagers that needed it, and he said that he would see you on his return. He does not expect to be longer than a few days, and will certainly be here for the ball.'

'Yes, of course,' Hester said, conquering her sense of loss. 'He will not be long—and my godmother will be here soon.'

'Yes, in time for tea, so her message informed me. She sent one of her grooms ahead to warn us of her arrival.'

'That was considerate,' Hester said. 'I do not think I am hungry, Mama. I shall go up and make sure her room is just as it should be—and arrange a few flowers.'

'You should eat, Hester.'

'Thank you, Mama. I shall have tea with you and Lady Ireland.'

Hester left the room and went upstairs to check that everything was perfect in the room her godmother was to occupy. It was her habit to check all the guest rooms and perhaps because of that she found it exactly as she would want it to be. After her inspection, she arranged some flowers, took them up and then went to change, ready for her godmother's arrival.

When she came down, she found Mr Knighton standing in the hall. He turned to look at her, smiling as she came to join him.

'How delightful you look, Hester. You grow more beautiful every day.'

'I do not think I am beautiful, sir.'

'Beauty is in the eye of the beholder and you have always been beautiful to me.'

'You are kind to say so, sir.' Hester was uncomfortable, because she sensed that he was working up to a proposal of marriage.

'Hester, will you walk with me in the garden for a moment? There is something I have been wanting to say to you for a while.'

'Mr Knighton, I…' Hester was saved at the last moment as she heard a knock at the door. The footman sprang to open it and Lady Ireland walked in. She nodded her thanks to the servant and then walked swiftly to Hester, gathering her into a warm embrace. 'My dearest girl! You look wonderful. I have been wondering how you would go on now that the heir has arrived, but I can see that it has not overset you. If anything, you thrive on it—or is it the country air?'

'I am sure the country air is very good for me,' Hester said, laughing as she kissed her cheek. 'I am so glad to see you, Godmother. It seems an age even though it was but a few days ago.'

'I have missed you, but then I always do when you leave after a visit,' her godmother said. She glanced at Lady Sheldon as she entered the hall. 'Judith, my dear, you are blooming. I do not remember seeing you look so well in an age.'

'It is the new viscount's influence,' Lady Sheldon replied. 'He has brought a breath of fresh air to this place, Sarah. He has taken all the worry from our shoulders and I am so grateful. Besides, I like him. He is good company and he makes me laugh.'

Lady Ireland looked at her for a moment. 'Do you not think he speaks a little…oddly?'

'Oh, you must not mind his funning,' Lady Sheldon replied. 'He is a great tease, is he not, Hester?'

'Yes, Mama, Cousin Jared likes to tease us all,' Hester said. 'Let me take you upstairs, ma'am. I am sure you must wish to refresh yourself after the journey.'

'How thoughtful you are, my love,' her godmother said, her bright gaze intent on the girl's face. 'Yes, do come up with me. You can tell me what Viscount Sheldon has done to deserve so much praise from your mama.'

'He has been most generous,' Hester said, tucking her arm through her godmother's as they walked slowly up the grand staircase together. 'He is rebuilding the village cottage by cottage, and he has promised that the fire damage will be restored.'

Lady Ireland looked astonished. 'I thought he had lost all his money! Did not Mr Birch say so in his letter? I am sure the viscount gave us to understand that he had hardly anything left.'

'I am afraid he was teasing us, ma'am. I believe he thought we deserved it for imagining that he needed to be taught how to go on in society.'

'Oh…' Lady Ireland's gaze narrowed. 'I see…so that accent…'

'A little charade for my benefit. You see, he had been told that I would teach him how to behave.'

'What idiot put it to him like that? His mother was a lady. I am not surprised that he was offended.'

'He was also angry because he thought the duke had behaved badly to his mother.'

'Well, in a way he did. I have always felt that he was too hard on her—but she was his favourite and he expected so much of her.'

'I think she broke his heart by running off,' Hester said. 'He was angry, but he ought to have replied to her letters. He knew that for himself when it was too late.'

'We all know what we ought to have done in hindsight,' Lady Ireland said. 'Where is the viscount at the moment?'

'He went to London on business,' Hester said. 'He promised to return in time for the ball.'

Her godmother nodded, then jumped as she heard a loud bang somewhere within the house. 'Goodness me! What was that?'

'The builders, I imagine. I hope they do not mean to make such a racket all the time.'

'Builders are always noisy,' Lady Ireland replied. 'We must hope that they do their work swiftly and well.'

'I shall ask them not to make too much noise for all our sakes,' Hester said. She opened the door for her godmother, following her into the guest room. 'It is the room you always have. I hope you will be comfortable here.'

'I always am, my dear,' Lady Ireland said, glancing at the flowers on a little desk by the window. 'Your work, Hester? How lovely!' She smiled at her. 'You may leave me to settle in now. I am sure you have things to do.'

'I shall go and see what those builders are up to,' Hester said. 'Mama will have refreshments waiting when you go down, ma'am.'

She was thoughtful as she made her way towards the wing that was under refurbishment. What on earth was Jared having done?

As she entered the first main parlour, which had been damaged by smoke but untouched by flames, she heard sounds coming from the next room and went to investigate. The sight that met her eyes was shocking, for almost the whole of the ceiling had been laid bare to the rafters.

'Oh…' she said and stared at the mess all around her. 'What is happening here?'

'Miss, you didn't ought to be in here.' A man came hurrying up to her. 'This ceiling was unsafe after the fire. Viscount Sheldon told us to take it down and re-plaster the whole thing.'

'I didn't realise,' Hester said. 'I thought it was just to be decorated and cleaned.'

'It wouldn't be safe in here, miss. Too much fire damage.'

'Have you much more to do? The duke's apartments are overhead…'

'Oh, it's quite safe, miss, he won't fall through a hole.' The man smiled at her. 'The bearing timbers were not burned, fortunately, but I'm sorry for the noise. We've only one last piece to take down and that is just above the door you entered. It would be best if you were to leave by the opposite door, miss—to avoid anything falling on you.'

'Thank you for the warning,' Hester said. 'I shall take your advice. Tell me, are any more of the ceilings due to come down?'

'No, miss—but there is some loose stonework at the back of this wing. I noticed it when I was making an inspection. I haven't told the viscount yet, but as soon as he comes back I shall do so because one or two stones could fall from the overhang and injure someone.'

'I shall be sure to inform everyone of the danger,' Hester said. 'Thank you for the warning, sir.'

'I've brought in all my men and hired some extra labour from the village for the rough work,' the builder told her. 'I promised the viscount I'd have this done as quickly as possible.'

'Then I shall leave you to get on,' Hester said. 'Goodbye.'

'Don't you worry, miss. In a couple of days you won't know it ever looked like this.'

Hester nodded and left him by a door at the far end, going up the back stairs to her grandfather's apartments. He asked her to go in as soon as she knocked, giving her a scowling look as she entered.

'What is that infernal racket downstairs?'

'I came to tell you,' she said. 'I am sorry if the noise has disturbed you. The ceiling of the green parlour had to come down, because it was badly damaged by the fire.'

'Damned racket,' the duke said but in a milder tone. 'Well, I suppose it cannot be helped. Viscount Sheldon did warn me.'

'It is a terrible mess,' Hester said, surprised that he had accepted it so easily. 'They tell me it is almost done, at least the noisy part. I suppose it may take some weeks to finish all the refurbishment.'

'That is what I would have thought, but Sheldon thinks otherwise. He says it will be habitable in a week or so, though we shall need new furniture apparently.'

'Yes, he did say something…' Hester waited for the outburst, but it did not come. 'I believe he intends to have his own things brought from America for his apartments.'

'Well, at least you won't have to see the stuff,' the duke said. 'I suggested that he should let you choose the new furniture, but he said he had it all under control. I hope he won't make a hash of it, but it can't be helped, I suppose. It's his money.'

'Yes.' Hester bit her lip. 'Try not to resent it, Grandfather. I know it must be hard to accept that we are dependent on his goodwill. We must be grateful he is prepared to do all this for us. He could have taken one look and gone home.'

'I don't resent it for myself,' the duke said and gave her a direct look. 'You know I've always loved you, girl— you're no blood relation and, if I'd been twenty years younger, I'd have married you and got myself another heir, but you don't think of me that way, and Jared will do. But I don't want you to feel as if you're being pushed out.'

Hester laughed softly. 'Grandfather! You old rogue! If I hadn't loved you as my grandfather for years, I would have married you, old as you are,' she teased. 'I like Cousin Jared, and I am not in the least put out that he has decided to do all these things without consulting me. I dare say I shall be able to live with whatever he does. After all, I have my own apartments.'

'You're a good girl, Hester,' the duke said. 'If I had my way, he would marry you, keep you here where you belong, but I can't order him to ask you.'

'If you did, I should go away and never speak to you again!' Hester was shocked at the suggestion. 'You must promise me you will never suggest such a thing to him!'

'You like him, girl, I've seen it in your eyes when you speak of him—and he likes you. It would be an ideal arrangement for all of us.'

'And am I to be given no say in this little plot of yours?' Hester eyed him wrathfully. 'I may like Cousin Jared, but that does not mean that I would marry him just to satisfy your whim.'

'Got a mind of your own, haven't you, girl?' The duke laughed deep in his throat. 'By God, you two would produce some splendid heirs for the family!'

'Now you are seeing me as a brood mare,' Hester said, torn between annoyance and amusement. 'You are a wicked old man, Grandfather. I think I shall go away and leave you to your dreams.'

'No, stay and talk to me for a while. I enjoy your company, girl. I promise I won't tease you any more.'

'Very well,' Hester said. She smiled, for she loved him too dearly to be angry for long. 'Shall I read to you for a while?'

'Yes, please. Nothing is more soothing than the sound of your voice when you read poetry to me, Hester. Forget my teasing. I dare say the viscount has ideas of his own.'

'Yes, I am sure he has,' she replied, looking more serene than she felt inside as she reached for a favourite book and began to flick through the pages. How long would Jared stay away? She hoped it would not be for too long, because he had only been gone a few hours and she was already feeling a sense of loss.

Jared looked at the agent his lawyers had hired to make inquiries for him, his gaze narrowing in thought as he weighed up the surprising information he had been given.

'You are certain of your facts, Mr Morrison?'

'Quite certain, sir. The family is very respectable, but there is a link…through a bastard.'

'Ah, yes, I see,' Jared said, nodding his understanding. 'So it would not be generally known… That clears up one point for me. It seems far fetched, but this could be a reason for him to want me dead.'

'It would not make him the direct heir, sir. As a bastard he could not inherit.'

'No, but I am not sure that is his aim,' Jared said, looking thoughtful. 'I believe that my death is incidental to his plan.'

'I am not sure I understand you, sir.'

'I believe the motive might be revenge rather than gain.'

'Revenge?' The agent lifted his brows. 'Forgive me if I am being stupid—I still do not see how.'

'I think this mystery mainly concerns another person,' Jared said. 'For the moment I prefer to keep my thoughts to myself, but I am grateful for your help. I was finding it difficult to work out why the attack on Mr Knighton took place, but now I see it very clearly.'

'What will you do, sir?'

'I must return to Shelbourne as quickly as possible,' Jared said. 'I think there is little danger for anyone until Mr Grant returns for the ball, but I might be wrong. I have left instructions with my lawyers and any further business I had here may be done through them.'

'Do you wish me to continue making inquiries for you, sir?'

'Yes, I shall need an agent now that I am to live in this country,' Jared said. 'But the inquiries I wish you to make now are of a different kind.'

He smiled at the man's surprised expression as he revealed the nature of the business he wished him to undertake. They talked for some minutes and then Morrison left. Jared followed him out into the street a short time later. He had decided on one last shopping expedition before he left the city to return to Shelbourne. It was as he was standing outside an exclusive establishment in Mayfair that he heard his name called and turned to see two ladies just behind him.

'Jared! Jared Clinton,' one of them cried, her face lighting up with pleasure. 'I was sure it was you.'

'Selina,' Jared said, grinning at her. 'I thought you never left Paris these days?'

'I came for the wedding of my niece, Annabel,' Lady Selina Mallard said, giving him a look from beneath her thick, fair lashes. In her youth she had been acclaimed as one of England's greatest beauties and had married well. Her husband had been several years older and had died leaving her a fortune only three years after their wedding. She had never remarried, choosing to live in Paris, where it was rumoured she took lovers and discarded them as easily as she would an old shoe. 'This is my sister Lady Raven. Now that all the pleasure of the wedding is over, we thought we would console ourselves by buying something pretty.' She arched her fine brow. 'Were you about to buy a love token, Jared? Do you have a new mistress?'

'You are as incorrigible as always,' Jared said. They had enjoyed a brief fling in Paris some years earlier, parting as friends by mutual agreement. 'I was considering a gift for a friend.'

'Did I not hear your name somewhere?' Lady Raven said, staring at him oddly for she had not met him previously. 'Clinton… Oh, yes, you are Shelbourne's American heir. Everyone is talking of you, sir.' Her brown eyes sparkled with mischief as her husband was many years her senior and this man was very attractive. The idea of an affair with an American was intriguing.

'I think you flatter me, ma'am,' Jared said, smiling at her in his lazy way. 'I hardly know anyone in London.'

'But the duke is giving a ball to celebrate your arrival,' Lady Raven said. 'I was not sure I would bother, though my invitation arrived yesterday—but now that I have met you, I shall certainly come.'

'I think I shall put off my return to Paris…if you will invite me?' Selina Mallard gave him a provocative look. 'For old times' sake, Jared?'

'Why not? Of course you are welcome to accompany Lady Raven,' Jared said. 'If you will excuse me, ladies, I have some business to complete before returning to the country.'

He smiled and went inside the jeweller's emporium, leaving the two ladies to look at each other meaningfully.

'He is exactly what you need to lift your spirits now that Annabel has gone,' Selina told her sister. 'You will find him a wonderful lover, Maggie. Believe me, he is worth the bother.'

'You don't want him yourself?'

'Oh, I wouldn't have minded a brief encounter, but you know I return to Paris soon—and Pierre is very jealous. No, dear sister, I shall let you have him this time. You need something to divert you…'

They walked on together, laughing as they plotted how Lady Raven could best entice the new viscount into her bed while staying for the ball at Shelbourne.

Unaware of their conversation, Jared took the elegantly wrapped packet from the jeweller, placing it in his inside breast pocket. It was a small gift, but one he thought Hester might accept. He had something else he wished to give her, but for the moment he would have to keep that

to himself. If his suspicions were correct, too much attention from him might be dangerous for Hester.

Hester was surprised and pleased at how quickly the
work was progressing. She visited the damaged wing
every morning to see what was happening, and she knew
that the ceiling had been completely re-plastered. All the
rooms had received a thorough cleaning and some deco-
ration had begun. At the beginning she had doubted that
the work could be finished in time for the ball, but now
she was beginning to believe that Jared had somehow
managed to achieve the impossible.

It was because he had told the master builder to bring
in extra labour, of course. There were so many men in and
out of the house that Hester thought they looked like ants.
However, they did not enter the main section of the house
and after the first day there were no loud bangs, only some
hammering and the buzz of people working.

'How do they go on, dearest?' Lady Sheldon asked her
daughter as they took tea together three days before the ball.
'Can it possibly be done before our guests start to arrive?'

'The first guests arrive tomorrow,' Hester replied. 'I do
not think it can be finished by then, but they will be housed
in the east wing. By the day of the ball we should be able
to throw the whole house open, though we may not have
much furniture as most of it was too badly damaged and
had to be taken away. I believe a few pieces may be
restored, but that will take time, for they cannot be done
as swiftly as the decorating, I fear.'

'No, indeed, the restoration of furniture is a delicate task.
However, I believe the viscount may have something in
mind.'

'You believe in him implicitly, Mama,' Hester said with
a smile. 'I do hope he will not let you down.'

'Viscount Sheldon is a remarkable man,' Lady Sheldon told her. 'I should not worry, Hester. I am sure he has thought of everything.'

'Yes, I dare say he has…' Hester would have said more, but at that moment the door opened and someone came in. She did not look round, but she guessed from her mother's expression that it was Jared and her heart took a sudden leap.

'Lady Sheldon, Hester.' Jared's voice made her spine tingle. She had been impatient for his return, but now she felt almost shy. 'I hope you will excuse me coming to you in all my dirt, but I wanted to let you know at once that I was back.'

'We are so pleased that you have come, sir,' Lady Sheldon told him. 'I do not fear the smell of the stables. My late husband often came to my salon without changing, for he was a great horseman. You are welcome to take a dish of tea with us just as you are.'

'You are very kind, ma'am,' Jared said. 'But I shall not join you until I have changed. I merely wished to let you know I had arrived.'

'Cousin Jared,' Hester said, getting to her feet and turning to greet him. Her heart leapt at the sight of him for he looked so good to her eyes that she wondered why she had not thought him particularly handsome when they first met. Seeing him now after a few days apart, he seemed to her the most attractive man she had ever known. 'I am pleased you are back. Have you visited the west wing? You will be pleased with the progress, I believe.'

'No, not as yet. Have they got the new ceiling in?'

'Yes, and the cleaning is done. It is just a matter of redecoration.'

'Good. I have arranged for the new furniture to be delivered the day before the ball. Hopefully, it will all be finished in time.'

'You employed an army to make sure that it would be,' Hester said and smiled. 'Would you care to look and see what has been accomplished in your absence?'

'If you would like to show me,' Jared replied, his eyes moving over her. 'I hope it has not been too disturbing for you—or the duke?'

'He was a little grumpy the first day when the ceiling made a noise as it came down, but it has not been too bad, thank you.'

'I am glad.' Jared stood back for her to precede him. 'I am sorry that I was so long. I had hoped to be sooner, but I was delayed.'

'Oh, I did not expect you to hurry,' Hester said, outwardly cool though her heart was racing. 'I dare say you had a great deal of business?'

'Yes, as it happens I did,' Jared said. 'Some of it concerns Shelbourne, but some of it was personal.' He had unexpectedly been forced to attend to some matters concerning his property in Paris, but as she knew nothing of his empire yet he kept the details to himself. 'However, I am back now and I do not intend to leave again for a while.'

'I see…' Hester's pulses were beating furiously, but she maintained her cool manner. 'I am sure Grandfather will be pleased, though he will not expect you to spend all your time here. I dare say you will make friends and wish to spend time with them—or at your club in London. If you are not a member, I am sure someone will put you up when you are ready.'

'Friends…' Jared hesitated, remembering something he had done in an unwise moment. 'I have invited an extra lady to the ball, Hester. I hope you don't mind. She is Lady Raven's sister and I met them together in town.'

'You know Lady Raven?' Hester was surprised.

'No, I know Lady Selina Mallard. Lady Raven said

that she had been invited and her sister asked if she might come with her.'

'Yes, of course. Do you wish to invite anyone else?'

'No, just Lady Mallard.' Jared hesitated—he knew that must sound as if he particularly wanted the lady to stay, but he had felt obliged to ask for the sake of their friendship. He had afterwards wondered if it might have been better to avoid it, but could not see how it could have been done without offence. 'I knew her in Paris.'

'Ah, yes, I believe you said you were in Paris last year.' Hester felt a pang, for she was aware of the lady's reputation, even though she did not know her herself. 'We have plenty of guest rooms, cousin. It will be no trouble to prepare another.'

'Perhaps I ought to have written.' He sensed that she was not pleased.

'No such thing,' Hester replied, lifting her head in what she hoped was a dignified way. 'As the heir, you are perfectly entitled to invite whomever you please, sir.'

'But I would not wish to offend you, Hester.'

'I am not offended. Why should I be?' She avoided looking at him, even when he was silent for a few seconds. 'I was pleased that you told the builders to keep to the original colours, for it was a beautiful house once.'

'Yes, I think it must have been,' Jared replied, following her lead. 'It will be again, I am sure. That pale blue the builder spoke of…what would you call it?'

'Some people call it duck egg blue, but it is a pale aquamarine when freshly done, as you will see.' They were about to enter the west wing. The first small salon had been the least damaged of all and was finished. It smelled new because the silk wallpaper was freshly pasted, and the ceiling had been whitewashed. 'This is a delightful room again now as the sun comes in here in the mornings rather than the afternoon.'

Jared stood in the centre of the empty room and glanced about him. 'I think it looks good, Hester. I hope you are pleased?'

'Yes, I am.' She smiled, some of her reserve melting when she saw the expression on his face as he sought her approval. 'In fact, I love it, cousin. I do not know what you have in mind for the furniture.'

'It is French, Louis XIV, but not too extravagant. Small pieces, the wood gilded and pale rose-and-cream satin-finish upholstery.'

'That sounds lovely.' She stared at him in surprise. 'Where did you find it at such short notice?'

'It already belonged to me. I sent for a load of furniture almost as soon as I came here the first time. It was waiting for me at a warehouse when I arrived in London. I have asked for it to be brought down with some other things…' He hesitated, looking at her seriously. 'I have made these arrangements so that it will all be respectable for the ball, but if you dislike what I have done you may tell me what you wish changed later, Hester.'

'Oh, no,' she cried. 'It is not for me to dictate to you, cousin. I am sure I shall like whatever you choose.'

'You shall have the choice when it comes to the rest of the house,' Jared promised. 'I am accustomed to doing what I think fit without reference to anyone. I did not mean to offend you.'

'You could not offend me,' Hester said. 'You have made this house live again, cousin. I can only thank you for all you have done.'

'But this is your home. I do not wish you to feel that I have swept away all that you loved and knew.'

'The fire did that here, sir. Besides, had I the money, I might have changed things sooner.'

'Then you are not angry with me?' He moved a step closer,

looking into her face. 'Hester, I—' What he was about to say
was forgotten as a man entered the room. 'Mr Knighton…'

'I heard voices and came to investigate, for the builders
left a few minutes ago,' Mr Knighton said. 'They said that
they would be here early in the morning to finish off. I
must say I think they have done very well. You are to be
congratulated, Sheldon. I would not have thought it could
be done in time. I dare say it has set you back a pretty
penny.'

'Not so very much as things go,' Jared replied easily. 'I
am glad you think it has turned out well.'

'Oh, yes, but I think you should get them to look at the
back of the house, Sheldon. There is some loose stonework
and, if it fell, it could cause a nasty accident.'

'Yes, that is true,' Hester said. 'Your master builder
told me that the day you left. He wanted your permission
to put it right.'

'I told him to do whatever needed doing,' Jared said.
'We cannot have that, for people may walk there and be
at risk. Would you show me where it is loose, Knighton?'

'Yes, certainly—would you like to go now?'

'I think we may as well. Hester, do not let me keep you.
I shall change after I have inspected the damage and see
you this evening.'

'Oh… Yes, of course,' Hester said. She was frowning
as she returned to the parlour where her mother was sitting.

'Back so soon?' Lady Sheldon asked. 'I thought you
would be longer. Is the viscount coming for tea?'

'No. He has gone to look at some loose stonework at
the back of the house.' Hester shivered suddenly, feeling
very cold. 'Excuse me, Mama, I must go…' She ran from
the room, flying through the house to the west wing. She
was panting and her heart was hammering wildly in her
breast, though she did not know why she was so fright-

ened. She could see the two men a little way ahead, staring up at the roof. 'Jared…'

Her cry made him hesitate. He turned and took a step towards her. At just that moment a large slab of stone began to fall. Had he not moved, he would have been standing right beneath it.

'Look out!' Knighton shouted. 'Good grief!'

The stone had smashed into pieces on the ground just behind Jared. He hardly noticed it as he moved to reach Hester, holding her as she flung herself at him, clearly distressed.

'What is the matter?'

'I don't know. I thought something would happen…that chunk of stone only just missed you.'

'It must have been very loose,' Jared said, seeming unperturbed. 'Knighton was right—it is dangerous.' He felt her tremble. 'It is all right, Hester. It missed me. I am not hurt.'

'Yes, but you might have been killed.' Her eyes were dark with despair, revealing more than she knew.

'Hester is right,' Knighton said, coming up to them. 'I know the builder was up there earlier looking at the damage. He must have dislodged it and it fell. It was a good thing you shouted, Hester. What made you come after us?'

'Instinct,' she said. 'I just felt that something awful was going to happen.'

'Just as well you did—that might have killed one of us,' Knighton said. 'I know the builder said it was loose, but I didn't think it was in such a dangerous condition.'

'He should have made sure it couldn't fall,' Jared said. 'You didn't go up there yourself?'

'No, but I saw someone coming from the stairway that leads up to the roof just before I came to you. I warned him that it was not safe to go up there and he gave me an odd look…a very odd look, come to think of it.'

'Who was that?'

'Mr Stephen Grant,' Knighton said. 'He arrived this afternoon, Hester. You knew that, of course?'

'No, I didn't know,' Hester said. 'I am not sure that Mama does.'

'Your mama did not mention it? How very odd…'

'You are certain it was he?' Jared asked, frowning.

'Yes…quite certain. I imagine the servants must have seen him arrive, but it is strange that Lady Sheldon did not know of it.'

'I think I shall go and ask her,' Hester said. 'Please go into the house, Cousin Jared—and you, Mr Knighton. I would not want either of you to be killed.' She had stopped trembling and walked away from them, head down. Her pulses were still racing, for the look in Jared's eyes had been so strange—almost as if he were warning her of something.

Hester returned to the salon to find that Lady Ireland had joined Hester's mother for tea. She took a deep breath, determined not to let either of them see that she had had a terrible fright.

'Mama, did you know that Mr Grant had arrived?'

'No, I did not.' Lady Sheldon looked puzzled. 'When was this, Hester?'

'I am told that it was earlier this afternoon.'

'Will you ring for Mrs Mills, please, my dear? He should have been announced. I would not show him any neglect, but I was not aware that he had arrived.'

'Yes, Mama.'

Hester rang the bell. A maid arrived and the housekeeper's presence was requested. She came in ten minutes, looking flustered.

'Forgive me, ma'am, I was busy with all the guests arriving tomorrow. Is something the matter?'

'Did Mr Grant arrive this afternoon?'

'No, ma'am. Not to my knowledge. I should have come to inform you at once.'

'Thank you, please do not let me keep you from your work, Mrs Mills.' Lady Sheldon waited until the woman had gone and looked at her daughter. 'Who told you that Mr Grant had arrived, dearest?'

'Mr Knighton thought he saw him,' Hester replied. 'He must have been mistaken.'

'Oh, well, it does not matter. I am sure he will be here for the ball. Unless he has changed his mind…'

'Yes, Mama. I am sure he will come.'

Hester accepted the dish of tea her mother handed her, taking a seat on one of the small, elegant sofas near the marble fireplace. She was thoughtful, her mind wandering restlessly as she listened to her mother and godmother making small talk about one of the many scandals concerning the Prince Regent that was currently circulating in town.

Someone had dislodged that heavy chunk of stone, hoping that it would fall and injure someone, but how could that person have known who would be standing nearby? Unless that person was still up on the roof and had taken his chance to make the attempt.

Mr Knighton thought he had seen Mr Grant near the staircase leading up to the roof, but the housekeeper did not know he had arrived. If he had entered the house, he had done so secretly, which meant he had come with the intent of doing harm. All the evidence pointed to Mr Grant as it must have been a chance thing. No one could know that Jared would be there at that time. Mr Knighton had known, of course, but he had gone with him—and there had only been inches between them. The falling stone could as easily have hit him as Jared. Besides, he had nothing to gain from Jared's death. Mr Grant had a great deal to gain.

Oh, how could he? How dare he! Hester was seething with anger. She could hardly believe that Mr Grant—a man of the cloth—had done such a wicked thing, and yet who else could it have been?

She would have to speak to Jared that evening alone. They must discover what was going on before someone else was killed!

Chapter Nine

Hester dressed in a dove-grey silk dress with a modest neckline and small puffed sleeves. She fastened a string of pearls about her throat, and added the bangle her godmother had given her. She was thoughtful as she went downstairs a little earlier than usual, hoping that she might find Jared alone. He was not in the drawing room, but something made her go to the library in search of him. He was there, an open book on the table in front of him. He looked up as she approached, but made no attempt to hide what he was reading.

'Your great-grandfather's journal,' she said, feeling surprised. 'I do not think I have read that volume.'

'It deals with the curse,' Jared said. 'I was looking for something, but it does not appear to be here.'

'Perhaps it is in one of the others,' Hester suggested. 'Was there something in particular that you wished to know?'

'It was rather a matter of confirming it,' Jared said. 'I have recently been given some information that may explain what has been happening here.'

'You think the accidents have something to do with the curse?'

'Not exactly,' Jared said. 'Nor do I think them accidents, Hester. Someone worked at that masonry to make it loose enough to fall. I went up to take a look myself before I changed, and I could see that a tool had recently been used to pry it forward.'

'But no one could have known that you would be there at exactly the right moment, Jared.'

'No, perhaps not. It may not have been meant to kill me, merely to warn—or to place the blame on someone by suggestion.'

'You mean Mr Grant?' Hester looked at him in concern. 'I thought that it must have been him. If Mr Knighton saw him near the stairs leading to the roof…'

'If he saw him there, it would certainly point the finger in Mr Grant's direction—but did he? Does it not seem curious to you, Hester, that no one else has seen Mr Grant this afternoon?'

Hester was thoughtful. 'He is not in the house. Mrs Mills went to the room he always uses when he visits to make sure, but his things were not there. I thought it meant that he had entered secretly in order to do harm.'

'That is one explanation,' Jared agreed. 'I know everything seems to point in his direction. He is the one who would benefit if I died. He might have had access to this house the night the fire was set and he could have fired that shot at me.'

'But you think otherwise?' She stared at him for a moment and then the sudden realisation of what he must be saying hit her. 'You cannot think…Mr Knighton? But why? He would not benefit if you died.'

'Directly, no, though he may be distantly related.'

'To my mother, but not the Shelbourne family.'

'If my information is correct, he may be related to my great-grandfather through a bastard-born son. I have learned that the child of the tragic affair your family thought had died, actually survived and was brought up in secret. He changed his name to Knighton when he was a man, and he married a relation of your mother's. The man you know is his son.'

'But he could not inherit the title even if that were true,' Hester said, feeling bewildered, because it was all so new to her. She had not once considered that Mr Knighton might be concerned in this horrid business. 'Besides, he was shot at.'

'Conveniently out of sight,' Jared said. 'We have only his word that it happened, Hester. The doctor told me that he was hardly bruised. He could have fallen deliberately and sent his horse off in a panic.'

'In order to make us believe that he was a victim,' Hester said. 'Surely not? He has been so concerned about all this business. I cannot think it—and why would he wish to kill you and blame Mr Grant?'

'A man convicted of murder could not inherit the estate. The duke would be able to break the entail—and leave the estate to you as he wished.'

'And if I married...' Hester shuddered at the thought. 'Oh, that is too horrible! It cannot be right. No one could stoop to such depths!'

'I may be misjudging him, of course.' Jared looked at her oddly. 'The agent I employed gave me the facts, but that proves nothing. I was looking for some clue that my great-grandfather knew the truth about the child actually surviving, but as yet I have found nothing.'

'But what made you suspect him in the first place?'

'You remember that I told you someone attacked me in London?'

'Yes, of course. It was not Mr Knighton!'

'It may have been he who paid to have the rogue attack

me,' Jared told her. 'I fought him off and persuaded him to tell me who had paid him. He did not know the name of the man, but he said he knew where the man went after leaving him. He took me there to show me—and that was to Lady Ireland's house. I asked you who had called that night and you told me Mr Grant had left his card; it is possible that Mr Knighton also called but you did not know.'

Hester stared at him, struggling to remember. 'Yes…he did,' she said after a moment. 'I did not find his letter until later, after you had asked me. I should have told you, but I forgot about it. I did not think it important.'

'You could not have known, Hester,' Jared said. 'The rogue who tried to attack me that night has been working for me since then. He told me that the man who had paid him was at this house, which meant that it could be Knighton or Grant. However, my instincts told me it was unlikely to be Grant, and when I was informed of Knighton's tenuous link with the Shelbourne family…'

'Yes, I understand why you think that he may be concerned, but…' She shook her head. 'It is too dreadful to contemplate. Mama's cousin through marriage. She would be so distressed if it were true.'

'Yes, I am sure she may be fond of him,' Jared said. He looked at her strangely. 'Perhaps you are too, Hester?'

'I have always thought him reliable, someone we could turn to if need be,' Hester said. 'But as a husband—no, I should never agree to marry him. You must know that I could not?'

Jared gave her his lazy smile, got up and came round the table to where she was standing. He reached out, drawing her close, gazing down at her anxious face. 'I have upset you, Hester. Forgive me. I should have kept my thoughts to myself until I was certain.'

'No, I prefer to know what you are thinking,' she said. 'If he paid someone to attack and murder you…' A shudder ran through her. 'How could he! The wicked man! Oh, I do not know how I shall ever face him again.'

'But you must, my dearest one,' Jared said. He leaned forward, brushing his lips over hers. Hester trembled, gazing up at him, a question in her eyes. 'What I have just told you is all supposition. I cannot prove any of it. I have no documents, nothing except the word of a rogue, which would be dismissed in a court of law.'

'Mama should ask him to leave! If she knew you suspected him, she would never wish to see his face again.'

'But she must not know,' Jared said. 'Much as I love your dear mama, Hester, she could never keep a secret. You, on the other hand, have a wonderful command of your emotions. You seldom show what you are thinking—except when you are overcome by anxiety or anger—and I am hoping that you will help me by playing your part a little longer.'

'What are you going to do?'

'I must find some way to provoke him into attacking me,' Jared said. 'I had thought it would be safe while Mr Grant stayed away, but after this afternoon…' He looked at her anxiously. 'You must be careful too, Hester.'

'Why? Surely if I am a part of his plan…' Her eyes opened wide. 'Yes, I see. You think that he might turn on me if I refused him?'

'What kind of a mind must a man have to kill others for revenge for something that happened so long ago? Yes, I think he might harm you if you made him angry, and that is the one thing I could not bear, my very dear Hester.'

'Oh…' She smiled at him a little uncertainly. 'I think I understand.' Her heart was racing wildly, for the way he looked at her seemed to promise so much. 'Thank you.'

'We must keep our feelings to ourselves for the moment,' he told her. 'If Knighton suspected something between us...'

'Yes, I do see that,' Hester said. 'You may rely on me. I shall be the same as always when I speak to him.'

'Good. I may be mistaken, but we shall see.' Jared touched her cheek once more. 'I think we had best join the others or we shall be missed. Please go ahead of me, Hester. I shall follow in a few minutes.'

'Yes, of course.' She turned and left the library. As she approached the drawing room where they assembled before dinner, she saw Mr Knighton walking towards it from a different direction. Her throat tightened and she was aware of a surge of disgust, which she had to fight to overcome.

'Hester,' he said as he saw her. 'I am so glad of the chance to speak to you alone. This is a bad business, you know. The builder assured me that there was no danger of any masonry falling for the moment and that the work was precautionary rather than urgent—and that means it must have been tampered with.'

Hester swallowed hard. How false he was! Had Jared not told her what he suspected, she might not have noticed, but the signs were there—his caring tone was assumed.

'Surely you cannot think it?' she said. 'Who would do such a wicked thing? Someone could have been badly hurt.'

'It must have been Grant,' he replied with an air of concern. 'It is hard to believe—but if the viscount were killed in an accident...'

'Mr Grant would inherit the title and the estate,' Hester agreed, because it was true. 'But do you think him the kind of man to do something like that, sir? Surely as a man of the cloth he would be above avarice?'

'His calling may not be a true one,' Knighton said, shaking his head. 'I agree that it seems unlikely, but who else could have done it—and why? Mr Grant is the only one who could benefit from Viscount Sheldon's death.'

'Yes, that is true,' Hester agreed again. His manner seemed just as it ought, and yet she sensed something hidden. Had it been there before or was she only aware of it now that her eyes had been opened? 'What do you think we should do, sir?'

'I think the viscount should tell him he is not welcome here.'

'Perhaps,' Hester said. 'But there is no proof of what he did—unless you are prepared to say in a court of law that you saw him near the stairs before the masonry fell?'

'Yes, if necessary I should be prepared to stand up in court,' Knighton replied, a gleam in his eyes. 'The viscount was shot at and so was I, though I do not see what he hoped to gain from that, unless it was because he was afraid that you would refuse his proposal in my favour.'

'Mr Knighton!' Hester said, taken aback. 'You have not proposed to me.'

'But you knew that I meant to? You must surely have known.'

Hester fought the surge of revulsion, taking a deep breath. 'I have thought, perhaps, and of course I am flattered—but you must give me more time, sir. There is so much to think about for the moment. Will you wait until after the ball and speak to me then?'

Knighton frowned, and then looked at her fondly. 'Of course. You have had a shock today and you must have so much to do, but since you know my intention now, please promise me you will consider it and give me your answer after the ball, Hester?'

'Yes, of course I shall,' Hester said forcing herself to

smile. 'I think we should go in now, sir. Mama will be waiting—and here comes the viscount.'

She went ahead of them, hearing the greeting between them. Jared's voice was casual, giving no sign of the emotion he must be feeling. She lifted her head as she went into the drawing room, knowing that she must continue to be careful.

Her mother turned to look at her. 'I was just thinking of sending for you, Hester. Where have you been?'

'I was talking to Mr Knighton,' she replied and kissed Lady Sheldon's cheek.

'It is odd that Mr Knighton thought he saw Mr Grant this afternoon,' Lady Sheldon said. 'He is not in the house and I have heard nothing from him. I expected that he would write to tell me when he is arriving. His behaviour is discourteous and it is not like him.'

'I dare say he will come tomorrow,' Hester said. 'He came quite unexpectedly last time, did he not?'

'Yes, I suppose he did,' her mother said, her brow wrinkled. 'It is inconsiderate, Hester. The house will be full of guests soon and if he isn't coming, his room might be used for someone else.'

'We have plenty of guest rooms,' Hester said. 'Do not worry, Mama. I am sure he will turn up sooner or later—' She broke off as Jared and Mr Knighton entered the room, but avoided looking directly at either of them. Had she done so, she would have seen that Mr Knighton was looking distinctly annoyed about something.

'Well, now that we are all here, we should go in,' Lady Sheldon said, standing up. 'Cook sent word ten minutes ago that she was ready to serve.'

Hester had hoped that she might have another opportunity to be private with Jared that evening, but he lingered over the port and then the two gentlemen went off to play billiards. The ladies decided to retire early since they would be having late nights once the guests for the ball started to arrive. Hester's mind was seething as she prepared for bed and she felt that she would never sleep.

However, after some tossing and turning she did sleep.

Waking early to hear the birds singing outside her window, Hester dressed for riding and went downstairs, heading for the stables. She had decided that she would not remain shut up in the house, but she would take the precaution of asking one of the grooms to accompany her.

Her ride was uneventful, but refreshing, and she had a pretty colour in her cheeks when she returned to the house to take breakfast. She discovered that Mr Knighton was at the table, though there was no sign of Jared.

'You have been riding,' Knighton said. 'I hope you took a groom with you, Hester? You cannot be too careful in the circumstances—though in the light of what Viscount Sheldon told me last night, things have altered.'

'Oh…' Hester was careful not to look at him, helping herself to bacon and scrambled eggs. 'What was that, sir?'

'Has he told you that he has a son? A bastard, it seems—but he intends to make him legitimate so that he can inherit the title if he should suffer an accident.'

Hester's hand froze in mid-air, the shock running through her. 'Cousin Jared has a son?' she asked incredulously and turned to look at him. 'I have not heard of this before.'

'I dare say he would not think it fit for a lady's ears, Hester. He must have had him hidden away, but now he intends to adopt him and make it legal—at least, that was what he told me last night, though as he was in his cups I could not say for certain.'

Hester swallowed hard. The knowledge that Jared had a son he intended to legalise was shocking. It was not so unusual for a gentleman to do that, but it must surely mean that he had some fondness for the boy—and it was a little hurtful that he had not told Hester of his intention. However, she maintained a cool indifference as she asked, 'Why does that alter things?'

'If Mr Grant imagines that killing the viscount means he will inherit, he will be disappointed. Unless he were to kill him before it could be done, of course.'

'Yes, I see,' Hester said. She took her seat at the table. 'It was a good thing that Mr Grant was not there to hear it last night, sir.'

'Yes, that is true, though he may learn of it some other way, Hester. These things have a way of becoming common knowledge, you know. If any of the servants heard him last night, it will be all over the house by now.'

'Yes, if they heard him, that would be the case,' Hester agreed. She got up to pour herself a dish of tea, her back towards him. 'But if he told you in confidence…'

'Oh, he was three parts to the wind,' Knighton said. 'Anyone could have heard in the next room—and one of the footmen was there, for I called him to help me get the viscount up the stairs.'

'I see…' Hester frowned. 'I have never seen Cousin Jared drink to excess before.'

'I dare say there is much you have not seen of him,' Knighton said with a sneer. 'He has been on his best behaviour so far to make an impression, I'm sure.'

Hester held back the angry retort that rose to her lips. She must be careful! Besides, there was some truth in what he said, because she did not know Jared well. Instinct told her that there must have been a reason for his behaviour that night and she frowned as she ate her breakfast in silence. She did not look up as Mr Knighton excused himself from the table.

He was clearly annoyed by what he had been told—as he must be if Jared was right about his intentions. A boy child legitimised would be another hurdle to surmount, another accident to arrange, though the child would not inherit if the documents were not signed. Hester was still frowning as she left the room, her thoughts in some confusion. Why on earth had Jared got so drunk that he had revealed something of that nature to a man he believed his enemy? Surely it was the last thing he wished him to know, for it would place the child in danger.

She was walking upstairs, intending to change into a morning gown, when the answer came to her. Of course he had not been drunk; it was merely a part of his plan to reveal the story to Mr Knighton. He wanted to force him into making an attack sooner rather than later. She smiled and shook her head, because she was not even sure that Jared truly had a bastard son—that might be a part of his plan too.

Hester changed into a pretty green morning gown. She had decided that she would begin to wear colours again and she dabbed a little perfume on her wrists, going downstairs just as the door was opened in the main hall. Two very fashionable ladies had arrived, one of whom she knew as Lady Raven. The other lady must be Lady Mallard—Jared's guest. She was a lady of perhaps just over Hester's own age, not in the first flush of youth but very attractive with pale blonde hair showing beneath her stylish hat. She was stripping off her pelisse, handing it to the maid who waited to take it, when Hester reached the bottom of the stairs, and she turned to look at her, her eyes appraising her frankly.

'Miss Sheldon,' Lady Raven said. 'May I introduce you to my sister, Lady Selina Mallard.'

'Lady Mallard.' Hester dipped her head slightly. 'I am happy to make your acquaintance. Viscount Sheldon told me he had invited you.'

'There you are,' Lady Raven said, smiling at her sister. 'I told you he would not forget. She was afraid she might not be expected, Miss Sheldon, and almost did not come.'

'Yes, you are expected. Your room will be ready for you. Shall I send for the housekeeper or take you up myself?'

'Perhaps we should speak to Lady Sheldon first?' Lady Raven said. 'I am sure she must wish to know immediately her guests have arrived.'

'Mama is not yet down,' Hester said. 'She is in her apartments, but will be down in an hour or so. I shall tell her you have arrived. If you would like to make yourselves comfortable, I shall order tea in the green sitting room—which is at the back of the house. I shall send Mrs Mills up to make sure you have all you need and she will direct you. If you would like to follow me, ladies.'

She led the way up the stairs and turned to the east wing, where the best guest rooms were situated. The ladies had come a day sooner than expected and Lady Sheldon would be upset that she had not been there to greet them, but it could not be helped.

After showing the sisters to their bedchambers, which were side by side, Hester went back to the main building to tell her mother. Lady Sheldon was immediately flustered, throwing back the bedcovers in a panic.

'Oh, Hester,' she exclaimed. 'I did not expect anyone before this afternoon.'

'Which would have been much better for everyone,'

Hester said. 'I told them you would be down in an hour, Mama, and that I would order refreshments in the green parlour. I am sure they must wish to change, which will give you plenty of time.'

'What should I do without your good sense?' Lady Sheldon said and rang for her maid. 'You said Lady Raven and Lady Mallard—I hardly know Lady Mallard. I believe she lives in Paris?'

'She is Cousin Jared's guest,' Hester said. She was conscious of a little ache in her breast, because the lady was so very beautiful, but she dismissed it. Jared had seemed to be saying he cared for her the previous night and she must not allow jealousy to sour her judgement. However, she could not help wondering if Lady Mallard could possibly be the mother of the bastard son…if there was one, of course. 'I believe he met her in Paris.'

'He has a house there, I understand,' Lady Sheldon said. 'And I think some kind of business, though I am not certain of that…but he must have a business to afford all those repairs, do you not think, dearest?'

'Cousin Jared is quite wealthy, Mama. I have not asked how that came about. I did not think it my affair.'

'You are perfectly right,' Lady Sheldon said serenely. 'I am content that he should have decided to stay here, and he has had everything done that we could wish for.'

'The new furniture is arriving for the west wing today,' Hester said. 'I must go and find him if I can, tell him that his guest is here.'

She left her mother to the tender ministrations of her maid and went in search of Jared. However, as she entered the west wing, she saw at once that the wagons must have already arrived. It was a hive of activity with floors being cleaned, carpets being laid, curtains hung and furniture carried in by an army of servants. She did not know some of the faces and could only think that Jared had hired them in London to help with the ball.

She found him in one of the rooms directing the arrangement of some extremely fine French furniture. She drew her breath sharply—she had never seen such magnificence as the inlaid cabinets that were being arranged at each side of the fireplace.

'Do you like them?' Jared asked as he saw her staring.

'They are wonderful,' she said, turning to look at him. 'I do not think this house has ever seen the like. Where did they come from?'

'Originally from the palace of one of the Sun King's mistresses,' he told her, a teasing smile in his eyes. 'But I bought them a few years ago for my own chateau in the Loire Valley. I sent for them because I thought they would go well here—and I have decided that I shall sell the chateau. I may keep the house in Paris if things go as I wish.'

If his mistress agreed to marry him when their son was legalised? Hester felt the sharp pain in her breast, but her expression did not change.

'Oh, I came to tell you that Lady Mallard has arrived. I have arranged to offer refreshments in the green salon, and Mama is coming down to entertain them, but perhaps you would wish to be there?'

'Yes, I suppose I should put in an appearance,' Jared said. 'In half an hour when I have finished here, perhaps.'

'Is there much more to do?'

'The furniture is mostly unpacked, but there are *objets d'art* to arrange in these cabinets.' He indicated a large chest a few feet away. 'Would you do that for me, Hester? Some of the pieces are delicate and rare. I would prefer careful hands—if it is not too much trouble?'

'Yes, of course. I shall come back later after I have welcomed your guests.'

'I am sorry they arrived a day early,' Jared said and frowned. 'I cannot recall what was said at the time I made the invitation.'

'It really is no trouble,' Hester said. 'I dare say some others may arrive later today.'

'Yes, of course.' Jared gave her an odd look. 'It must mean a lot of work for you…this ball?'

'I enjoy it,' she told him. 'The house has been empty too long. Besides, these rooms look so lovely now it would be a pity not to show them off.'

'Yes. Hester….' Jared hesitated and then shook his head. 'No, it does not matter.'

She turned away, going back to the main house. The ladies would be down soon and it was time to order refreshments brought for them. She was glad to be busy because it stopped her thinking about things that would only make her unhappy. Jared was selling his house in the Loire Valley, because he now had a big country house here—but he was keeping his house in Paris. Was that because Lady Mallard preferred to live there? Hester put the thought away from her. Jealousy was a horrid thing and she would not let it invade her thoughts. She had too much to think about with so many guests, and all the while the shadow of fear that someone might be planning to kill the man she loved was there at her shoulder.

Hester was not long alone with the guests for Lady Sheldon came in just as she had begun handing out glasses of sweet wine and small almond biscuits. Lady Sheldon brought the scent of flowers with her, her gentle fragile air immediately charming the ladies as she gave them her smile and apologised for not being there to greet them.

'We were a little early,' Lady Raven admitted. 'But Selina was impatient to see the house. She knew Lord

Sheldon when he was Mr Clinton, you see—but she has never visited here and was curious.'

'Oh, you must ask him to show you the west wing later,' Lady Sheldon said. 'It has all been refurbished and is quite lovely.' She glanced at her daughter. 'You may leave us, Hester dear. I am sure you have much to do.'

'Thank you, Mama. I shall see you later, Lady Mallard—Lady Raven.'

Hester was pleased to be relieved as she had not yet seen to the flowers that day and there was also the matter of the precious *objets* Jared wanted arranged in the beautiful French marquetry cabinets. She decided that the flowers could wait, partly because she was curious about what was in the box.

When she returned to the salon where the cabinets stood waiting, she discovered that the box had been opened, though no attempt had been made to unpack it. The room now contained an elegant sofa and matching elbow chairs, also some pretty wine tables and a torchère in the corner with a magnificent bronze figure holding gilded candelabra aloft.

It was a room for entertaining, fit for the palace it had come from, and Hester realised a little ruefully that it made the rest of the house a little shabby by contrast. She would not wish to spend her mornings here when alone, but it was exactly what the house needed when there were guests.

She bent to start unpacking the treasures in the box, discovering first some gold boxes with engraved lids, some of them set with precious stones. After that came several pieces of Sèvres china, delicate figures and small ornamental pieces that had been made for display and not for use. Each piece seemed more expensive than the next, and Hester lingered over the work, handling the delicate treasures with care. She had just set a beautiful enamelled box in its place when she heard voices in the next room.

'Well, this is more like it, Jared, my darling,' a woman's voice said teasingly. 'I had begun to wonder what you were doing in this dreadful mausoleum, but now I see that you have made a start. Surely I know some of these things? Were they not at your house in the Loire Valley?'

'Yes, Selina. How clever of you to recognise them, but then you always had good taste.'

'That was how we came together,' Selina reminded him, the tinkle of laughter in her voice. 'We both wanted the same table, do you not remember? When you discovered that I wanted it, you bought it and gave it to me.'

'Yes, of course. I had not forgotten.'

Hester closed the door of the cabinet and turned the key, slipping it into her pocket to give to Jared later. She left the room by the far door before he and Lady Mallard could enter and discover her there. Hot tears were burning behind her eyes, but she lifted her head proudly, because it would be so foolish to cry.

Jared was a man. She had known that he must have had mistresses in the past, but it was hurtful that he had invited the lady he was currently having an affair with to this house. He was entitled to do as he pleased, of course—but why had he made Hester fall in love with him? She would not have minded if he hadn't kissed her, arousing the passion she had not known was in her and the foolish hope that he intended to ask her to be his wife.

Of course he would not ask! Why should he when Lady Mallard was so very beautiful?

She must not let anyone see how much she was hurting inside! Hester raised her head, fighting the ache inside her as the tears threatened to fall. She had far too much to do to worry about silly things! The flowers needed to be arranged for all the public rooms. She must send some up to the guest rooms now occupied, and then find the gar-

deners and make sure that sufficient blooms were sent up
the next day. Then there were all the menus for the next
few days. She had already agreed them with Mrs Mills,
but it would be best if she looked at them again, and she
hadn't even been to see her grandfather that morning…

She certainly did not have time to dwell on her foolish
thoughts!

Somehow, Hester managed to get through the day
without giving in to the pain building inside her. She hoped
that her smiles did not seem false, and to compensate she
laughed a little more than usual. She caught Jared looking
at her oddly once, but he was fully occupied looking after
both Lady Raven and Lady Mallard, who seemed to be
vying with each other for his attention. Had Hester not
been feeling so upset, she might have found it a little
funny, because it was obvious that Lady Raven was
annoyed with her sister for demanding so much of his attention.

Hester gave her attention to her godmother and Mr
Knighton, who seemed to disapprove of the other guests,
though he was unfailingly polite whenever one of them
noticed him, which wasn't often.

It was a long evening and Hester could not help feeling
relieved when Lady Ireland announced that she was tired
and intended to retire. It gave her the chance to escape for
a while and she rose to go up with her godmother. Lady
Ireland looked at her as she kissed her goodnight.

'You should not let their behaviour upset you, Hester.
It is often the way with married ladies of a certain kind and
the viscount is far too sensible to become entangled with
either of them. I think he finds their behaviour amusing.'

'I am not upset,' Hester lied. 'I just have a little headache.'

'Ah, I see,' Lady Ireland said. 'Why do you not go to bed, my dear? I am sure no one will mind.'

'I shall go back to say goodnight to Mama and our guests, ma'am.'

'Yes, my dear, if you wish.'

Hester kissed her again and went back down. She hesitated outside the drawing room and then turned away, seeking out the library. She thought that she would like to take a book up with her, because she felt that she might not be able to sleep. Going into the library, she discovered that Mr Knighton was there, looking through the shelves. He turned as she entered.

'Hester. I was looking for something to read. I think I shall go up. I do not care for that kind of behaviour, though it is often the case at country house parties—but to make it so obvious...' He pulled a face. 'I believe the viscount is beginning to show his true nature. Regrettable, but I suppose it was to be expected with his upbringing.'

'I think you are unfair, sir,' Hester said. Her nerves were strained and she forgot caution as she spoke in Jared's defence. 'It is the ladies who will not leave him alone. You should not judge him by their behaviour!'

'But I told you there is a bastard child, did I not?' Knighton said. 'I dare say she has got him to promise that he will make her bastard legitimate.'

Hester turned and left the room, taking a volume from the shelf without looking at it in her hurry. She was angry and distressed and she knew that if she had stayed longer she would have betrayed herself. How dare Mr Knighton say such things? Hester was angry on Jared's behalf, for he had done nothing to deserve it. He had been courteous and attentive to the ladies, it was true, but they were guests, and since they insisted on having all his attention he could hardly have done otherwise without causing offence. He had, in fact, behaved as a gentleman ought and she could find no fault with him.

After what she had heard in the west wing, Hester could not doubt that Lady Mallard had been—might still be—Jared's mistress, but she would still not allow that he was capable of the loose behaviour Mr Knighton was suggesting.

Just why was he going out of his way to plant the thought in Hester's mind? As a gentleman he ought never to have spoken of something Jared had said in his cups, and he certainly ought not to draw her attention to what had been going on earlier. The two ladies might have been hoping to arrange an assignation for that night, but a man of Mr Knighton's character would not normally have mentioned it to an unmarried lady. It must be part of his plan to discredit Jared, though what lay behind it she could not guess.

She was tempted to go straight up to her own room, but good manners prevented it. She returned to the drawing room and discovered Jared in the act of finishing a glass of brandy. He was alone.

'Oh, has everyone gone up?' she asked. 'I came to say goodnight.'

'I do not think Lady Sheldon expected you to return,' Jared said. 'The others went a few moments ago.'

'I came to get a book,' Hester said. 'Goodnight, sir.'

'Have I offended you, Hester?' Jared looked at her oddly. 'Forgive me if I have, but…' He hesitated as Mr Knighton came back into the room. 'Goodnight, Hester. Knighton, care for another game of billiards?'

'I think not, sir. I am for an early night. The ball is tomorrow and we must all be fresh for that—do you not agree?'

Hester did not stop to hear Jared's reply. Her heart ached, though she was trying not to be foolish. She would not condemn Jared without a hearing, and, as she had told Mr Knighton, the ladies had been the ones pursuing him.

If she thought of it that way, the situation became almost amusing and some of the tension left Hester as she entered her bedroom. She would not break her heart just yet, she decided, practical as always. Now that she was calmer, she discovered that she had picked up one of Jared's great-grandfather's journals.

It would be interesting to read it, she thought, and placed it on the little table beside her bed. Glancing out of the window, she saw that it was a clear, bright night, the sky lit by the full moon. She pulled the curtains tightly shut, undressed, brushed her hair and got into bed. Picking up the journal, she began to flick through the pages. The date was towards the end of the second Duke of Shelbourne's life and she turned the pages until she came to an entry that made her sit bolt upright.

Jared was right! She read the entry again, discovering the old man's feelings on finding that his dead son's bastard child was still alive.

I regret that the child was ever born, but since it still lives I feel it my duty to do something for him. He has been given only a modicum of education. I shall fund his advancement in a profession, perhaps the army, for I doubt that the church would take him...

The child had not died at birth as she had been led to believe. The second duke had obviously known of it, but he had kept it a secret, refusing to acknowledge the bastard as his blood, though by this entry he had clearly intended to help the child—or the young man at this point—to find a career for himself. Hester realised it was the proof that Jared had been looking for with no success. With this he could challenge Mr Knighton and perhaps force him to confess.

Had she known where to find him, Hester might have gone in search of him then and there, but she could not go wandering about the house at this hour, particularly when there were guests. She got out of bed and placed the journal in the bottom of a tallboy, covering it with pieces of clothing. It should be safe there until she had a chance to speak to Jared about her discovery.

Turning, she leaned over and blew out her candle, snuggling down into the softness of her feather bed. Her mind was still busy with things that were bothering her, but she did her best to dismiss them and was soon drifting into a peaceful sleep.

Hester left the book where she had placed it when she went down to breakfast that morning. She had forgone her usual ride, because it would be a busy day. She had arranged to have the flowers brought to the house early so that she could prepare vases for the guest rooms and the reception rooms. Hester would fill them herself, leaving it to the maids to deliver them to the right rooms. Once that was done, she would visit all the guest rooms with Mrs Mills, making sure that everything was as it ought to be.

The morning flew by and it was soon time to join her mother and the other guests for luncheon. She found that five ladies and four gentlemen had already arrived, and another fifteen guests were expected at some time that afternoon.

Hester looked for Mr Grant, but discovered that he was not at table. She detained her mother as she was leaving the room.

'Have you heard nothing from Mr Grant, Mama?'

'No, my dear,' Lady Sheldon replied, wrinkling her brow. 'I was certain that he would come for the ball; he was so particular when he left.'

'Perhaps he will come later,' Hester said and frowned.

'Have you seen Cousin Jared or Mr Knighton this morning, Mama?'

'I saw the viscount just before luncheon,' Lady Sheldon said. 'He told me that he had been sent a note that meant he must go out for a while, but I have not seen Mr Knighton.'

'I see…' Hester was thoughtful as she left her mother. She needed to check that everything was going as it ought in the kitchens, and that the ballroom was ready for the evening. After that, she would go up and change into a pretty gown, for her work would be done and she need do nothing more until it was time to dress for the evening.

Chapter Ten

An atmosphere of excitement had built up during the day with guests arriving at regular intervals. By the time that everyone went up to change for the evening, the house had come alive with the sound of voices and laughter. Jared had returned to the house just before tea, and Mr Knighton joined them in the parlour in time to be served by Hester.

'Thank you,' he said, accepting the dainty dish of fragrant liquid. 'I think you have been very busy today, Hester. Everywhere looks very nice.'

'Thank you,' she said. 'The gardeners have worked hard to furnish us with all the beautiful flowers for the house.'

'It is your personal touch that brings such serenity to the house,' he said, smiling at her. 'I hope you will save a dance for me this evening?'

'Yes, of course,' Hester replied easily. 'You must put your name down for one of the country dances, sir.' She caught sight of Jared looking at her from across the room. He raised his brows, but made no move to come to her, turning almost at once to listen to something Lady Raven was telling him. He said something to her, which made her laugh and tap him on the arm with her fan, apparently delighted with his attentions. Hester looked away, telling herself that she should not feel hurt or neglected. Jared was simply carrying out his duties as a host, and doing it very well too. She thought his society manners exceptional, and it was obvious that he was already popular with the ladies.

Jealousy would be ridiculous! Hester raised her head, determined to remain as composed as ever. He was her cousin through marriage and she had no right to mind if other ladies enjoyed flirting with him!

Going upstairs to change a little later, Hester found her maid waiting to assist her and took as little time as she could dressing in the pretty yellow silk gown she had had made especially for the evening. She went to the duke's apartments as soon as she was ready, discovering that he was already in his evening clothes and the footmen were preparing to carry him downstairs.

'Are you ready, Grandfather?' she asked. 'Everyone has been asking for you. I think they realise what an event it is for you to come down to dinner.'

'Go ahead of me, Hester,' he told her. 'These fellows will see me right and there's nothing you can do.' He surveyed her appreciatively. 'You look well in that, girl. I shouldn't wonder if you're as pretty as anyone here this evening.'

Since the majority of guests were the duke's friends and therefore of a similar age, Hester was amused by the compliment. She had invited some of her own friends, of course, and there would be daughters and grand-daughters, but in the main the guests were the duke's contemporaries.

'You are a flatterer, sir!' she said and laughed.

Hester kissed his cheek and then left him to the care of his valet and the footmen. She was a little early, but she wanted to make sure that the table was set correctly, and she went first to the grand dining room. It was a large room in the main building with a lofty ceiling; they seldom used it when it was just the family as there was a more comfortable parlour in the east wing. Mrs Mills was taking a last look round as she entered.

'Will it do, Miss Hester?'

Hester's eyes moved over the gleaming silver, fine porcelain and beautiful cut glass and nodded her satisfaction. 'It is perfect,' she said. 'Please tell everyone that I sent my grateful thanks for all the work they have put in.'

'It was a pleasure to do it for you, miss,' the housekeeper said. 'Oh, the viscount said as I was to tell you he was in the library if you came down before the others.'

'Thank you,' Hester said. She left the dining room, making her way to the library. Jared was standing with his back to her, a book open in his hand. He turned, letting his gaze move over her with deliberate intent. The expression in his eyes brought heat to her cheeks. She felt a tingling sensation at the nape of her neck, and her insides seemed to melt as their eyes met and held. She averted her gaze, for another moment of looking into his eyes would have had her near swooning, such was the intensity of her feelings.

'You look beautiful, Hester. That shade of yellow suits you well. You should wear it more often.'

'Thank you, but I am not beautiful, you know.'

'You may not think it, but I find you beautiful.'

She smiled at the compliment, but decided to turn the subject. 'You asked for me?'

'Yes. I wanted to give you this trinket,' he replied, taking a little box from his pocket and holding it out to her.

It was a leather ring box and she took it in silence, opening it to find a pretty little ring with a mixture of small, semi-precious stones.

'Oh, how lovely. This is kind of you, cousin, though I do not know what I have done to deserve it.'

'Do you need to do anything?' he drawled, a look of amusement in his eyes. 'I believe the jeweller called it a friendship ring—the first letter of each stone spells regard.'

'Yes, I have seen them before,' Hester said. She took the ring and slipped it on to the third finger of her right hand, where it fitted perfectly. 'I love it and I shall treasure it always.' She put the box on the table, planning to retrieve it before she went up that night.

'It is a trinket, no more. Perhaps one day—' He broke off. 'It is difficult to say what I mean at the moment, Hester. I do not wish to bring you into danger.'

'That reminds me,' Hester said. 'I have been wanting to tell you that I have found what you were looking for, Jared, the journal you hoped to find.'

His head came up at that. 'Indeed? Did it confirm what I suspected?'

'The child was not mentioned by name, but it states that the second duke had discovered his existence and intended to set him up with an army career.'

He nodded, looking thoughtful. 'Then I believe we may have found our missing link. Knighton's father was in the army for a time, though I believe he may have left under a cloud. I trust you have put it away carefully?'

'Yes, of course. I knew at once that you must be right.'

'Be careful, Hester. It is best not to speak of these things. You might be overheard.'

Hester nodded, accepting what he said, but still thoughtful. 'Does it seem odd to you that Mr Grant has not come for the ball?'

'Perhaps he felt he was not welcome,' Jared said with such a casual air that she immediately suspected him. 'No, do not look at me that way, Hester. I shall not tell you—but believe me, it is for the best that Mr Grant stays away.'

'You are up to something!'

'Whatever happens, Mr Grant cannot be blamed if he is not here.'

'Yes, I see,' she said, her gaze narrowing. 'I thought when Mr Knighton told me—' She broke off, her cheeks warm. 'But it is not my business.'

'Damn him for his loose talk,' Jared said, a dangerous glint in his eyes. 'I knew something was wrong. A gentleman would not have told you. It concerned the bastard child, of course.'

'I did not regard it,' Hester replied, a faint flush in her cheeks. 'You are an attractive man in the best of health. You could not have been expected to live like a monk.'

Jared stared at her for a moment in silence and then chuckled deep in his throat, laughter dancing in his eyes. 'You are priceless, my very dear Hester! Believe me, everything will be explained in time.'

'I did not doubt it,' she said. 'Besides, you are not obliged to explain anything to me.'

'Obliged, no,' he said. 'Nevertheless, I shall tell you the whole—but not yet. He must not doubt what I do or say…do you understand me?'

'Yes, of course,' Hester said and smiled. A warm curl of happiness had begun to spread through her. She ought to have known that the tale of his bastard was a part of his plan to trap Mr Knighton. 'I think I should go to the drawing room now, and you should not be long in following, cousin. I must be there to welcome Grandfather down.'

'Yes, go now,' he said. 'You will save a dance for me, if you please—a waltz, the first of the evening, I think.'

'Yes, of course.' Her cheeks were a little pink as she turned away, because the thought of dancing in Jared's arms was sending little spirals of happiness throughout her body.

She saw Mr Knighton coming down the stairs as she went into the hall leading to the drawing room. He called to her and she paused, turning to look at him as he approached her, a polite smile on her lips.

'Hester,' he said. 'I was looking for you. Did you receive my gift?'

'Oh…' She hesitated, for she did not wish to accept anything from him, but it was difficult to refuse without giving offence. 'Really, you should not, sir.'

'It is merely a spray of flowers, which I asked to have sent to your room. I thought you might wish to wear them this evening.'

'How thoughtful of you,' Hester said. 'Unfortunately, they did not arrive before I came down. I must hope that they have been placed in water so that I can see them later. I do not think I can spare the time now to find them. Shall we go in? I do not wish to keep Grandfather waiting.'

She preceded him into the drawing room, where she found her grandfather seated in a rather grand chair, which had been provided with large wheels so that when the time came he could be moved easily from one room to another and would not suffer the humiliation of being carried. Her mother was with him and so were several of the guests. He was surrounded by his older friends, who seemed very pleased to see him downstairs again, and there was a little buzz in that area of the large room.

'Have you seen Viscount Sheldon?' Lady Raven said, coming up to Hester at that moment. 'I have saved the supper dance for him, as he asked, and I wanted to remind him that he is engaged to me for supper.'

'I am sure he will not forget,' Hester said. The smirk on Lady Raven's mouth was rather irritating and it took every ounce of her willpower to remain calm and composed. 'I have found Viscount Sheldon very reliable.'

'Oh, my dear,' Lady Raven trilled, a look of contempt in her eyes, 'I swear you make him sound positively dull. He is far more than reliable, I do assure you. A man like that is not easy to find—' She broke off as Jared entered the room. 'Oh, there he is! I must speak with him.'

Hester watched as she sailed majestically across the room to corner her quarry. She was about to join her mother and grandfather when Mr Knighton came up to her.

'Do you not think it a little odd that Mr Grant has not turned up?' he asked, frowning. 'He told me most particularly that he intended to come for the ball.' He glanced across the room to where Jared was standing, joined now by Lady Raven, Lady Mallard and one or two other ladies. 'Do you have incontrovertible proof that he is actually who he claims to be?'

'Whatever can you mean?' Hester asked, startled by the question. 'He has made no claims, but he looks very like his mother—and it was Grandfather's lawyer who approached him.'

'Yes, but you know nothing of him, Hester. He might be any sort of man…a gambler and a rogue…'

'I think you should be careful what you say,' Hester replied. She had to curl her nails into the palms of her hands to stop herself showing her anger too plainly. 'Viscount Sheldon has already done more for this family than we could possibly have hoped for. I must tell you that anything he gains from this situation is far less than he has given.'

'Well, I dare say, but I still think it is very odd that Mr Grant hasn't come,' Knighton said, a scowl on his face. He was clearly angry and had forgotten to be careful when speaking of Jared. 'He would be the heir if the American was proved an impostor.'

'Since he isn't, I think this conversation has gone far enough, sir,' Hester said crossly. 'Excuse me, I must join Mama.'

She had fought her anger as best she could, but knew that it must have shown. Had they been alone, she might not have been able to control her temper, for his words had been malicious and she had wanted to defend Jared in a much stronger manner. Only his warning that she must be careful had held her tongue, but it really was too much! Knighton was obviously hinting that something had happened to Mr Stephen Grant, and that the viscount was to blame. Had she still been in doubt of Jared's character, it might have led her to think all kinds of dreadful things! Fortunately, she had only one question left in her mind and that was personal.

'Ah, there you are, dearest,' Lady Sheldon said as her daughter came up to her. 'Your grandfather was just asking after Mr Grant. I told him that I had no idea why he hasn't come. It is a little strange, do you not think so?'

'Oh, perhaps he had another engagement—or he may not be well,' Hester said. She was relieved as the house-keeper came in to announce that dinner was served. 'I am sure he will be in touch with us soon.'

'Yes, I am sure you are right. I told his Grace that he must either be a little unwell or have some important business elsewhere.'

Hester smiled and nodded to one of her grandfather's oldest friends, listening to him as he proceeded to tell her a very long story about the fox that had recently got in amongst his chickens.

Dinner was a light meal that evening since no one wished to eat too much before the ball, and after three courses with a selection of removes had been served, Lady Sheldon led the ladies from the room. They all went upstairs to tidy themselves, coming down again as the guests invited simply for the ball began to arrive.

The long gallery had been cleared of furniture for the dancing, and three reception rooms were thrown open, the impressive double doors fastened back out of the way, so that the guests could move freely. Footmen were circling with large silver trays and glasses of champagne, and there was a buzz of laughter and excited voices when the music began.

Jared asked Lady Sheldon to open the dancing with him. Flushed with pleasure at being singled out, she claimed that it was so long since she had danced that she would tread on his toes, but it was a false claim and they twirled around the floor for a few minutes on their own before being joined by other dancers.

Hester found herself surrounded by gentlemen asking to be her partner and it was not long before her card was filled. Many of the gentlemen were old enough to be her father, but she was equally happy to dance with them, as with the younger gallants, for they were all so kind to her.

Her dance with Mr Knighton was fortunately a country dance, which meant that they did not stay together all the time, but changed partners, and she was relieved when it was over. She was afraid that her reluctance must have shown, because when she glanced at him later, she saw he was watching her and his expression was brooding.

However, she put the slight feeling of anxiety from her as Jared came to claim her for the first waltz of the evening. He smiled down at her as he placed his gloved hand at the small of her back, sweeping her into the throng of swirling dancers, proving that he was well skilled in the art and had needed no tuition from her. He was, in fact, accomplished in all the arts he needed to carry out his duties as the duke's heir, and had already proved popular with both the ladies and the gentlemen.

'Are you enjoying yourself, Hester?'

'Yes, very much,' she replied. 'It is a long time since I have had such a pleasant evening. I like to see Grandfather looking so well.'

'I like to see you happy, and to hear you laughing.'

'Oh…' Hester replied, a faint colour in her cheeks, because his words made her heart race. 'I am happy and much of it is because of what you have done for us, cousin. Are you having a pleasant evening?'

'To be in company is always pleasant,' Jared replied. 'But I would rather keep company with some people than others.'

Her eyes quizzed him, but she shook her head as he would have spoken, 'No, do not tell me. I believe I know what you mean.'

'Yes, I dare say you do. I have always found you intuitive and intelligent, Hester.'

'I hope that is a good thing?'

'Oh, yes, I believe you may take that for granted,' he replied, his eyes alive with devilment. 'I have observed that Mr Knighton seems to be a little out of sorts this evening. Would you have any idea why?'

'I think he is puzzled because Mr Grant did not come. He made some rather unfortunate remarks earlier and I may not have received them as he hoped.'

'Ah…' Jared nodded. 'That would explain it.'

'He tried to cast aspersions on your character, cousin.'

'Yes, I dare say he might. His options are narrowing.'

'What do you mean?' Hester was asking as the music came to an end. She stood looking up at him for a moment, attempting to read his mind, but finding him as inscrutable as ever.

'We shall speak of this tomorrow, Hester. Be wary of finding yourself alone with him—for my sake.'

She caught her breath as she saw something in his eyes, watching him walk away, her heart racing madly. However, in another moment Hester's next partner claimed her and she was forced to give him her attention, bringing her thoughts back to the present.

The evening passed pleasantly as Hester went from one partner to another. She ate supper with her grandfather and some of his friends, her laughter ringing out again and again as they showered her with extravagant compliments, teasing her and making a great fuss of her. If she had not taken during her first Season, she certainly had admirers enough that evening and more than one gentleman turned his head to look at her as she flirted prettily with her grandfather's friends.

'Well, girl, I think it has been a success,' the duke said to her after supper. 'I shall let them take me upstairs in a few minutes. I'm satisfied that they have accepted him. He will do well enough now. If I die tonight, I know the family is in good hands.'

'Oh, Grandfather,' Hester cried. 'Please do not say such a thing! You will live for a long time yet.'

He smiled at her ruefully. 'I'm not ready to go just yet, girl, but I know that you will be all right. He will take care of you and your mother—and that is all I really care for now. When I was younger I was proud and I thought of the family's good name, but I know now that nothing but love and the people you care for matter a jot.'

Hester bent to kiss his cheek, wishing him a good night before returning to the gallery, where the dancing had begun again. Some of the guests were still dancing, but others had begun to leave. Hester helped her mother to see them off, sending for cloaks and their carriages. She went back to the ball after bidding farewell to the last of those who were returning to their homes, finding that only a handful of couples were dancing, though some ladies and gentlemen lingered, drinking a last glass of champagne before going upstairs. There was no sign of her mother or godmother, and she guessed that they must have gone up. Jared was still talking to a group of three gentlemen. She glanced round the room, but could not see Mr Knighton. Indeed, she had not seen him since before supper.

Hester went up to Jared. She smiled at the gentlemen, who turned to her with friendly greetings. 'Is there anything more I may do for anyone?' she asked, but was met with smiling refusals. 'Cousin Jared, if you do not need me for anything else, I think I shall go up now.'

'You go up, Hester. I dare say you are tired.' Jared gestured towards her as he said, 'Miss Sheldon has worked tirelessly these past few days to make the evening a success, gentlemen.'

'Very well done, Miss Sheldon. You've brought this place back to life again. It was sad to see it as it was.'

'You must thank Lord Sheldon for that,' she said.

'You make a good team, Miss Sheldon.'

'Yes, we do,' Jared agreed with a look that made her drop her gaze. Her cheeks were warm as she walked away from them, but her heart was thudding with excitement. Jared had been saying things recently that made her believe he truly cared for her and she looked at the ring on her finger, smiling to herself. She had been about to go straight upstairs, but, remembering the box for her ring, she turned towards the library.

As she went in, she saw him at the far end of the room. He was looking through the books there, which she knew were family journals and should be of no interest to anyone outside the Shelbourne family.

He turned as he saw her and frowned. 'Hester? Has the ball ended?'

'Yes, Mr Knighton, it has,' she said. 'Are you looking for something in particular? I do not think you will find much to interest you there—they are family journals.'

'I was merely browsing,' he said. 'You are a great reader, I believe? Have you read all these family histories?'

'No, not all of them,' Hester replied. 'Was there something you wished to know?'

'Oh, no,' he said, struggling to appear casual. 'But I find family histories fascinating. One discovers so many secrets. The skeletons in the cupboard, so to speak.' His eyes narrowed. 'A family like this must have many secrets, bastards, tragic deaths. Do you not think so?'

'Yes, perhaps,' Hester said. 'Excuse me, I came to retrieve a box.' She picked it up. 'Goodnight, sir.'

Knighton's eyes were intent on her now. 'I suppose that contained the ring you are wearing. I have not seen you wear it before, Hester.'

'It was a gift to me…for the work I have done helping to prepare for the ball.'

'From *him*, I suppose?' Now there was something almost frightening in the way he was looking at her. 'You should be careful, Hester. He will hardly marry a girl like you when he can take his pick of society. As the duke's heir, he will look higher.'

'I dare say you may be right,' Hester said, maintaining her dignity. She gave him a cool, proud look. 'Goodnight, sir.'

'You would not have been so proud a few months ago,' Knighton said to her, suddenly vicious. 'Be careful you do not fall into his trap, Hester.'

She was so angry that she did not dare to reply, but walked from the room, her head high and her back straight.

She had tried not to show her dislike, but it seemed that she had failed. He was aware of her preference for Jared and it had made him angry.

Hester discovered that she was very tired as she undressed and got into bed. It had been a very long day, and she had danced for most of the night. She was on the verge of falling asleep when she thought of the journal in her drawer. She got up, went to the door leading to the hallway and locked it. She was not sure why she had done so, but some instinct told her that, if Mr Knighton was the man Jared thought him, she could be in danger.

Hester slept well despite some worrying thoughts. She slept in a little later than usual, but because the maids had been told to leave her to rest, no one had discovered that her door was locked. She had unlocked it by the time her maid brought her a tray of chocolate and croissants with honey.

'The viscount said you were to have breakfast in bed today, miss.'

'Oh, thank you,' Hester said, yawning as she sat up against the pillows. 'I am a lazy stayabed this morning!'

'It will do you good, miss,' the maid told her with a smile. 'Most of the ladies have slept in this morning, though some of the gentleman have gone out riding.'

'Did the viscount go with them?'

'Yes, miss. Him and some of your neighbours. I think he said he wanted some advice about the land, miss.' The girl blushed. 'I wasn't listening, miss, but it was my job to take in the toast.'

'You could not help overhearing, Maisie,' Hester said. 'Do you know if Mr Knighton went out at all?'

'Not with the others, miss. I haven't seen him this morning so I don't know for certain.'

'Thank you,' Hester said. 'Would you lay out the grey gown with the lace insets this morning please?'

'Oh, yes, miss. I like that one. It's pretty.'

Hester drank a dish of chocolate as her maid did some tidying and then left her to finish her breakfast. She ate one of the croissants and then got up to wash and dress herself. As the grey gown fastened at the front she had no need of help, and she brushed her thick, glossy hair, winding it into a double knot at the back of her head. She loosened a couple of strands about her face, then glanced at herself once more before leaving the room. She would have liked to go riding, but there were still guests in the house, which meant that she ought to be on hand if she were needed.

Downstairs, the clearing up had begun. Servants were returning furniture to its proper position, and discovering crystal glasses that had been carelessly left in peculiar places the previous night. Hester went to inspect the flowers she had arranged the previous day. Some of them seemed to have drooped and she carried them to the flower room to refresh them. As she was carrying one large container filled with huge blooms, she almost collided with a young maid holding a pot of silver polish. Somehow, it splashed on her gown, making a large greasy stain on the skirt.

'Oh, miss,' the girl exclaimed, looking horrified. 'I am so sorry. I've ruined your gown. Silver polish won't come out.'

Hester was a little disappointed that it should be one of her favourite dresses, but, seeing how upset and anxious the maid was, she smiled at her.

'Do not look like that, Susie,' she said. 'It was as much my fault as yours. Please go and ask Mrs Mills if she knows what to do for the best. I shall go upstairs and change.'

'Yes, miss. I am so sorry.'

The girl ran off in a hurry and Hester went up the stairs and along the landing to her own room. The door was slightly open, and, hearing something inside, she paused for a moment before she entered. As she did so, she saw that a man was standing near the bed and he had a book in his hand. It was the journal she had put in one of the tallboy drawers, and he had obviously been hunting for it, pulling out her possessions and leaving them scattered about the room.

'What are you doing here, sir?' she asked coldly. 'I did not give you permission to come to my room and that book belongs to the Shelbourne family. It is private. Please give it to me.' She held out her hand for the journal, but he did not pass it to her.

'You know what is written here, don't you?' Knighton said, turning to look at her. The expression in his eyes chilled her because it was so very odd. 'You know that my father was named a bastard...the child of a man who would have been the master here had he not died.'

'I suspected it,' Hester said, because the time for deception was past. 'I did not know for certain until you told me, sir.' She raised her clear eyes to his. 'You know that you have no claim here because your grandfather did not marry your grandmother.'

'That isn't true,' Knighton told her, a flash of anger in his eyes. 'My father told me that they were married secretly. Both families denied it because they quarrelled, but it was so.' His gaze intensified. 'My father was denied his birthright. He was bitter because of it and took to drink. He made my mother's life a misery and mine.'

'I am sorry,' Hester said. 'But if what he told you were true, there would be proof...do you not think so? If you have proof of the marriage, you should present it.'

'The proof was lost,' Knighton said. 'That is why I

have looked for it here, because he knew—my grandfather knew the truth. Why else would he have tried to buy my father off with a commission in the army? Besides, it isn't the title I want. I would not be able to support a house like this.' He glared at her. '*He* has all the money… that upstart from America!'

Hester felt a chill at the nape of her neck, because in that moment she knew for certain what he had done. 'What did you hope to achieve by trying to kill Viscount Sheldon? You could not hope to inherit his fortune?'

'Damn you! I knew you had fallen under his spell,' Knighton said, advancing on her with malicious intent. 'I thought you would marry me. If the others were dead, the old man would have left the place to you. I should have had my revenge then. I was going to wait until you gave me a child. Imagine his face when I told him who I was, Hester.' His mouth twisted with bitterness. 'If he survived the shock, he would have had to live with the knowledge that he had no right to all this…his life has been a lie. My father should have inherited the title when his father died and my child would be the master here one day. The perfect revenge, do you not think so?'

'Grandfather would not have cheated you,' Hester said, too angry now to care what she said. 'I do not believe that your grandparents were married. You have been fed on lies and supposition. Your father had no right to the title and nor do you.'

'Damn you!' Knighton raised his fist, advancing on her, his purpose obvious. 'I was waiting for Stephen Grant to come so that I could get rid of him, but he changed his mind.' His eyes glittered with something dark and dangerous. 'But I'll have my revenge now and be damned to this place! Your death will hurt them both more than anything else.' He reached out to grab her by the throat. 'With you dead, the old man won't have the heart to live.'

'No!' Hester put out her hands, trying to push him off as he came at her. He looked so strange, and had a queer, blind look in his eyes. At this moment he was not capable of rational thought. 'No! Stay away from me! Do not touch me! Help me…help me!' Hester struggled against him, but he had her by the throat. His hands closed about her throat as she tried desperately to throw him off, but he was very strong and she knew that she did not stand much chance against him. 'Help me!' she screamed again in desperation. Surely someone must hear her!

'Miss Hester!' The shout from behind her alerted her that Mrs Mills had arrived, clearly come to see the damage to Hester's gown in person. 'What do you think you are doing, sir? Take your hands off Miss Hester…'

Hester screamed again, struggling to throw him off, but he seemed impervious to the fact that his attempt to murder her was being watched by the housekeeper. He had lost all control and she doubted that he truly knew what he was doing. She did not see what was happening in the room until Mrs Mills loomed up behind him with a large, heavy brass candlestick taken from the desk in the window. She launched herself at his back, striking him a blow on the side of the head. It was not sufficient to floor him, but it threw him off balance and Hester managed to break free. She moved away from him as Mrs Mills brandished her weapon. For a moment he held his hand to his head as if surprised and then his eyes fixed on the housekeeper, narrowed and angry.

'Now don't you try anything, sir,' Mrs Mills warned. She brandished her weapon determinedly. 'I saw what you were doing to Miss Sheldon and I'll swear to it in a court of law. I shouldn't wonder they'll hang you. At the least you'll be transported.'

'Damn you,' Knighton snarled. His malicious gaze came back to Hester, who was holding her throat, which felt tender where his fingers had pressed into her flesh. 'I haven't finished with you or this cursed family yet…'

Hester drew a breath of relief as he turned and rushed from the room. She sank down on the edge of the bed, beginning to tremble as the horror of what might have happened overcame her. The housekeeper put down the candlestick and came towards her.

'Are you all right, miss?' she asked in concern. 'What was wrong with him? He didn't seem the sort of man to drink too much. Did he hurt you badly?'

'Not very much,' Hester said. 'I think you were in time. If you hadn't come…' She drew a sobbing breath. 'Thank you so much.'

'It's just as well Susie spilled that polish on your gown, miss,' Mrs Mills said with a look of satisfaction. 'Not that it excuses her for her carelessness—and that dress one of your favourites as well.'

Hester gave her a faint smile. 'I think it is of very little consequence in the circumstances, Mrs Mills. Mr Knighton has tried to have Lord Sheldon killed twice now and he might have killed me but for the accident to my gown that brought you here.'

'Oh, my lord!' the housekeeper cried, horrified. 'I never heard of such a thing! The wicked man! And him a guest in this house.'

'I think he was not entirely in his right mind. I cannot thank you enough for helping me so bravely. It was fortunate that you came when you did.'

'I was cross with Susie,' the housekeeper said, shaking her head. 'I came to see what I could do, Miss Hester, though I cannot hold out much hope of rescuing the gown.'

'It really doesn't matter, because I dare say I may have

another made like it in another colour,' Hester told her. She touched the woman's hand. 'I am very grateful for what you did—but could you keep it to yourself for the moment, please? Mama will be very distressed when she discovers what Knighton did. He is her cousin by marriage and she thought him a man she could turn to in need.'

'She will be distressed, miss—but more because of what he did to you than any feeling for him. I dare not think what the master will say.' Mrs Mills shook her head. 'If anything had happened to you…'

'His Grace must not be told,' Hester said. 'Please keep this to yourself, Mrs Mills.'

'I was speaking of the viscount, miss,' Mrs Mills told her. 'Strictly speaking, his Grace is the master here, but the viscount has done so much that we've started to think of him as being in charge here.'

'Yes, of course, he is,' Hester said, realising that it was true. The duke had as good as acknowledged it the previous night. 'I believe he has gone out, and I shall tell him when he returns—but until then I must ask you to say nothing.'

'Well, as long as you tell him what happened, I dare say he will know what to do for the best.'

'Yes, I am sure he will,' Hester told her, smiling inwardly.

'Why don't you pop into bed, miss? I'll send one of the girls up with a nice soothing drink for your poor throat.'

Hester went to the dressing table, looking at herself in the mirror. 'He has bruised my neck, but otherwise I am not hurt,' she said. 'I shall change my gown and come down in a few moments.'

'Make sure you lock your door, miss,' the housekeeper said. 'Not that he will dare to come here again, but it is best to be sure. Would you like me to wait while you change?'

'I'll take my gown off,' Hester said, going behind the screen. She threw her dress over the side and Mrs Mills took it down. When Hester came out she discovered that the thoughtful housekeeper had put out a similar gown for her. She put it on, pleased to see that it had a high neck to hide the bruises on her throat. She would have to be careful what she wore for a day or two, because she did not wish to distress her mother or the duke.

Having tidied her hair, she went out and began to walk along the landing just as Jared came racing up the stairs. His expression was harsh, his features set in grim lines. He stopped as he came up to her, his keen eyes going over her in such a way that she knew Mrs Mills must have seen him and told him of the incident.

'Hester! Are you all right, my love?'

Hester smiled at the endearment. 'Yes, of course I am, Jared,' she said. 'Mrs Mills arrived in time. She very bravely attacked him with a candlestick and he ran off.'

'Damn him!' Jared said, looking rueful. 'I have done my best to entice him to attack me; I have provoked him several times, but unhappily he chose you instead. I did not want that to happen, Hester, though I was afraid it might if he understood you would never marry him.'

'It isn't the title or the estate he wants,' Hester said. 'Though I dare say he would have taken them if his plan had worked—it was revenge. Just as you thought. He claims his grandfather married his grandmother. He says his father should have inherited the title after his grandfather died and he wanted revenge because this family refused to acknowledge the marriage.'

'I doubt it ever took place,' Jared said. 'He was obviously obsessed with the desire for revenge, Hester. He wasn't mad, but he had that strange intensity about him at times that made me think he wasn't mentally stable.' He

reached out to touch her cheek with his fingertips. 'I tried
to hide my feelings for you, and I warned you to be careful,
because I feared it might tip him over the edge if he
realised all his plans were doomed to failure…and it seems
that it did, my poor love.'

His words soothed Hester's frayed nerves as nothing
else could. She smiled at him, reassured by his presence.
He was such a strong man, both physically and in character, and she knew that he would not fail her.

'I am afraid that may have been my fault. I went to
retrieve the box for my ring last night and discovered
him going through the family journals. Something I said
must have angered him. He came here to find the book
I had hidden, hoping that it would give him the proof he
needed, but of course it did not. His father had fed him
on stories about his right to inherit Shelbourne, but it
was all lies.'

'Yes, it was a lie,' Jared replied. 'I have had the records
checked thoroughly and I can assure you there is no record
of a marriage having taken place. If there was one, it must
have been clandestine and was probably not legal.'

'I accused him of having tried to kill you and he did
not deny it. When he knew his plans had no chance of
succeeding, he tried to kill me in the hope of having his
revenge that way.'

'He would have succeeded had Mrs Mills not arrived
when she did,' Jared said. 'You are much loved by us all,
Hester. If he had murdered you, it would have killed your
grandfather and destroyed this family.'

'Oh…' She blushed and looked down. 'I know Grandfather and Mama…'

He moved towards her, tipping her chin with his finger
so that she looked up at him. 'Surely you know that I
would have felt your loss as much as anyone?'

Hester's eyes were very bright as she gazed up at him. 'I have thought…but I wasn't truly sure…'

'Foolish Hester. Sometimes so wise and yet so foolish.' He bent his head to kiss her softly on the mouth. Hester moaned as her body was pressed against him and she felt herself melting with a surge of fierce desire that raced through her. 'You must have known how I felt when we kissed?'

A little smile touched her mouth. 'I knew how I felt,' she told him truthfully. 'I wanted you to go on kissing me and never stop. I wanted…so much more…' Her cheeks were pink as she met his hot, teasing gaze. 'I think it is very immodest of me to say so, Jared, but had you asked, I might have been yours before this.'

'Did you imagine I wanted you as my mistress? Oh, Hester, you shock me, you really do. There was I thinking you a perfect example of a well-behaved English lady, and you—'

'Don't!' she implored him, putting her hands to her face. 'I know it was shameless, quite shameless…'

'It was adorable and exactly what I had hoped for,' he replied. 'I would have asked you to marry me even if you had not responded so delightfully, my dearest love—but to know that you have such passion in you makes me think that we shall be very happy together.'

'Jared…you really do want to marry me?'

'Yes, of course.' He took her face between his hands, gazing down at her. 'You may have thought I was interested in certain other ladies, Hester, but I was trying to lead Knighton astray. I thought that if he believed I was going to marry the mother of my bastard son and make him legitimate, it would force him out into the open. I needed him to attack me himself so that I could bring the force of the law to bear. Unfortunately, my plan misfired for it made him realise his could never work—so he attacked you instead.' A shudder went through him. 'I cannot believe that you came so close to death.'

'Mrs Mills and her candlestick saved me,' Hester replied, a hint of mischief in her eyes now. 'I think I am safe for the moment for he will have fled, but we must take care, Jared. Until he is caught and arrested he remains a danger to all of us. I believe that he would not hesitate to kill any member of this family.' She stared at him as a thought came to her. 'Grandfather! We believed he must have fled…but it must be his Grace he hates the most.'

She began to run along the landing, fear catching at her heart. When Knighton ran away after the housekeeper attacked him, she had thought he would leave the house immediately, but intuition was telling her that he would take one last chance to be revenged on the family he hated.

'Hester, come back,' Jared said, catching up with her. 'Leave this to me. If he is there, he will be dangerous.'

'Grandfather may be hurt,' Hester said, refusing to falter. 'You cannot stop me, Jared. I must be there.'

'Let me handle him if he is there,' Jared said, taking a small pistol from his coat pocket. 'Just keep out of his way. I do not want him using you as cover to make his escape if…'

Hester threw him a desperate look and ran faster. She was terrified that they would be too late. The duke was an old man and vulnerable! He would be no match for a man who was eaten up by bitterness and the desire for revenge.

Jared caught up with her again as they reached the door of the duke's apartments. He grabbed her arm, pulling her back and thrusting her behind him as he went into the duke's private parlour, then gave a muffled curse at what he saw. The duke was sitting in his bathchair, a small pistol in his hand, and it was pointing straight at the chest of the man in front of him.

Knighton's head turned as Jared entered, followed by Hester. His eyes sparked fanatically as they centred on her. 'Now you are here, you can ask him for the truth, Hester. Make him tell you what he knows before he kills me. I know that is what he wants…what the family has always wanted…to be rid of the evidence of their scandal.'

She moved closer to her grandfather for she had seen that his hand was trembling. Facing Knighton, she gave him a scornful look. 'I do not need to ask,' she said. 'I know that his Grace would never have cheated your father of his birthright if he had had a legitimate claim to the title and the estate.'

'Thank you, Hester,' the duke replied. He looked grey and very tired. 'Yes, I knew that my elder brother had a son. The story went that the child had died at birth, but my father discovered the truth before he died, and when Jack died, he told me. I had extensive inquiries made, but there was no record of a marriage ever having taken place. If one took place, it must have been a sham, to pacify my brother's lover. Jack was capable of that, but he never spoke of it to his family. Your father changed his name when he was thrown out of the army in disgrace, Knighton. I knew who you were when you first came here, but for Hester's sake, and her mother's, I received you and said nothing.'

'You are a liar!' Knighton cried and made a lunge towards him. The duke raised his arm, but he hesitated, and before he could fire his pistol, Jared had tackled Knighton from behind, bringing him down to the floor.

A short but fierce struggle took place, ending with Jared straddling the other man's body as he lay face down on the floor. A footman hurried to give him the cord from a window curtain and he trussed Knighton's hands behind his back. Getting to his feet, Jared dragged Knighton up with him, still struggling and cursing, shouting that he had been cheated of his rights. Two burly footmen had now joined the first and they took hold of his arms, looking at Jared as they waited for orders.

Jared looked at the duke. 'What do you want done with him, sir?'

'You tell me what you would do with him, for I'm damned if I know.'

'It will cause a scandal, but I think he should be made to stand trial for his crimes, sir. He has tried to have me killed twice, but, more importantly, he attempted to strangle Hester not half an hour ago.'

'Curse him!' the duke cried. 'Had I known, I would have shot him.' His eyes moved over her anxiously. 'Are you all right, girl?'

'Yes, Grandfather.' She bent down to kiss his cheek, feeling the papery softness of his skin beneath her lips. He looked so frail and anxious that her heart caught. 'Please do not worry, dearest. But I agree with Jared. I do not see what else we can do but have him arrested and tried for his crimes.'

'Take him away,' the duke said wearily. 'Do what you wish with him. I do not want to set eyes on him again.'

'Stay with Grandfather,' Jared said to Hester. 'I think we should ask for his Grace's doctor to call.' He was so clearly in charge that one of the footmen immediately went off to do his bidding. 'Henderson, Briggs, take him down the backstairs, if you please. We will have him confined in one of the outbuildings until the constable comes to take him away. I shall join you in a moment.'

He waited until they had left, and then looked at the duke's valet, who nodded in answer to his unspoken question. 'You can leave him to Miss Hester and me, sir. His Grace has had a bit of a shock and he will do better in his bed for a while.'

'I shall see you later,' Jared said, glancing at Hester. 'Excuse me, I must see what is going on.'

They all heard the shouting at that moment and Hester threw him an urgent look. 'Go quickly. Something is happening.'

Jared nodded and strode from the room. He was in time to see the two footmen beginning to run up the stairs at the far end of the landing. Immediately, he understood that Knighton had somehow broken free from them and was heading for the stairs that led out to the roof. Something told him what the man was intending and he ran up the stairs, reaching the top seconds after the footmen, who were standing watching as Knighton walked precariously along the ridge between the west wing and the main part of the building. With his hands tied behind his back he had no balance, and he swayed precariously, in danger of falling.

'Stop,' Jared said as he saw that one of them was preparing to follow Knighton. 'You are too heavy, Briggs. Some of this stonework is still unstable. The builders told me the problem was much bigger than they first suspected. Let me try. I have more idea of the danger spots than you.'

'Be careful, my lord,' Briggs said. 'It's unstable and cracking. Best to let him go. We'll get him if he makes it down to the ground.'

'But he may fall,' Jared said. 'He may not be aware of the danger here.'

The look the footman gave him spoke volumes. He obviously thought it would be the best for all concerned, but Jared knew he must at least try to save Knighton from his folly. He put one foot out on to the ridge, walking slowly and carefully towards Knighton, who seemed to have come to a standstill just ahead of him. He appeared dazed, as if he were unsure of what he was doing up on the roof.

'Come back,' Jared called. 'It isn't safe to go any

further. Those slabs are loose. The builders are coming back next week to finish repairing the roof. If you go any further, they may give way and take you with them.'

Knighton looked back at him, his eyes glittering wildly. 'Stay away from me,' he said. 'You want me dead. You're like all the others—liars, cheats, refusing me what was rightfully mine.'

'You know that is a lie,' Jared said. 'For God's sake, man, I never wanted all this. I had a life of my own. If you were the rightful heir, Shelbourne would have told you. He's a hard man, but fair.'

'Stay away from me!' Knighton was standing right at the edge of the ridge. 'You're just like all the others. You're cursed…cursed…do you hear me?'

'Come back, you fool!' Jared shouted but already he could see what Knighton meant to do. He stood helplessly as the other man took a step forward into space, letting himself fall from the edge of the roof straight down like a stone to the ground. As he did so, a chunk of masonry went tumbling after him and smashed into pieces only inches from where his body lay. It was obvious that no one could have survived such a fall, and the angle of Knighton's neck indicated that it had broken on impact.

Jared stood staring down at him, an expression of horror in his eyes. The man's mind had clearly cracked under the strain of his delusions, but even so, it was a violent and desperate act to take his own life in that way. Surely there had been another way to solve this mess? Jared felt sickened by the waste of life. Why had Knighton not listened to him? He would have saved him if he could.

'Come back, my lord,' Briggs called, breaking his train of thought. 'Don't go any further, sir. It's all cracking up there. You must come back now! It could give way at any minute.'

Jared turned. He could feel that more of the stonework

had cracked beneath his feet and he had to edge his way back carefully. The masonry was unstable, splintering as he stepped on it. He knew that at any minute it could fall and take him down with it to certain death. He slowly inched his way back to the door where the footmen waited helplessly, watching him, knowing that they could not do more, for any further weight could cause the structure to collapse. Two strong hands reached out to hold him as he reached them, drawing him back into the safety of the stairwell.

'We saw what happened, sir. Mr Knighton took his own life deliberately.'

'Damned fool,' Jared said. 'He killed no one and might have served his sentence in the colonies if he had stood trial. He could have made another life for himself.'

'Perhaps he preferred death,' Briggs suggested. 'Seemed a little unwell, if you ask me, sir. Something turned his mind, perhaps? It was a tragic accident, my lord, wouldn't you say so? Poor Mr Knighton was obviously not himself. He must have come up to look at the stonework and turned dizzy.'

'Are you implying we hush it up and hide it under the carpet?' Jared asked, looking doubtful. 'If someone had brought all this business out into the open years ago this might never have happened…but perhaps you are right. Knighton was obviously ill.'

'Yes, sir, exactly what all of us was thinking.'

Jared looked him in the eyes. 'You are a good man. What makes you—all of you—so devoted to a family like this?'

'We are part of the family, my lord. You have your place and we have ours, but it is all the same family.'

'Yes, yes, it is.' Jared smiled, because suddenly he understood what the lawyer had been trying to tell him when they first met. He did have a duty here, not just to his blood relations, but to the extended family that relied on the estate. 'Thank you, Briggs. I think his Grace is lucky to have people like you about him.'

'It is a pleasure to serve this family, sir. I've been here since I was a lad and I hope to stay until you pension me off.'

'You do, do you?' Jared grinned. 'Well, that means I shall have to stay around to see that your loyalty is rewarded, doesn't it?'

'Just so, sir. I think it is what Miss Hester would like, sir.'

'Yes, I dare say you are right,' Jared said. 'Well, we had better get this mess cleared up, don't you think?'

'Exactly so, sir. If you don't mind my saying, you were very brave risking your life for Mr Knighton, sir. I am sure everyone will think so.'

'The fewer who know about it, the better,' Jared said. 'I had better go and reassure the ladies.'

Chapter Eleven

'Hester, dearest,' Lady Ireland said as Hester came downstairs later that afternoon. 'Your mama has gone to lie down for a while—this is a terrible business. I always knew that Mr Knighton was a little intense, especially where you were concerned, but he must have been dreadfully ill to go up on the roof like that. Mrs Mills told me that the viscount went after him, tried to save him, but it was no use. He was determined to jump. The poor man must have been out of his mind.'

'Yes, I am certain he was unwell,' Hester said. She knew of the story that was to be given officially to the remaining guests, though of course every one of the servants would know the truth, because it was already being talked of downstairs. 'I think he must have been under a strain for some time.'

'It is as well you did not marry him,' Lady Ireland said, shaking her head over it. 'This is a terrible upset for everyone. And the ball was such a success. I am afraid all your guests have gone, my love. They were told his Grace was unwell and I think they did not wish to be in the way.' She raised her brows. 'How is Shelbourne?'

'His doctor says it was merely a little turn. He is no better and no worse than he was before.'

'I dare say it was all the excitement of the ball,' Lady Ireland said, for she had been told nothing of the attack on Hester or the scene in the duke's chambers. 'He will be better once he has rested for a day or so.'

'That is exactly what he told me,' Hester replied with a smile. 'So everyone has gone?'

'Except me, of course. I stayed on to see if I could be of help to you, my love—and your poor mama. She is rather distressed over this, as you may imagine.'

'Yes, she must be,' Hester agreed. 'Thank you for staying on, but you are one of the family, of course. I think I shall go and see how Mama is, and then we must change for dinner. I hardly know where the day went.'

'Yes, you do that, Hester,' Lady Ireland said. She was about to kiss Hester's cheek when the door opened and a man entered. She frowned at him, lifting her lorgnette to peer at him in disapproval. 'Mr Grant…we expected you yesterday for the ball.'

'And I should have been here, ma'am,' Mr Grant said, looking indignant. 'Except that I had an urgent message that took me to London three days ago.' His eyes snapped with temper. 'I was told that my lawyer wished to see me on a matter of business—something of life-and-death importance!—and when I arrived it was no such thing. I had the whole journey for nothing! I was never so put out in my life. The letter was a forgery and had never come from him at all!'

'Oh…' Seeing his expression of outrage, Hester felt an urge to laugh as she realised what Jared had done to keep him out of the way for a few days. 'That was most unfortunate, sir.'

'Indeed it was,' Mr Grant replied. 'Someone sent me

that letter deliberately and I think I know who it was.' He glared at her. 'Is Knighton still here? I want a word with him!'

Hester's desire to smile left her at once. 'Mr Knighton had a terrible accident, sir. He was unwell…suffering from anxiety, we think. He went up on the roof for some reason and fell to his death.'

'Fell from the roof?' Mr Grant's face was a picture of astonishment. 'Good gracious! What on earth was the fellow doing there?'

'That is the question,' Jared's voice said. He stood in the doorway, looking at Mr Grant, his expression registering nothing but polite concern. 'I am glad to see you here again, sir. We were sorry you did not come for the ball. Hester, your mother is asking for you. Grant, come and have a drink with me in the library. There are some things you should be told…something that would be distressing for the ladies.'

'Oh, right.' Mr Grant looked surprised and then pleased that he had been invited to share a confidence. 'Yes, of course. I shall see you at dinner, ladies. Please excuse us now. I am at your service, my lord.'

Hester met Jared's eyes for a moment and smiled. He was showing his true colours now, his air of command one that even Mr Grant was bound to respect. She realised that he would very soon have them all hanging on his every word, and the thought made her want to giggle. It was so very different from what they had all expected.

'I shall go up to Mama. Gentlemen, I shall see you both this evening,' she said and went out, followed by Lady Ireland.

Hester spent half an hour with her mother. Lady Sheldon was a little tearful, for, not knowing the whole story she regretted the loss of her cousin. She was propped up against a pile of pillows, a lace kerchief in her hand. However, she recovered her spirits after Hester took her one of the housekeeper's tisanes and smiled wanly at her daughter.

'Jared was something of a hero, you know, my dear. Mrs Mills told me that he didn't want it spoken of, but apparently he went after Mr Knighton and tried to bring him back. The poor man, he must have been quite ill to do such a foolish thing. I had noticed he was a little off colour these last few days.'

'I think he must have been worried about something.'

'Perhaps he was in debt,' Lady Sheldon said, nodding her agreement. 'I do not think he has any living relatives other than us. I do not know what arrangements should be made for the funeral and everything.'

'I think you may leave safely these matters to Jared,' Hester told her. 'He will do whatever needs to be done.'

'Yes, of course,' her mother said and gave a sigh of satisfaction. 'It is so good to know that we have someone to lean on, Hester. I really do not know how we managed without dear Jared.'

'No, Mama,' Hester said and hid her smile. 'Nor do I.'

Leaving her mother to rest for a little longer, Hester went to her own room to change. She spent some time arranging her hair, letting it wave softly about her face instead of scraping it back as she often did when in a hurry. She put on the pale blue, heavy silk gown her maid had put out for her, fastening her pearls about her throat and adding a scarf of lace to hide the bruises to her skin. Satisfied that nothing was showing, she left her room and went along the landing, up the stairs to the west wing to her grandfather's room.

His valet answered the door, inviting her in to see for

herself that his Grace was resting. He lay propped up against a pile of pillows, looking at some papers, but smiled and put them down as she entered.

'Hester, my love. I was just sorting out a few things for when I've gone. I shan't be here for ever and I want to make sure you are taken care of.'

'Oh, Grandfather,' Hester said, 'I have enough for my needs. Besides, I have my allowance—and the inheritance from my father's aunt.'

'It's just as well, for I haven't much to leave you, but there are a few things—personal items I want you to have.'

'That is different,' she said and smiled. 'Though I need nothing to remind me of your kindness. I shall never forget you took me in as your own.'

'And you have been more than any daughter could ever be,' the duke told her. 'All I want now is to see you happy, Hester.'

'I am happy,' she said, turning as the door opened to admit Jared. Her pulses raced at the sight of him. He had an air of sophistication in his evening dress, clearly a man at home in his element, and her heart caught with love. 'Have you come to talk to Grandfather? Do you want me to leave?'

'No, of course not, my love,' Jared said, smiling as he came to stand at her side. 'I have some news for you both. The builders have been up to the roof, examining the damage, and hidden under a ledge they found a valuable chalice wrapped in soft cloth. It has tarnished a little, but I am sure a good jeweller will be able to restore it to its former glory.'

'The chalice—hidden here all that time?' The duke was astonished. 'You know the tale, of course? But if it was here all the time…'

'The family made its own fortune,' Jared told him. 'The

curse was never more than words said in anger. If the old scandal had been dealt with years ago, Knighton would never have been led to believe that he was the rightful heir.'

'True enough,' the duke said. 'If there was a curse, it was broken when you came here, sir. I think that the fate of my family lies in your hands—and they are capable hands, I believe.'

'I shall do my best, sir.' Jared turned to Hester. 'Give me your hand, my love.' He took her left hand and slid something on to the third finger, smiling as she opened her eyes at him, because it was the most magnificent emerald-and-diamond ring she had ever seen, the emerald square cut and flawless. 'I may not have asked you properly yet, but I thought it was time we made it official.' He turned his steady gaze on the duke. 'I trust this meets with your approval, sir?'

The duke's eyes narrowed, intent on Hester's face, satisfied with what he saw there. 'What would you say if I said I did not approve?'

'I would tell you that I was very sorry, but I intend to marry Hester if she will have me—and I believe she will?' He grinned as she inclined her head. 'But I hope that you will give us your approval, sir?'

'With all my heart,' the duke said and grinned back, looking much like his grandson might in later years. 'I couldn't have arranged matters better myself if I had tried.'

Jared raised his brows. 'Do not tell me that it never crossed your mind, sir, for I should not believe you.'

'It would do me little good to lie to you,' the duke said. 'You would see right through me. I hoped you might fall in love with my girl, but I knew if I said a word it might send you right back where you came from, so I kept my silence.'

'Grandfather!' Hester exclaimed. 'You told me I had to

teach him how to behave in society so that he could find a rich wife!'

'Well, he ain't got a need of one,' the duke said, his eyes twinkling. 'Got enough to build another dozen houses like this if the truth were known, I dare say.'

'I have sufficient for my needs and those of my family,' Jared replied with a lazy smile. 'I am afraid you may not like the source of my wealth.'

'Gambler like your father?' the duke barked.

'As a matter of fact, I make most of my money importing goods from one country to another and selling them,' Jared told him. 'I have ships, warehouses and quite a bit of property. I started off with tobacco and wine, but then I became interested in fine furniture, works of art... I bought a lot of goods that were stolen or displaced in the French Revolution. I rather like French furniture, you see. But I buy from anyone that has something of interest to sell. Some of it I keep and some of it is sold on at a profit.'

'In trade, are you?' The duke frowned at him. 'Best keep it to yourself, sir. You might find some of the high-minded society ladies would turn their noses up at you if they discovered your secret.'

'I rather think my business has gone beyond that, sir,' Jared told him with a little smile. 'I have found that if there is enough money people tend not to bother too much where it came from.'

'Got that much, have you?' the duke growled. 'Well, I can stop worrying about my girl, then. You'll make a decent settlement on her?'

'Of course,' Jared replied easily. 'Hester is welcome to anything I have. I hope she knows that she means everything to me?' His eyes rested on her tenderly, bringing tears of joy to her eyes.

'I would marry you if you were as hard up as you would

have had us believe at the start,' Hester told him, taking his hand and pressing it to her cheek. 'You are the only man I have ever wanted to marry.'

'You've got good taste,' the duke growled. 'He'll do very well, Hester. Now take him downstairs and show your ring to your mother. She has been telling me for weeks this was going to happen, but I wasn't sure. Come and kiss me first, girl.'

She bent her head, kissing him affectionately. 'You are a wicked old man, sir.'

'Can't teach an old dog new tricks,' he grunted. 'But I'll die happy if I see my first great-grandchild in your arms, Hester.'

'You'll see him grow to a lad,' Jared assured him. 'You've nothing to worry about now that I am here, and no reason why you shouldn't live for a good few years yet.' He smiled at Hester. 'Go down now, my love. I'll follow in a few minutes.'

Hester nodded and went out, leaving the two men together. The duke gave him a hard look.

'Everything sorted, then?'

'I've confided in Grant. I thought he had the right to know.'

'Yes, I dare say. He had nothing to do with any of this?'

'Nothing at all, but he was the key to Knighton's plans, sir. Knighton knew that two sudden deaths would be suspicious. He didn't want an investigation into his background. He meant to kill me, but he wanted the blame to fall on Grant, leaving the way clear for you to leave this place to Hester. Once she had given him a child, he would have delighted in telling you the truth.'

'Knowing that I could do nothing for her sake.' The duke nodded. 'The man was mad. Believe me, he never had a true claim to the title. My elder brother was a womaniser and went through more than one sham marriage

with innocent girls, besides pestering some of the maids—
but keep that to yourself, please. There has been enough
scandal in this family.'

'I had the old story thoroughly investigated,' Jared said.
'I wanted to know the truth before I made up my mind to
stay here.'

'You will stay?'

'It is Hester's home,' Jared said. 'I would give her
whatever she wanted—and I know she loves this house.'

'But she loves you more,' the duke said. 'Ask her—
decide between you. I have no right to demand that you
give up your own life for us.'

'You may not have,' Jared said. 'But Hester does.'

'Everyone is delighted,' Hester said as they walked
together in the garden later that evening. 'Mama says that
she has known it for an age. Lady Ireland was surprised,
but pleased—and even Mr Grant wished me happiness.'

'I think you will find he is content with the situation,'
Jared said. 'I have some influence that may lead to a pre-
ferment for him, a first step on the way to becoming a
bishop perhaps.'

'Yes, he would make an excellent bishop,' Hester said,
eyes dancing with laughter. 'I thought you handled Grandfather very well, Jared—but you should never have risked
your own life for Mr Knighton the way you did.' She
stopped walking, her hand pressed to his chest as she
looked up into his eyes. 'If you had slipped and fallen…'

He bent his head, brushing his lips lightly over hers,
hushing her with a kiss that left her breathless, her body
melting with desire. 'It is over, my love. Nothing
happened and the builders will be here again tomorrow
to finish their work. I have no intention of going
anywhere…except on my honeymoon with you.' He

touched her cheek with his fingertips. 'Where do you wish to go—Italy, France…America?'

'I should like to see where you were brought up one day,' Hester told him. 'But a short trip to Paris would be enough for me. I do not want to leave Grandfather for too long.' She gazed into his eyes. 'I know it is asking a lot of you to give up your home and live here. It is only while he lives, Jared. I could not leave him alone here—but one day, when he is no longer with us, I will go anywhere that you wish. My life is with you. I do not mind where we live once Grandfather has gone.'

'But you love this house. Would you not hate to leave it?'

'I love Shelbourne,' Hester agreed, reaching up to touch her lips to his. 'But I love you more, Jared.'

He touched his fingers to her lips. 'When I was a child, my home was in many places. My father was a gambler. Sometimes we lived in the best places, sometimes we lived anywhere we could find a roof over our heads. In the end he made enough money to invest in a small business and we began to prosper. He gave me a good start and I have multiplied that money many times over—but I have never had a real home. Yes, I have houses—more luxurious than this, as it happens—but the one thing I didn't have was a home. I have found my home here, Hester—with you.'

'Jared…' She pressed herself against him, feeling the burn of his need throbbing against her through the silk of her gown. 'I love you so much, want to be yours so much…when will you marry me?'

'As soon as it can be arranged,' he told her, bending his head to kiss her once more. His eyes were alight with amusement. 'If you are impatient, my dearest heart, just imagine how I feel.'

'Oh, Jared,' she said, laughing now as she saw the hunger in his face. 'If you can arrange it, I will marry you tomorrow.'

'I could arrange it,' he said. 'But I want a big wedding with lots of important guests, my darling. You are not to be married in some small, hurried way, but with all the pomp and ceremony I can arrange.' His hand moved down her throat, moving the lace aside, his lips pressing against the bruising he found there so gently that it felt like a soothing balm. 'You tried to hide it, my love, but I knew he had hurt you.'

'It is nothing,' she said, lifting her face for his kiss. 'Nothing can harm me now that I know your love is real and true.'

'Nothing will harm you,' he promised. 'While I live, I shall do all I can to protect you and make you happy.'

'You do that every time I look at you,' Hester said. 'You know that I am yours whenever you want me?'

'I want you now,' he said huskily, his hand moving down to caress her breast through the softness of her gown. 'But I shall wait for our wedding night, Hester. It may drive me to distraction, my adorable one—but I shall wait.' He kissed her again. 'You know there have been other women in my life, but there is only one I want to wake up next to every morning of my life.'

Hester lay in her husband's arms, her face pressed into the salty warmth of his chest. She felt safe, relaxed and loved, her body still tingling from his lovemaking. Raising herself on one arm to look down at him, she traced the line of his cheek with her finger.

'What should I have done if you had refused to come when Grandfather summoned you?' she asked. 'You had no reason to comply with his wishes—what made you do it?'

Jared's hand stroked the satin arch of her back, his

other hand tangling with her long hair as he thought about the question she had asked. She was a beautiful, sensuous woman, and they had found intense pleasure in each other last night.

'I am not sure,' he said. 'At first I meant to play a trick on the lawyer and send him back with a false tale, but then something he said made me wonder…'

'What did he say to you?' Hester asked, her lips against his ear so that her breath tickled him.

'He talked about family loyalty and tradition,' Jared told her simply. 'He told me about the family, about my ancestors and the things they had done to win honours and wealth long ago. He talked about a special bonding between master and men that was not often met with these days and it made me curious.'

'Was that all—curiosity?' Hester looked down at him. 'No, there was more, surely? You wanted to see your mother's home—to tell the duke what you thought of him.'

'Yes, that too,' Jared replied thoughtfully. 'I came with anger in my heart, Hester—but then I met you.'

'You were angry when we first met,' she said. 'It wasn't just what the lawyer said to you, was it?'

'I'm not sure,' he said. 'Perhaps it was because you looked so beautiful—so sure of yourself—and you were prepared to teach me how to behave so that I could find a rich wife.' He lowered his head, kissing her thoroughly. 'That made me angry—how could you promise to help me find a rich wife when I wanted only you? I thought you were indifferent to me, despised me for being an American upstart.'

'Oh, Jared,' Hester said, a little break in her voice. 'At first I behaved towards you in the manner I knew was expected of me. We needed the money so badly for the estate—but even then I wished that you did not have to marry for money. I wanted you to love me.'

'I was never sure,' he said, his eyes burning into her with such intense passion that she trembled, her body arching towards him as he drew her closer, beginning to ache for him again, to need him inside her once more. 'I knew quite soon that I loved you, as I had never loved another woman—but you were always so proper, so much the English lady.'

'It was my upbringing,' Hester whispered against his ear. 'I did not dare to let you see how I felt, for I was not certain you cared for me as I cared for you. I was jealous of those ladies you invited to the ball.'

'Selina was my mistress for a while, but that was long over—and I did not care for her sister. She was too demanding for my taste, Hester. I was merely being the perfect host—and trying to deceive Knighton, to deflect his attention from you, my love.' His hand tangled in her hair, bringing her face closer so that he could kiss her again.

'And there was never a bastard son?' she asked when she could, her eyes searching his face. 'No other woman you wanted to marry? No secret love that still haunts you?'

'Never,' he promised her. He reached out to touch her cheek, his fingers trailing the line of her face, moving over her soft mouth. 'Believe me, I never wanted to make a child with any other woman, my love.'

'But you do with me?' Hester's eyes dwelled on his face, searching for the answer she needed.

'I do with you,' he said, turning her over on to her back so that he gazed down into her eyes. He kissed her softly on the lips, his eyes gazing into hers so intently that she thought he must be able to see into her very soul. 'I hope we shall have children one day, but for the moment all I want is you. Forgive me, but I cannot seem to have enough of you.'

Hester reached up, bringing him down to her, her legs parting as she welcomed him, her body throbbing with the desire he could so easily arouse. She arched towards him, giving herself up to the pleasure of his seeking hands and tongue.

'And I can never have enough of you,' she whispered as his lips found her breasts, making her whimper with pleasure. 'Never, never, never…'

And after that there was for some time no more need of words.

* * * * *

The helicopter swung abruptly sideways in a dizzying arch, setting Jack McCall's fever-ravaged brain spinning.

His friend's voice sounded tinny, coming through the earphones. "You belong in a hospital," he said. "Not some backwater bed-and-breakfast."

All Jack really knew about the virus raging through his system was that it wasn't contagious, and there was no known treatment for it besides a lot of rest and quiet. "I don't like hospitals," he responded, hoping he sounded like his normal self. "They're full of sick people."

Vince Griffin chuckled but it was a dry sound, rough at the edges. "What's in Stone Creek, Arizona?" he asked. "Besides a whole lot of nothin'?"

Ashley O'Ballivan was in Stone Creek, and she was a whole lot of somethin', but Jack had neither the strength nor the inclination to explain. After the way he'd ducked out six months before, he didn't expect a welcome, knew he didn't deserve one. But Ashley, being Ashley, would take him in whatever her misgivings.

He had to get to Ashley; he'd be all right.

He closed his eyes, letting the fever swallow him.

There was no telling how much time had passed when he became aware of the chopper blades slowing overhead. Dimly, he saw the private ambulance waiting on the airfield outside of Stone Creek; it seemed that twilight had descended.

Jack sighed with relief. His clothes felt clammy against his flesh. His teeth began to chatter as two figures unloaded a gurney from the back of the ambulance and waited for the blades to stop.

"Great," Vince remarked, unsnapping his seat belt. "Those two look like volunteers, not real EMTs."

The chopper bounced sickeningly on its runners, and Vince, with a shake of his head, pushed open his door and jumped to the ground, head down.

Jack waited, wondering if he'd be able to stand on his own. After fumbling unsuccessfully with the buckle on his seat belt, he decided not.

When it was safe the EMTs approached, following Vince, who opened Jack's door.

His old friend Tanner Quinn stepped around Vince, his grin not quite reaching his eyes.

"You look like hell warmed over," he told Jack cheerfully.

"Since when are you an EMT?" Jack retorted.

Tanner reached in, wedged a shoulder under Jack's right arm and hauled him out of the chopper. His knees immediately buckled, and Vince stepped up, supporting him on the other side.

"In a place like Stone Creek," Tanner replied, "everybody helps out."

They reached the wheeled gurney, and Jack found himself on his back.

Tanner and the second man strapped him down, a process that brought back a few bad memories.

"Is there even a hospital in this place?" Vince asked irritably from somewhere in the night.

"There's a pretty good clinic over in Indian Rock,"

Tanner answered easily, "and it isn't far to Flagstaff." He paused to help his buddy hoist Jack and the gurney into the back of the ambulance. "You're in good hands, Jack. My wife is the best veterinarian in the state."

Jack laughed raggedly at that.

Vince muttered a curse.

Tanner climbed into the back beside him, perched on some kind of fold-down seat. The other man shut the doors.

"You in any pain?" Tanner said as his partner climbed into the driver's seat and started the engine.

"No." Jack looked up at his oldest and closest friend and wished he'd listened to Vince. Ever since he'd come down with the virus—a week after snatching a five-year-old girl back from her non-custodial parent, a small-time Colombian drug dealer—he hadn't been able to think about anyone or anything but Ashley. When he *could* think, anyway.

Now, in one of the first clearheaded moments he'd experienced since checking himself out of Bethesda the day before, he realized he might be making a major mistake. Not by facing Ashley—he owed her that much and a lot more. No, he could be putting her in danger, putting Tanner and his daughter and his pregnant wife in danger, too.

"I shouldn't have come here," he said, keeping his voice low.

Tanner shook his head, his jaw clamped down hard as though he was irritated by Jack's statement.

"This is where you belong," Tanner insisted. "If you'd had sense enough to know that six months ago, old buddy, when you bailed on Ashley without so much as a fare-thee-well, you wouldn't be in this mess."

Ashley. The name had run through his mind a million times in those six months, but hearing somebody say it out loud was like having a fist close around his insides and squeeze hard.

Jack couldn't speak.

Tanner didn't press for further conversation.

The ambulance bumped over country roads, finally hitting smooth blacktop.

"Here we are," Tanner said. "Ashley's place."

* * * * *

Will Jack be able to patch things up with Ashley,
or will his past put the woman he loves in harm's way?
Find out in
AT HOME IN STONE CREEK
by Linda Lael Miller
Available November 2009
from Silhouette Special Edition®